Shenandoah Nights

Winds of Change

* * *

Shenandoah Nights

Shenandoah Crossings

Shenandoah Dreams

WINDS OF CHANGE

SHENANDOAH NIGHTS

LISA BELCASTRO

www.oaktara.com

Shenandoah Nights

Published in the U.S. by:
OakTara Publishers
www.oaktara.com

Cover design by Yvonne Parks at www.pearcreative.ca
Cover image © Alison Shaw at www.alisonshaw.com
Author photo © 2013 by Heidi Wild Photography

Published in association with Les Stobbe, Literary Agent, 300 Doubleday
Road, Tryon, NC 28782; www.stobbeliterary.com

Scripture quotations are taken from The Holy Bible, New International
Version®, NIV®. Copyright © 1973, 1978, 1984 by Biblica, Inc.™ Used by
permission. All rights reserved worldwide.

ISBN-13: 978-1-60290-378-4 ▪ ISBN-10: 1-60290-378-6
eISBN-13: 978-1-60290-428-6 ▪ eISBN-10: 1-60290-428-6

Shenandoah Nights is a work of fiction. References to real people, events,
establishments, organizations, or locales are intended only to provide a sense
of authenticity and are used fictitiously. All other characters, incidents, and
dialogue are drawn from the author's imagination.

Printed in the U.S.A.

* * *

To Betty Belcastro

Encourager, supporter and friend, my mom

1

"I'M NOT GOING, MARK. Please don't force me."

"Rebecca, please? I wouldn't ask if you weren't my last hope."

"No way. You're the principal, why don't you go?" Rebecca O'Neill paced from the kitchen counter to the dining-room table and back again while contemplating the sanity of the person who invented the cell phone. Who wanted a device that allowed one's boss to track her down during summer break?

"Rebecca, I'm begging."

"Absolutely not. The last thing I want to do during the final week of my summer vacation is spend *my time* on a haunted boat with sixth graders and ghosts of teachers past."

"I thought only Catholics believed in the Ghost?"

"Funny, Mark, very funny. And I think they believe in the Holy Ghost, not ghosts, which has nothing to do with the *Shenandoah*. I don't believe in ghosts, I just don't feel like revisiting the scene of the crime."

Rebecca heard her boss sigh. "Not you, too. There was no crime five years ago. No ghosts. No haunted boat."

"I don't care, Mark, I'm not going."

*

Rebecca threw another sweatshirt on the bed and assessed her clothing inventory. She grumbled to herself once again as she replayed the previous day's conversation in her head. How many times had she said no? Obviously not enough because here she was, packing for a trip she didn't want to take.

"I've got to learn to be more convincing," she said as she stomped down the hall for her raincoat and flip-flops. She slammed the closet door and wished right then that she owned a pet so somebody could see how annoyed she was with herself. A startled jump or yip would be comforting, a little affirmation at least.

Rebecca threw the flip-flops on the bed and then tossed the raincoat behind the T-shirt pile. She could think of a hundred reasons she shouldn't be going on the trip. Her boss telling her no school chaperone meant no school trip was downright unfair. Mark knew she wouldn't let the kids be disappointed or their parents lose the money.

Sometimes Rebecca hated living in Tisbury, where everyone knew what everyone else was doing. The small town on an island off the coast of Massachusetts had a hotline for news and secrets that traveled the eighty-seven square miles with alacrity.

Hello? Of course Mark knew without asking me that I had no off-island vacation plans. Probably heard from Jessica at the post office that I was going to the beach every day.

Rebecca had argued, without enough conviction, that her days at the beach collecting sea glass and walking miles of the Vineyard's shoreline were the best vacation she could think of anywhere in the world. She lived on Martha's Vineyard, vacation paradise for a hundred thousand people every summer, including presidents—why would she want to go anywhere else?

In the end Mark had promised her five days off whenever she felt the need to escape to the beach. She picked up a picture of her parents. "Mark knows full well I will probably never use those days. Heck, the only time I've taken any time off during the last four years was in April after Gram died." Rebecca put the picture back on the desk and walked to the bed. "Unless, of course, I go missing like Melissa Smith, and then I'll be taking a lifetime off."

She shook off a chill, squared her shoulders, and clenched her jaw. She pushed the thoughts of Melissa and her disappearance to the far recesses of her mind. Rebecca had enough negative energy to deal with without adding death and disaster to the list. She thought about the deal and the potential for five free days on an Indian summer day. The thought was sweet, yet she knew she wouldn't, couldn't, take off and leave her classroom to a substitute without feeling guilty. And Mark knew it, too. Rebecca guessed he only offered those vacation days to make the chaperone job sound more like a compromise. Some compromise. Blackmail was more like it!

Complaining would get her nowhere, though, and there was a lot to do. She needed to swing by Jackie Walker's and pick up all the supplies and the daily activity sheets Jackie had planned for the kids before she threw her back out and earned a ticket off the *Shenandoah*. She also needed to call Jeff and cancel their date to the gallery opening on Friday night. They'd been dating for a couple of months, but Rebecca knew in her heart it wasn't going anywhere. She'd avoided saying anything during the last month because she hadn't wanted to hurt Jeff's feelings.

The summer was Jeff's busy season. While Rebecca walked and soaked up the sun at the beach, Jeff was managing his tour company by the harbor in

Oak Bluffs. His crazy schedule had kept their dates limited to Friday nights, which was enough for Rebecca. She shrugged. There was one plus to the trip, and she was thankful.

The cell phone's reggae ring tone interrupted her thoughts. "Tell me it's true. Tell me the gossip I heard while ordering my morning cappuccino is true."

Rebecca rolled her eyes. She knew Tess was going to love the fact that her friend would be the teacher chaperone sailing with her father on her favorite ship. Rebecca knew she should have called Tess yesterday and asked her to let her father know she'd be sailing with him on Sunday. She wasn't ready yesterday to deal with Tess' enthusiasm. Tess loved the *Shenandoah* more than any other ship. All her life Tess had wanted to take over the helm from her father. Captain Roberts wouldn't even let her work onboard, never mind captain.

"All rumors are true. The Vineyard Gossip Mill is still fully functioning with the latest boring news of my life. I am officially sailing on the *Shenandoah* as the teacher chaperone despite every effort on my part to convince Mark that I did not want to go."

Tess squealed into the phone. "I can't believe it! Why didn't you call me? I wish I could go with you. Any chance they'll let me bunk in your cabin? Heaven knows my father won't let me sail with the all-male crew. Maybe if I can finagle a job as school chaperone he'll discover how indispensible I am and hire me on next summer."

"If I could take you, you know I would."

"I know, Becca." The pain in Tess's voice was as clear as the blue sky out Rebecca's window. Her friend had longed to sail on her family's beautiful old ship, the *Shenandoah,* since they were in high school. Captain Roberts, Tess' father, had told his only daughter year after year that she couldn't work as a member of the crew because she would be the only female on an otherwise all-male crew. The fact had cut Tess to the bone, especially since all three brothers had spent their summers working on one of the family sailboats. Jack, her eldest, now captained the *Lady Katherine.* Todd had little interest in the ships, while Andy managed the family business and sailed whenever he wanted, which was often. The best Tess had managed was to work in the crew on the sunset sails or the day cruises.

"I wish you could go instead of me. You know me, Tess, I'd rather walk the Island than sail any day. On the other hand, I have an excuse not to go out with Jeff on Friday night."

Rebecca heard Tess chuckle. "When are you going to have that talk with him? The summer's almost over, the tourists are gonna leave, and Jeff's going to have more free time to spend with you. You'd better spill the beans before fall arrives."

"I don't want to hurt his feelings. Jeff's a decent guy. I just don't feel 'it' for him."

"You've always been a softie, Becca. If you're not careful, he's going to ask you to marry him and you'll end up saying yes because you don't want to hurt his feelings."

Laughter filled the phone line. "That happens, you'll be standing beside me in one of the frilliest dang dresses I can find."

Tess only laughed harder. Rebecca joined in.

"I'm going to go beg my father to let me sail with you. Don't hold your breath, though. I'll call you back if he says yes. If he says no, I'll be sulking Up Island on Sunday night trying to console myself at Brendon's barbeque. Have a great time."

After talking with Tess, Rebecca called Jeff and left a message on his cell phone. He wouldn't be happy, but at least Rebecca had a valid excuse. She took one look at the clothes on her bed, grabbed her bathing suit, and headed to the bathroom. The packing could wait till later. She wanted to swing by the post office and ask them to hold her mail before they went on lunch break. Most of all, she had to get an attitude adjustment. The beach was the only place that would happen.

Rebecca walked over to her computer, pulled up the *Shenandoah*'s company website, and printed out the "Suggested Packing List" as well as the "Chaperone Guide" and "History of the *Shenandoah*." She could read the last two at Bend In The Road Beach and hope the salt air, warm summer sand, and rhythmic roll of the waves would make the words more palatable.

An unsettling thought compelled her fingers to Google: "Melissa Smith, missing teacher, *Shenandoah*." She found hundreds of news stories. Rebecca clicked on a dozen of them and scanned the articles. She printed out three, including a controversial account given by the then galley boy, Pete Nichols, which had run in a less-than-reputable newspaper.

Rebecca had little recollection of the stories and gossip after the accident. She had just left the Island to start her senior year at Boston College when Melissa disappeared. She'd scanned the newspaper clippings her Gram had sent her and listened to the tidbits of speculation her Gram had shared during their phone conversations, but she hadn't known Melissa and hadn't retained many of the details.

Everyone knew Melissa had boarded the *Shenandoah* with her sixth-grade class five summers ago for a weeklong sail. On the fourth morning of their trip, while anchored off of Cuttyhunk, Melissa hadn't come up on deck to supervise morning chores. The stories after her disappearance told how a student had gone below and knocked on her door but had gotten no response.

Rebecca sorted some of the printed papers, her thoughts swirling. Lizzie Rubello, the girl who had gone below looking for Melissa that morning, was in high school now and she still talked about that day. Lizzie would have known in a minute something was wrong when Melissa didn't answer her door, which was the main reason she'd run to find John Masters, the biology teacher at school and the boys' chaperone that week.

A quick phone call to John could answer a few questions. Rebecca stared at her cell, debating whether she wanted to hear the answers. One minute turned into five. She kept staring at the phone. Curiosity finally won out. Rebecca walked to her desk and looked up John's phone number.

Four rings later, her call went to voicemail. "Hi John, it's Rebecca. Listen, I got roped into going on the *Shenandoah* instead of Jackie. I don't want to sound like a wimp, but I've got some questions, and I'd love to talk with you if you have a minute. Feel free to call my cell any time. Thanks."

Still frustrated, Rebecca picked up another article and searched for clues. According to the story, John had knocked and eventually jimmied open the door to Melissa's cabin to discover she was nowhere to be seen. A thorough search of the boat had also turned up empty. The captain had called the Coast Guard, who had conducted a full search of the small island and its surrounding areas in the Elizabeth Islands archipelago. Neither Melissa, nor Melissa's body, was ever found, and no one had ever heard from her again. Those were the facts.

Dread rippled through Rebecca's body like a thrown stone shattering the stillness of a pond. She practically hit the ceiling when her phone rang. Startled and catching her breath, she recognized the number as John Masters'. "Hi, John."

"Hey, Rebecca. So Mark convinced you to sail next week, huh?"

"Blackmailed is more like it, but we'll keep that between us so I can keep my job."

They both chuckled, and then Rebecca got serious. "Listen, John, I have little memory of Melissa. I probably shouldn't be giving this a second thought, but I am, so I've got to ask: What do you remember?"

"Everything, I remember everything like it was yesterday. Worst vacation of my life. I never figured Melissa to be one for a midnight swim, but I guess we never really know anyone."

"So you think she went swimming?"

She heard John chortle. "Well, I don't believe Pete Nichols, if that's what you're asking. Is that what's got you spooked?"

Rebecca rolled her eyes. She was being silly. John was absolutely right. "I just printed out his story. I haven't read it yet. I guess I wanted to hear from you what went on that night."

"Listen, Rebecca, I don't know if we'll ever know what actually happened to Melissa. I can tell you that, when Lizzie first told me Melissa wasn't answering her door, I figured she was overtired and had slept in. After the sixth knock—and I was banging by then—I suspected something was wrong. Even then I wasn't thinking she drowned. I thought I was going to open her door and find her dead from a heart attack. When I finally got in after working the latch with a putty knife, I was stunned to find her bunk empty."

"Did Pete say anything then?" Rebecca interrupted, fingers tapping on the desk. "While you were searching for her? After the Coast Guard arrived?"

"He was mumbling something, but I was focused on Melissa, calming the kids down, and calling the school and all the parents. You can't begin to imagine how chaotic it was. The Coast Guard didn't want anyone to leave the boat, and all the parents wanted their children shuttled home immediately. It took all day to get the kids transported back to the dock and safe with their parents. I had to return to the boat while the search continued. Mark arrived in the early afternoon. Whatever happened that night, whether she went swimming or fell overboard, she was gone."

"I take it there was no note or anything like that?"

She heard John sigh. She stood and went to the window.

"I wish, Rebecca, there had been some clue, any clue. There was nothing. She vanished."

"Um, thanks, John. I guess you've answered all the questions you could."

"Have fun, Rebecca. The *Shenandoah* has been sailing every summer since without incident. Melissa's accident was a freak event. Don't let it spoil your trip."

"I'll do my best. See you after Labor Day. Thanks again."

Rebecca hung up the phone and stared at the papers on her desk. She inched across the floor and sank into her padded chair. She rolled the pages and tapped them against the wooden legs. The Pete Nichols story rested in the printer's out tray. She had never given heed to his sci-fi version of Melissa's disappearance—after all, who believed in time travel and vanishing teachers? John hadn't believed it, either, and he had been there.

The Coast Guard had given a perfectly logical explanation: accidental drowning. Melissa had either fallen overboard or had decided to take a moonlight swim. She had drowned, and her body had been pulled into the current and carried out into the Atlantic. Though no one knew for certain, the Coast Guard's conclusion suited Rebecca.

Nevertheless, her natural inquisitiveness and a slight case of nerves took hold as she sat on the edge of her bed and skimmed the Pete Nichols story, "Teacher Dreams Her Way Back to Colonial Boston."

Rebecca scanned the story, her eyes focusing on "excited and agitated," "talked about strange dreams every morning," "pestered everyone, especially the captain, for information on the *Shenandoah*'s history," and "asked about captains from the 1800s, specifically 1770."

Rebecca shivered. John hadn't mentioned any of that. She could call him back. Maybe she would later. She continued reading. She drew in a sharp breath two paragraphs later. "Nichols stated Melissa stayed in Cabin 8 and that she was curious if anyone else had ever mentioned hearing voices or having visions of sailors in Colonial Boston." A chill slithered down Rebecca's spine. She remembered Jackie telling her that she would be staying in Cabin 8 and how Jackie had made a joke out of it.

Great—now I'll not only be cooped up on a boat with hyper students, but when I finally get them to bed, I'll then have to deal with the Ghost of Christmas Past and his Colonial friends!

Rebecca jammed the story into her beach bag nestled in the corner of the room by the bookcase. She turned and swiped a scrunchie out of the pile on the bed, gathered her unruly brown curls back into a ponytail, and then grabbed the beach bag off of the floor. She marched through the house, pausing to snag a bottle of water, a bag of trail mix, and the book she'd left overturned on the kitchen counter yesterday when Mark had called. Her grandmother no longer present to yell at her, Rebecca slammed the new screen door as she headed to her car.

Five days? Huh! Mark was going to owe her a month at the beach for this one.

2

REBECCA inhaled the scent of the sea. She ran her hand along the smooth, painted railing and looked about the ship. Twenty-six years old, she was standing on the *Shenandoah* for the first time. She'd grown up watching the great ship glide by the beaches on her summer cruises, her majesty obvious to all who viewed her regal sails catching the wind. Rebecca could still hear her father saying, "There's no ship in all the harbor as fine as she, Lass."

Tourists on a catamaran departing on a sunset cruise waved as they passed. Rebecca returned the greeting, then glanced at her watch. She had an hour before the kids boarded. While she could easily spend the entire sixty minutes soaking in the atmosphere, she gave herself ten minutes to explore before she had to inspect the cabins and check off the list she'd been given. She moved slowly across the ship from rail to sail to rail.

Like a child, Rebecca wanted to touch and investigate every inch of the neat and tidy boat. The wood felt strong and sleek under her fingers...the sails as crisp as heavily starched linen. Walking toward the front, she caught a whiff of gasoline. Rebecca figured the generator used for morning chores was stored in what looked to be a large chest.

As she approached a hatch, she heard voices. She guessed she'd found the crew's quarters and did an about-face. Then she walked the length of the boat to the wheel, covered by a piece of sailcloth. Rebecca could imagine how happy her father would be if he could see her. Surely, she thought, he must be looking down from heaven and smiling. She noticed the gleam of the brass bell on the captain's roof and nodded. "The bell tolls for me," she said with a glance up toward her father. "No time for this now. I've work to do."

With a clipboard in hand listing eleven cabins below deck to inspect, leisurely appreciation would have to wait until after her work was done. She went down the ladder at the back of the ship to search for the first mate or one of the crew members who had rowed her over. She walked from one end of the boat to the other and found no one.

Rebecca returned to the deck and stood by the side. Where was everyone? An evening ferry was pulling away from the dock, and the *Shenandoah* rocked in the ferry's wake. Rebecca closed her eyes and let her mind carry her back fifteen years to the days she had stood on the deck of her uncle's fishing boat. She saw her father and uncle casting and hauling, talking and laughing. She pictured herself at eleven sitting on an overturned bucket singing or standing by the rail fishing with her pink rod and reel.

She had loved going out with her dad and Uncle Paddy. The days had always been filled with laughter and song. The two men she loved most would drop the net and haul it back in, telling her and each other stories of Ireland, some true and some pure fantasy. Rebecca had enjoyed each and every one.

They'd had a few lobster traps, too, and Rebecca would wait expectantly for one of them to mention it was a good time to check the traps. As their blue, green, and orange buoys came into view, her mouth would water at the thought of grilled lobsters dipped in her mom's lime butter.

"You look lost in thought," a friendly male voice said.

Startled, Rebecca swiped at the tears forming. "Remembering."

"Wild sailing adventures?"

Rebecca turned toward the crew member. "Nope, I've never sailed. But my father was a fisherman and used to take me with him sometimes. He loved the sea. My mom called the ocean 'the other woman,' though she, too, loved the salt waters and sandy beaches of the Island." She extended her hand. "I'm Rebecca O'Neill. I'll be the teacher chaperone on this voyage."

He reached out a strong, calloused hand. "Nice to meet you, Rebecca O'Neill. My name is Hawk. I'm the first mate on this vessel."

"Hawk? No last name?" Rebecca grinned.

He winked. "Hawk will do."

Rebecca scanned the ship, took in the gorgeous late-summer afternoon, and sighed. "My father would have loved to be standing here today. He'd see the *Shenandoah* in the harbor and comment on her beauty. He never tired of watching her, nor of telling me she was a fast-vanishing breed and I should take a good, long look. After a dozen or so good, long looks, I had enough. My father never did."

Rebecca toyed with a piece of rope tied to a pin-like thingy on the rail. "I remember when she was painted white. He never appreciated Captain Roberts' color choice. He loved her black and sleek, like she was sailing through the turbulent waters of the Revolution. He would tell me tales of her stealth and speed, outrunning the British and carrying much needed cargo to the Patriots along the coast. He loved this ship. I wish he could see me aboard her today. I hope he can. He died before Captain Roberts repainted her black."

Mr. Rather-Good-Looking flashed a grin. "He sounds like a great dad. You must miss him. You'll have to tell Captain Roberts about him. Anyone who loves *Shenandoah* is a friend of the Captain's."

9

Rebecca moved toward a large chest. "Oh, the Captain knows. My father told him many times he owned the best ship in the harbor. I do plan to ask the captain about the history of the boat so the kids can learn while they're here, and I can bring it back with me into the classroom for the other grades. I brought my camera to take pictures, too."

A gull flew low overhead, searching the deck for food. Finding none, he squawked and flew on. Rebecca watched him fly away before returning her attention to the man beside her.

"Once you get the captain started, it would be easier to tame the wind than slow his tales of all things *Shenandoah*. By the end of the week you'll have more than enough history for your classroom." He peered at the evening sky. "You should have a good trip, too. The weather is supposed to be perfect."

"Wonderful."

Hawk's eyes roamed over Rebecca in a subtle but obvious appreciation. Her stomach flipped and she averted her eyes. "You're younger than most of our chaperones."

Rebecca took in the well-muscled, sun-bleached blond and knew they were about the same age. "That's why I got the job—young and single with no family to care for. You could say I teach sixth grade happily, but I'm a rather reluctant chaperone."

Hawk chuckled. "We get a few of those each summer. Hard to take a week off from your summer break and spend it with the little monsters again, huh?"

Rebecca laughed before catching herself and clamping a hand over her mouth. "Sounds horrible, but that about sums it up."

"Well, if you have any questions or problems, let me know. I may not be able to keep the kids in line all day, but I can sure work them hard enough that they'll drift off as soon as their heads hit those pillows."

"That's a promise I'm going to hold you to," Rebecca said.

"We both need to get ready for your students. I'll leave you to check the bunks." Hawk turned and walked toward the front of the boat. He was about ten feet away when he stopped and glanced back. "Oh, and Rebecca, asking about the *Shenandoah's* history will bring a sparkle to the captain's eye. But do us all a favor and don't ask about Melissa Smith or the mystery surrounding the boat. The captain's mood will shift faster than a hurricane's wind."

Rebecca waved him off. "No problem, though I am a wee bit curious. Maybe you could tell me one night. Were you part of the crew five years ago?"

He shook his head. "Except for the captain, no one on the boat today was onboard five years ago. As for the story, perhaps, but no promises. Even the crew gets spooked, and some things are best left in the past. If you'll excuse me." He walked away, leaving Rebecca itching to know more.

Hawk moved along checking ropes and gear and finally stopping to speak with a crew member who had climbed out of the opening at the front of the boat. Rebecca took in the beautiful woodwork, the polished brass and tidiness of the ropes and masts. Everything was perfectly kept. She knew the ship had undergone another heavy renovation during the winter months, but the *Shenandoah* still looked as though she hadn't been covered in salt water and sea air for the last two months, never mind carrying a passenger list of eleven- and twelve-year-olds each time out.

Rebecca nodded. The kids really were going to work and swim themselves into exhaustion over the next week. Hawk would easily be able to keep his promise. And she would surely get a good night's sleep.

Rebecca headed midship and went down the companionway, remembering to face the ladder and descend backwards. She reached the floor and found herself staring at a beautiful, old pot-bellied stove. "Ooh, you're gorgeous," she said to the huge black antique. Rebecca walked around to the front and tried to open the firewood door. "Obviously you're just for looks," she said after a third attempt to open the door failed. "I bet you kept plenty of sailors warm in your day, though, didn't you?"

Rebecca patted the stove affectionately and continued toward her cabin. After opening the door to the head, she gagged on the first whiff of powerful toilet-cleaning chemicals and covered her mouth, waving her left hand back and forth furiously, trying to move the fumes in any other direction. She was about to make an amusing comment when she noticed a shadow moving across the hall. Her body tensed, every word of the Pete Nichols' story scrolling across her brain.

"Calm down, Becca, you're imagining things." She gently closed the door to the head and tiptoed the twenty or so feet to her cabin. She hugged the clipboard to her chest. Logically, she knew it simply had to be someone walking by overhead.

Inches from her door, she stopped and slowly poked her head around the doorframe, peeking into the room with her left eye. Seeing nothing, she stepped forward and stood square in the center of the doorway. Nothing jumped out at her. The cabin appeared pretty empty. But, just in case, she decided it couldn't hurt to look around, completely and totally around.

Rebecca knew she wasn't fooling herself. The cabin was maybe ten by ten; if she couldn't see anybody in the doorway, there was no need to investigate. *Everything looks normal.*

Still, she opened all the footlockers, peered behind the door, and even lifted the blankets placed on the bed. "Of course it looks normal; it *is* normal. I'm being ridiculous," she told herself aloud. "Cabin 8 is just a room like any other room on this ship. Get a grip, Becca, get a grip!"

Laughing at herself for being spooked, Rebecca picked up her clipboard and headed down the corridor to inspect the children's cabins. The girls were bunking in the front with her, while the boys were rooming at the back of the boat through the saloon and past the galley.

Cabins 9 and 10 were perfect. Cabin 11 was missing a washcloth and blanket. Rebecca looked at the clipboard and realized her pen must have fallen off when she put her stuff down on the bed.

She walked back to Cabin 8 and searched her room. No pen on the floor, on the bunks, or even between the bedrails and mattress. Always a planner, she had a few extras somewhere in her backpack, which one of the crew had brought down to her bunk with her luggage, most likely while she was nosing around on deck.

Sitting on the bunk, she rummaged through her stuff. That's when she heard footsteps and hushed voices, as though they were whispering in her ear.

"We should ready the cannons."

Rebecca jumped up. "Hello? Who's there?"

No one answered.

She peeked up into her porthole and couldn't see a soul. Sitting back on the bunk, she listened. Only the rhythm of the sea moved against the boat. No voices.

I heard someone, I know I did!

Moments passed. The only sound was her own shallow, rapid breathing. Rebecca mumbled, "No! No! No! I am not hearing voices. That's what I get for reading that ridiculous Pete Nichols story. Serves me right."

She stood on shaky legs. Enough. Brushing her jeans off—she didn't know what she was brushing and didn't care as long as the voice was gone—she rolled her shoulders to release the tension. Back to reality...and work.

In cabin 11, Rebecca made her notes and then moved down the corridor to finish the job. She inspected each room, making sure all the bunks had two sheets, a blanket, a pillow, a towel, a washcloth, a wash basin, and a cup placed on each bed.

No showers or baths on this cruise. There were two fresh water pumps on deck, primarily used to fill water bottles and wash hands and faces and brush teeth. They were only waist high and had one selection for water temperature—cold. Not exactly a shower setting. Rebecca chuckled, knowing the boys would simply ignore bathing completely, thereby resolving all issues of cleanliness, as well as the care and rinsing of the basin and cup or the proper way to hang the wet towel and wash cloth. The girls would either try to sponge bathe using the basin, or they'd jump into the ocean with a bar of soap and a bottle of shampoo and clean up.

Rebecca listed the missing items in the boys' cabins and scanned her list of needed supplies while walking through the dining room, or saloon as it is known on a ship. She looked up when she reached the stove. Her cabin loomed in front of her. Again, shivers skittered down her spine.

She seriously had to get a grip, and soon. The kids would be there in twenty minutes. She needed a cup of tea. Chamomile would be great, but anything would do. Maybe they'd even stock honey for baking or to drizzle over the chef's famous biscuits.

Rebecca headed back to the galley, hoping the cook or galley boy would be able to tell her how or where to get a cup of tea.

Five minutes later, mug of green tea sweetened with honey in her hand, Rebecca climbed up the ladder through the cook's galley and meandered over to the side of the boat facing the docks. She leaned against the rail, placed her mug between two pegs to keep it from falling overboard, and took out the *Shenandoah* information packet. Now would be the perfect time to figure out what was left, what was right, what was front and what was back.

She had wonderful memories of fishing with her father, but he had never stood on formality, nautical or otherwise. The most he ever said was "pick up the bucket over there" or "go back and bring the blue line up to me." This would be a first for bow and stern.

Rebecca clicked her pen cap repeatedly as she learned that forward and aft meant toward the bow or the stern. Starboard was the right side of the ship when she faced forward and port was the left.

She took a sip of tea. Bow and stern referred to the front and back of the boat. She could tell the students to, "Take a bow on the front of the stage with the stern teacher at the back." They'd like that one.

Amused at her joke, she lost focus. She stood when she heard the crew talking loudly to each other. "Come on," was yelled a couple of times on deck.

Rebecca glanced around and noticed some of the crew was disembarking.

"Where are we going?" Rebecca asked.

"Oh, not you, Miss," replied a lanky man with jet-black hair. "'Come on' is the cue to start picking up the kids. Means all the gear has passed inspection, been stacked by the icebox on the dock, and the yawl boat should come get them. Already got one rowboat headed toward us."

Rebecca heard a motor start and gave Jet Black a quizzical look. He chortled. "Yup, that's a motor. The yawl boat is Captain Roberts' one concession to modern boating. A yawl boat was originally meant to be attached to or carried by a schooner and then lowered to the water and rowed when needed." He pointed to the shoreline on the far side of the harbor toward West Chop. "The captain loves to bring his dogs sailing, which creates a stinky problem, if you know what I mean. In order to get the dogs to shore quickly a few times each day, the captain outfitted the yawl with a motor. Makes life a lot easier once we get out of the harbor."

Rebecca watched as the first group of students approached, along with a couple of parents who desired to see the ship. "Hopefully the parent chaperones have gone through everyone's gear. I don't want to find forbidden cargo and be taking away swimming privileges the first night."

"I hear that," Jet Black said.

All of the kids were instructed to leave cell phones, Gameboys, iPods, and all other electronic equipment at home. They were allowed to bring a flashlight and camera. While most of the kids followed the packing instructions, every Sunday brought a few shouts of, "Brian, you know you can't bring this iPod," or "Karen, where is your toothbrush?" that resulted in: "Wait right here. Do not get into the skiff before I get back from the grocery store."

Rebecca had taken Jackie's advice and had packed a few extra toiletries just in case someone's parent didn't catch a missing necessity. She had also packed a box of granola bars and a bag of nuts in case one or two students forgot to eat dinner before boarding. Rebecca chided herself for not packing a sandwich for her own dinner, then realized excitement and curiosity had consumed her appetite. She, too, would be snacking on a cinnamon-raisin granola bar or almonds and pecans if she got hungry later.

Checking the time on her watch, she noted she had three hours before curfew. She thought of the voice she heard, or thought she'd heard, this afternoon talking about cannons. Goosebumps rose on her arm. She didn't want to wait three hours to talk to Hawk.

Rebecca could just hear Tess telling her to give it up and get focused on the kids before laughing about her sudden interest in ghosts. And Tess would be right; she had twenty-five students depending on her to be sane.

3

"HELLO, HOLMES HOLE. Are you ready to sail?" Hawk called out like a rock star starting a concert.

The kids pounded on the tables and whooped and hollered.

"Well, I see we have an enthusiastic bunch. Let's get this meeting started so you can enjoy some milk and cookies."

Cheers erupted again. Hawk smiled. Rebecca joined him.

The meeting got underway. Hawk introduced himself and the eight crew members on board. He told them Captain Roberts would board tomorrow after lunch with the week's supply of fresh meat, vegetables, and ice to keep it all cold. Dozens of questions were asked and answered while Rebecca sat impatiently waiting for a chance to speak with Hawk. When the milk and cookies were gone, she hurried the kids back to their cabins to make their bunks and be ready for bed by the 9:30 curfew.

"Move along, girls. Don't dilly-dally," Rebecca said as she escorted a herd of girls up on deck for evening rituals and then back down and into their cabins. She listened to the girls whispering and giggling but knew it would do no good to nag them. This time tomorrow they would be begging for sleep after a day of Hawk's chores.

Rebecca was eager to find Hawk, but she knew she should check in with Sharon Butler, the girls' parent chaperone, before finagling a ghost story. She knocked on Sharon's open door. "Hi, Sharon. Have you settled in?"

The woman who resembled a Ralph Lauren model wannabe lifted both hands palms up. "I think so. My eyes are adjusting to these dim lights, but I doubt my head is going to tolerate the bumps and bruises. I don't want to complain, but every time I bend over and stand back up, I hit my head on something. I had no idea the cabins were so small. The description should have stated the cabins were closer in size to a coffin than a bedroom."

Rebecca leaned against the doorframe and tried to look sympathetic. A week with a cranky parent could be worse than a week with a couple dozen rambunctious kids. "I know what you mean," she consoled. "I keep trying to visualize sharing my cabin with four, five, or even ten people, as they must have two hundred years ago. I feel spoiled having a room to myself knowing the kids are three or four to a cabin. Then again, they actually want everyone in their cabins. I guess we're lucky to have our own space, no matter how small it is."

The tall, elegant blond emitted a small snicker as she refolded and laid a pink polo shirt on top of two others in varying shades of pink. Sharon's entire wardrobe lay on the top bunk sorted by color, and separated into shirts, shorts, pants, sweaters, and underwear.

Rebecca's jaw dropped. She counted six shades of pink, five blues, three greens, two yellows, and that was just the polo shirts.

Sharon continued on, oblivious to Rebecca's shock. "You're right, I know it. I promise not to whine the entire trip. I don't want to sound like a prima donna, but I feared a week with twenty-five children, no shower, no gym, no massage, and questionable sleep would push me toward the brink. I can't believe I let Casey talk me into this. I envisioned a larger space to escape to. If I retreat to my bunk at night, please don't take it personally. Coffin quarters or not, I'll be glad for some quiet time." She paused and eyed Rebecca, who was still gawking at the piles of clothes. "Thanks, Miss O'Neill."

Rebecca shook her head. "Don't give it a second thought. Escape as necessary. And please, call me Rebecca. I'm going up on deck for a little stargazing. Would you like to join me?"

"No, thanks. I'm going to lie down and pray for sleep. Be careful up there. I don't want to be knocking on an empty cabin door in the morning."

If Rebecca hadn't heard, or thought she'd heard, that voice this afternoon, she might have laughed at the reference to Melissa Smith. She wondered if Sharon knew her teacher chaperone was staying in the same cabin. Better not to feed that superstition.

"Trust me, Sharon, I am not going swimming, and I will be here tomorrow."

The evening air was sweet. A soothing wind caressed Rebecca's sun-soaked skin. She loved summer nights—the cool ocean breezes that carried the scents of the sea, sand, and marsh grasses; the lingering aromas of oils and lotions; and her favorite flowers, beach roses.

Rebecca gazed at the heavens. She loved looking at the stars. Until she went to college, she thought everyone lived with millions of stars illuminating the sky on clear nights. When she went up to Boston, she was stunned to discover how the city lights erased the stars. The sky looked lonely there, empty like a vacant hotel. Tonight the stars seemed especially bright, yet Rebecca knew she was in for a treat the further out to sea they went.

She noticed a few of the crew gathered around the cook's doghouse. She didn't see Hawk. "Perhaps he's in his doghouse," she mused, chuckling at the

16

thought. Rebecca had laughed when she'd read the description of the two doghouses on deck. The cook and the first mate each had private quarters, much coveted on a ship. These quarters, though, were merely four walls surrounding a cot-like bed, a small nightstand, and a strip of floor space. The doghouses made the cabins look like suites at the Ritz-Carlton.

Rebecca walked over to the men. "Is Hawk around?" she asked Tim Connors, whom Hawk had introduced as the ship's bosun, or second-in-command.

Tim stood, ran a hand through his jet-black hair, and motioned to his left. "He's in his doghouse, probably trying to sleep. Best keep it down. Brian Little went ashore, so Hawk has to do Brian's middle watch tonight from midnight to 4 a.m. Can I help you with something?"

Rebecca knew she shouldn't stretch the truth, but after the cannon comment this afternoon she *had* to know more. "I asked Hawk earlier if he would tell me about Melissa Smith. Were any of you around back then?"

Silence. You could hear a pin drop. The crew peered around like children about to steal sweets from the forbidden cookie jar. Josh peeked over his shoulder toward the captain's cabin. The man wasn't even on board, and the taboo subject shut down all conversation. Rebecca's sense of apprehension grew. For a second or two she wondered if she shouldn't forget the whole idea and go to bed.

Josh glanced back at Hawk's closed door before opening his mouth. He spoke in decibels barely above a whisper. "None of us were working for Captain Roberts then. Some say he fired the whole crew, some say the entire crew quit. Captain told us the crew needed to find new jobs after the Coast Guard shut him down that summer. I believe the captain. If he shut down now, I would need another job and wouldn't spend much time waiting around to find one."

Curiosity piqued, hesitation tossed to the wind, Rebecca stepped closer. "So, when did you start working on the *Shenandoah*, Josh?"

"Four summers ago, when Captain started sailing again."

Rebecca surveyed the guys, all of them fit and rugged. "Were any of you nervous? Worried about ghosts or disappearing like Melissa did?"

Josh snorted. "Are you joking? I don't believe for a second Melissa Smith was flying to Boston each night in some Jules Verne time capsule. Talk to Mikey, there, if you want to hear about aliens and space ships."

Mike Natale, an Island native, was the youngest crew member, though one of the bigger guys. Rebecca could feel the tension between the two men. "Give it a rest, Josh. I knew Melissa. She didn't drown."

Rebecca's ears pricked up. Here was the juicy stuff. "Was Melissa your teacher in elementary school, Mike?"

"No, she was friends with my mom."

"Oh, gosh, I'm sorry. I shouldn't have brought this up."

"Don't worry about it."

"Can I ask why you came to work on the boat?"

"I talked to Pete Nichols."

A few groans from the other crew members let Rebecca know how little respect they had for Nichols and his version of Melissa Smith's disappearance. The *Shenandoah* crew wasn't the only group of people who thought Pete was crazy. Other than a few Island eccentrics and the one alternative newspaper, no one on the Island had given Pete or his story the time of day.

"That guy is a joke," Josh snapped.

Rebecca noticed the others elbowing each other, clearly taking their lead from Josh.

Rebecca moved closer to Mike. His telephone-pole arms were crossed and his eyes locked on the equally burly Josh. She didn't want to stir up trouble, but the door was open, and she was ready to walk. "I read Pete's story yesterday for the first time. I confess it was a stretch for me to believe the rumors years ago when I first heard them. Now that I'm staying in the same cabin it's unsettling to think the room might be haunted. I have to admit..."

Mike softened his stance, lowering his arms. "It's not haunted, Rebecca. Pete never said anything about ghosts or spirits or anyone being haunted by anything. He told me Melissa never left her cabin at night. Pete was one of the guys on watch the night she disappeared. People said he fell asleep during his four-hour shift and didn't hear her fall or jump in and made up his story to cover his butt. Pete swears he was awake every second of his watch. I think folks wanted to believe Pete fell asleep so they could believe Melissa fell overboard or went swimming and drowned. I believe Pete. That's why I joined the crew. I want to know more."

"If Mike disappears, we'll know he jumped, too," Josh joked, though no one looked as though they thought it was funny.

Mike sent a scathing glare at Josh, then directly met Rebecca's eyes. "It's the cabin, not the water. If anyone goes missing, it won't be me."

"Enough!" Hawk slammed his sliding door open. "Not another word from any of you. If you don't need sleep, or you don't have work to do, then you can polish brass!" Hawk glared at each one of them, his gaze settling on Rebecca. "The party is over. Get to work, or go to bed. Now!"

18

4

IT'S GOING TO BE A LONG WEEK IF I KEEP THIS UP! Rebecca slid between the sheets, feeling the sting of Hawk's anger and a twinge of guilt for involving the crew. Obviously, Mike had more questions than she did. Had he discovered anything over the summer? She would love to get him alone and talk about Melissa when Hawk wasn't around. As soon as the thoughts bounced around in her head, twinges of guilt chased after them. If Tess or Captain Roberts thought she believed Mike, they'd both be angry with her. *Give it a rest, Becca. You're a teacher chaperone, not Nancy Drew.*

Rebecca climbed into the top bunk with far too much on her mind, most of which she knew she shouldn't be entertaining. After ten minutes of counting sheep, Rebecca reached for her flashlight and a book. She heard the ship's bells chime and made a mental note to ask someone what they meant. She turned the pages of the book methodically, half focused at best. The bells rang a few more times before she finally drifted off to sleep, thoughts of time travel and Colonial Boston swirling in her brain.

*

Men's voices awakened her. She didn't want to know what the guys had to do this early. Too little sleep left her wishing for hours of nighttime. Rebecca patted the bed, wanting to pull the sheet up over her head for a few minutes. When her hands came up empty, she opened her eyes to see if she'd kicked the sheet and blanket onto the bunk below. Panic spread as she stared at the floor, not the bunk that should have been beneath her. She sat up and realized she wasn't in her room. She remained motionless, trying to figure out where she was without alerting anyone to her presence. She didn't want to freak out any of the kids if she'd developed a sudden habit for sleepwalking.

"I suspect we shall need to make another run shortly after we unload. They are extremely low on ammunition."

Rebecca held her breath, trying to figure out who was talking and where they were. She slid off the pallet she was on and crouched behind a large barrel, almost like the huge pickle barrels the penny candy store had years ago before they went out of business.

"Where will we find more gunpowder?"

"I am not worried about finding powder. My concern is maneuvering in and out of the harbor. The King's Men have control of the harbor and the city."

"I do not believe what happened. I wish we had arrived sooner. If we had been there, we could have fired on the *Lively*."

"We would have given it our best shot, Jonah. I pray Father and Magnus are safe. Mother fretted enough over our sailing south."

Rebecca slinked left and crouched behind a crate, hoping to get a glimpse of who was speaking. She had no idea how she'd walked into the storage room during the night, but she knew these two men were meeting in secret. Who were they? She didn't recognize either one of their voices. And what did they mean by firing on the *Lively?*

She had taught her social studies students about the British ship, *HMS Lively*, and its significance in the Battle of Bunker Hill, but these men could not be talking about that *Lively*. She tugged the back of her T-shirt down to keep the cold wood off her back and listened for any movement from above.

The only sound was the swish of the waves against the ship.

"How many were wounded? I heard the lads on the dock say we lost hundreds of men. Do you think it is true, Ben?"

Rebecca tensed. First Jonah and then Ben. She hadn't heard either of those names mentioned last night at the welcome meeting. Hawk had commented that one of the guys had an early morning doctor's appointment and was staying in town. He hadn't said anything about a Ben or a Jonah sailing with them. She tried to peer around the edge of the crate to see if she recognized either of the men. She could only see the backs of their heads.

"I do not know. It is hard to imagine the bloodshed. It does sound like the Bloody Backs suffered great casualties, even though they declared victory."

"Lexington pales in comparison. How are we going to survive long enough for a petition to reach the king?"

A shiver ran down Rebecca's spine. *What are they talking about? What king? What petition?* She was getting nervous and a little scared. Something wasn't right. She needed to find Hawk and let him know about these two. If only she could get a good look at them. The light of their lamp was all she had to see by in the dark room. She searched both pockets of her sweatpants for her flashlight and came up empty-handed.

"I think the time for petitions has passed. I heard tell John Adams was in Philadelphia weeks ago to elect a general to lead the Continental Army. I believe war is inevitable."

"A battle with Britain? David had a better chance with Goliath."

"Jonah! You know better. Father would tell you right quick the Good Lord is with us as He was with David. Our fight for freedom will not—cannot—be in vain."

Rebecca sucked in her breath, a burst of panic permeating her mind more swiftly than the oxygen filled her lungs. A battle with Britain? *There is no way Britain attacked the United States. These men must be terrorists.*

Rebecca tried to see around the stack of crates without any luck. If only she could catch a glimpse of one of the men, she could point him out to Hawk.

At that instant a loud boom sounded, followed by a clanging. Rebecca jumped up and smashed her right knee into another crate.

"Who's there?"

"Present yourself at once!"

Heart pounding, Rebecca searched for an escape and noticed the door behind her. If she made it out the door, she'd get to Hawk before they got to her. Shooting a glimpse at the two men, she dashed for the door, screaming Hawk's name....

*

Rebecca sat bolt upright at the loud boom, whacked her head on the ceiling, and slouched forward, her legs hanging over the bunk. Blood pumping, she rubbed her head and then her eyes. Feeling the bump of her flashlight under her right leg, she shone the beam around the room.

Her cabin. She was in her cabin! How did she get back here? Where were the men she'd heard? She had not imagined those voices. She squinted upward and noted that her porthole was open. Had she dreamed the whole thing? Maybe some of the crew had been talking on deck? Maybe she'd imagined two men talking about gunpowder?

Or maybe I'm losing my mind?

Rebecca listened for voices and heard the clanging again. She eased herself down to the floor and inched open her cabin door. Peering through the main saloon, she noticed a light shining from the galley. As she tiptoed down the hall, the noise grew increasingly louder. Right as she was about to enter the galley, Dave, the ship's cook, walked out. Rebecca screamed.

"Whoa. Sorry to startle you. Didn't know anyone else was up yet. Did the old stove wake you?" Dave's brown eyes sparkled with amusement.

Rebecca struggled to regain her composure. "Is that what's making the noise?" she asked between gulping gasps for air.

Dave's grin let her know she wasn't the first person to be startled out of sleep by the kitchen stove. "She's a loud one when you fire her up. You'll get used to the banging and clanging. She usually wakes a few people the first morning. I feed her some coal around 5 a.m. every day so she's ready to start breakfast at seven. Sometimes she bangs, sometimes she clangs, sometimes she grunts, and sometimes she does a bit of everything. She's a beauty, though, real antique."

Rebecca shook her head. "I thought I was dreaming. I thought I was in a battle."

"Just the battle to fire up Bessie." Dave glanced at his watch. "You've still got over an hour of shut-eye if you can get back to sleep."

"Thanks, Dave. I think I'll throw on a sweatshirt and head up on deck and wait for the sunrise. I'm awake now and doubt I'd fall back to sleep even if I tried."

Rebecca staggered back to her cabin. Grabbing her hoodie sweatshirt and yoga mat, she headed topside. As she stretched and performed her salutations, she replayed the evening's events. What had happened to her? Never in her life had a dream seemed so real. She would have sworn she was in a room with two terrorists. Their voices were as clear as a bell. Nothing about it, even now on deck with the sun starting to rise, seemed like a dream.

"Best keep this one to yourself, Becca, or Hawk will have you locked in your room 24/7," she mumbled as she exhaled and lowered her hands to the floor.

5

"Beautiful," Rebecca whispered through her final cleansing breath. The pinks and oranges of the early morning sunlight gave way to a bright blue sky. The ship's bell chimed six times, and Hawk started the generator. It was exactly seven o'clock. Rebecca rolled up her mat just as twenty-five children stampeded onto the deck. Hawk blew a long shrill whistle, instantly stopping all chatter. He explained the morning chores.

"Each of you will pick a scrub brush, sponge, or broom. When I turn the water pump on, follow behind me as I spray down the deck." He stopped by a bucket of brushes and picked one up. "Scrub every wooden surface. When the deck is spotless, get a handful of Always Bright Silver Cloth and start polishing all the brass. I want to see the glint of the sun bouncing off the bells and trim when you're done." Hawk grinned and passed the brush to Starr Gates.

A collective groan preceded the race for a broom. Seemed nobody wanted a scrub brush or sponge. Rebecca chewed on her lips so she wouldn't laugh as she watched the students start the first of their chores. Most of the girls were still in their pajamas. Images of young women begging to turn in early brought another chuckle to Rebecca. She would relish an early bedtime tonight if the girls were too tired to talk all night long.

After an hour of getting the ship into shape, the galley boy, Brian Little, rang the breakfast bell. Three dozen people greedily grabbed seats at one of the two long tables on either side of the saloon.

"Hey," Dave snapped as he placed a platter of biscuits on the beautiful cherry tabletop, "no arms or elbows on the table. They're gimbaled, boys and girls, which allows them to move and balance should the ship be in rough waters. It also means that if one of you leans on the table, everyone else could be wearing their breakfasts."

Arms jerked back and the students began passing the platters of food around. Rebecca was amazed how hungry she was. She noticed she wasn't the only one who filled a plate with scrambled eggs, biscuits, fresh fruit, and even the forbidden bacon. When she cleaned her plate and reached for a bowl of yogurt topped off with Dave's famous granola, Ashley Burns elbowed Starr Gates.

"Wow, Miss O'Neill, you never eat this much at school."

"Must be the sea air, Ashley. I'm famished. I noticed you've put a dent in those biscuits."

"Yum," Ashley mumbled while swallowing a mouthful. "They're sooo good. My brother sailed two years ago and didn't stop talking about the food for weeks. My mom got sick of him mentioning it every night at dinner."

Tess had told Rebecca numerous times that Dave made huge batches of granola on Sunday mornings before a cruise. She said it was pure torture to walk by the kitchen windows in the office and smell the tempting aromas of maple, cinnamon, and vanilla cooking with the nuts and oats. Rebecca knew firsthand that Tess had stolen more than her fair share of spoonfuls from the pans cooling on the racks.

Rebecca eyed her bowlful of yogurt and granola. "If this is a sample of what we have in store, we're all going to be talking about the food onboard."

Ashley shook her head. "I better not. My mom already told me not to come home asking for biscuits every day."

The conversation ended when Hawk sat at the head of portside table where Rebecca and the girls were eating. The captain always sat at the head of starboard table and the first mate on the left. "Good morning," Rebecca said without looking him in the eyes.

"Good morning, Rebecca. Did you sleep well?"

She faltered momentarily. "Ah, not too badly."

"What time will we sail today?" Jennifer interrupted.

Hawk stood. "Jennifer has just asked what time we will sail today. Does anyone remember from last night what rule number one is?"

A dozen voices shouted, "Never, ever ask what time we will sail."

"Good," Hawk said, sitting back down.

Jennifer blushed.

Rebecca mouthed, "It's okay," then turned to Hawk. "So, what *is* on the agenda for today?"

All ears pricked up in anticipation. Spoons stopped midway to mouths.

"The five on breakfast duty will clean up the dishes and tables while everyone else prepares their cabins for inspection. By ten we should be gathered on deck for a knot-tying course, and then I imagine everyone will be ready for a swim."

Cheers went up. A few boys took bites of food, stuffing as much into their mouths as possible while Hawk waited for the room to quiet down before continuing.

"As I said last night, Captain Roberts will arrive after lunch with the fresh fruit, vegetables, meat, and ice we'll need for the week. Once everything is unloaded and stored, the captain will decide if we sail. Everyone is expected to help store the goods. The more hands we have on deck, the sooner we're done with the work and the sooner we can sail or swim."

Rebecca raised her hand. "Sounds great. What happens at night?"

Hawk paused, staring into Rebecca's eyes.

She smiled, then squirmed, remembering last night. *Oh great,* she thought, *I hope he doesn't think I was asking about ghost stories. Better get this back on track.* "Is there a set time for supper or an evening routine?"

She watched his shoulders relax before he looked around at the kids. "We normally have dinner around seven. During dessert the captain will talk to you and the students about sailing, the *Shenandoah,* and what life was like for a sailor two hundred years ago. He'll usually spend about half an hour on a topic. Sometimes the kids play games after, though most nights they take off to their cabins as soon as the captain is done speaking."

Brian rose from the table and called the five students on galley duty to start clearing. Everyone else dispersed to their cabins. Rebecca, who was still in her sweats, took the opportunity to change into her swimsuit and pull on a pair of shorts and a T-shirt over it.

"Eh, gad!" Rebecca exclaimed when she saw a bruise on her knee. "Where the heck did that come from?"

A knock on the door shifted her focus. "Miss O'Neill, I can't find my hairbrush."

Rebecca opened her door. "Did you pack a comb, Kayla?"

"Well, I thought so, but now I can't find anything."

"Maybe one of the girls borrowed them without asking. Go check it out, and then come back if you need either. I have a few extras. Please remind your friends to go up and brush their teeth. I'm heading up now. I'll be back in five minutes if you need me."

Back in her cabin, Rebecca ran a brush through her brown locks, then wove the length of it into a braid. A blue Sox scrunchie matched her favorite Boston Red Sox T-shirt. A little sunscreen, and she was ready for the day.

She tidied up her cabin and left to check on the kids. Kayla had found her hairbrush, the girls' cabins were presentable, and Sharon had managed to dress casually elegant with a hint of makeup. Rebecca thought the sail would undoubtedly be a long journey for her.

"Morning, Sharon. I didn't see you at breakfast. How did you sleep?"

"Good morning, Rebecca. I never eat breakfast. Hope you don't mind if I skip it and put my face on instead. I expected dark circles this morning, but I actually slept fine, excluding a bit of tossing and turning and bumping into the side bars. From the looks of your leg you bumped around a bit, too."

Rebecca looked at her knee. "I have no idea what I did or when. I guess I must have bumped it in my sleep."

"Perhaps a little padding on the bedrails would save us all. Any chance you've seen Kevin Cohan this morning?" Sharon asked.

Rebecca wondered what Sharon wanted with the boys' chaperone. "Sure. He was at breakfast. He's probably with the boys now, helping them get their cabins cleaned up."

Sharon turned, waving as she went. "I'm off to find him. I told my husband I would chat with Kevin about the new clubhouse at the golf course. Randy has been after him for years. The board finally okayed the construction, and Kevin is still dragging his feet."

Rebecca cringed inwardly. She didn't need the chaperones fighting. "Ah, well, good luck. Be on deck at ten for a knot-tying course."

"I guess I must," Sharon called over her shoulder as she set forth on her mission.

*

Tying knots was fun. Rebecca remembered a couple of them from her Girl Scout days. Five crew members each took one of the five-member, student work groups and taught the kids a figure eight, a bowline, a clove hitch, a square knot, and a rolling hitch. If she practiced every day, Rebecca thought she'd be a pro by Friday.

"Last one in is a rotten egg," Tim yelled as he jumped off the starboard side.

Shirts went flying in all directions as the boys raced to the rail for their first jump. Most of the girls went below to grab a towel and change out of their shorts. Rebecca spied Kevin and Sharon chatting toward the bow. She caught Kevin's attention and let him know she was going in, too.

She dove in, welcoming the shock of the cool water, loving the refreshing jolt of the first dive. She knew many folks who couldn't stand the cooler temps of the New England waters, but she had grown up in this ocean. By the end of August the temperatures were as good as it got. Rebecca swam from June through September with occasional plunges in May or October if the weather hit seventy-five, which it sometimes did. All winter she'd walk along the shoreline counting the days till summer swimming began. She toyed with the idea of joining the Polar Bear Club, but somehow the concept of swimming in freezing cold water never won her over.

"Miss O'Neill, let's swim around the boat," Scott Jeffers challenged.

"Sure thing, but you'd better keep up!"

Twelve bodies surged through the water for multiple laps until exhaustion took over.

Laughing, Rebecca pulled up and treaded water. "I think we just worked off breakfast."

"All I care about is lunch," said Nick Gossage, heading up the ladder as the dinner bell rang. "Score! Chicken sandwiches, clam chowder, and salad for you girls who love green stuff. You all better get up here quick before the food is gone."

A delicious bowl of clam chowder and a salad carried Rebecca through the afternoon. The crew and kids made light work of storing the supplies. Captain Roberts boarded with his two Corgis, Carrot and Ginger, so named for his favorite carrot-ginger soup. The girls gathered the tailless duo in their arms and carried them around like dolls. Captain Roberts assured Rebecca the dogs expected nothing less than pure adoration.

"Get ready to sail," Tim whispered as he walked over.

"How do you know?"

"Captain just took the cover off the wheel. Whenever the cover comes off, the sails go up," Tim said with a wink.

A few seconds later Hawk bellowed, "All hands on deck."

Three dozen crew members, the hired ones and the newly enlisted smaller versions, stood at attention waiting for Hawk and Captain Roberts to dispense orders. "Form two lines, one on port side, one on starboard. We're going to raise the mainsail first. When the lines are laid out and I've given the order, pick up the line with two hands like this. Pull hand over hand," Hawk said, demonstrating the motion of holding tightly with one hand while the other hand grasped firmly further up and both pulled back together. "Keep pulling until I say 'hold.' When the crew ties up the lines, someone will call out 'up behind.' That is your command to drop the line immediately. I want to hear the line hit the deck in one loud crack."

Eager faces grabbed the lines and hauled as the mainsail and foresail went up. The captain maneuvered the ship out of the harbor and the crew raised the additional sails. Rebecca unknowingly held her breath.

"Have you been on a boat since your father died? I know Tess tried numerous times to take you out with her."

Rebecca turned to look at the kind old man, weathered from years of sailing, yet still handsome and proud, like her father had been. "No. Other than the ferry, I never went fishing on a boat again, never mind a sailboat.

Tess did try many times. I...well, I guess I wasn't ready."

"First-time sailing can change your life."

"Yes!" Rebecca tilted her face to the sun and exhaled. "I can't believe I waited so long to get back on a boat, and sailing to boot. My father is smiling down on me now. You know he loved the *Shenandoah*. I finally understand why. She's beautiful. The sails alone are splendid. I think I'll just sit here and let the world drift away."

Captain Roberts nodded as she sat on the rooftop. The sails collected the wind and the Island shrank as they moved out into the Sound and toward the Elizabeth Islands. Everyone seemed in awe. Even Sharon wore a somewhat serene expression. Kevin looked as happy as a kid on Christmas morning.

You were right, Da, Rebecca thought as she watched cumulus clouds shape and shift in the sky. *This boat is magic. I feel like I'm floating back in time. I wish I could, you know. Ride one of those clouds back to you and Ma and Gram. I would take you all sailing.*

A couple hours passed before Rebecca knew it. Captain Roberts had tucked them into Tarpaulin Cove for the night. Hawk called for the sails to be lowered. After the anchor was dropped, Hawk told the kids they could jump in. Rebecca was too peaceful to play. She sat on the rail and watched the swimmers till they were called in.

They consumed a hearty lasagna dinner with gusto before Captain Roberts called for everyone's attention and shared the history of the *Shenandoah*. His rough, gravelly voice brought forth images of sailors and pirates from long ago.

"The *Shenandoah* is a square top-sail schooner, one of only a few left. When I purchased her in 1958, I had hoped to remodel her and save the original ship, which had sailed for George Washington during the Revolution. The ship builders, the best in the business, told me she was beyond repair. I didn't want to lose her, but I knew she would rot and return to the sea if I didn't take drastic measures."

Captain Roberts paused and stood, his tall lanky frame nearly reaching the ceiling in the saloon. He moved sideways and put his right hand on the old black stove. "See this stove? She's an original. Oh, I don't believe she was the original stove, but somewhere in the *Shenandoah*'s history this stove served her captain and crew. The anchor was salvaged off the bottom of Boston Harbor. We don't know who she belonged to, but we know she's old. The swords you see overhead are also originals. The third one down on the starboard side belonged to Captain John Taylor, the *Shenandoah* captain from 1854 to 1868," Captain Roberts stated before sitting back down.

"Cool. Did he kill anybody with it?" Nick asked.

"I don't know, young man. I imagine that is possible as he sailed during the Civil War. More importantly, the boat you're on today was reconstructed as much as possible to the original plans, even reusing some of the same wood. I wanted to authenticate the *Shenandoah* as best I could. I asked the shipbuilders to make a detailed drawing of her and then they could take apart the original ship board by board and number the boards."

Nick interrupted again. "You numbered every board? That sounds nuts. I hate numbering the pages of my schoolwork. I wouldn't have wanted that job."

Almost everyone laughed. Nick appeared rather pleased with himself.

The captain nodded in agreement. "You weren't the only one who didn't want the job, son. Some people said I was crazy, said the process would take too long and cost too much. Those naysayers didn't understand what was important. If I couldn't have the original *Shenandoah*, I wanted as much of her as possible."

Scott Jeffers shot his hand up in the air repeatedly, drawing the captain's attention. Captain Roberts pointed at him.

"What did you do with the old boards? Did you build a house or a fort?"

"Every reusable board is on this ship today."

"No way" and "awesome" were uttered around the tables.

"Some of your cabins are reconstructed with original boards. Cabin 8 is completely whole, each board reused in the exact same location, though the room has been relocated to fit the new floor plan."

"Did you hear that, Miss O'Neill? That's your cabin. You can pretend you're two hundred years old and living during the Revolution, just like you talk about in school," Alexis said.

Rebecca shivered involuntarily. "I haven't reached thirty yet, Alexis. Let's not rush me into old age," she said, catching sight of Mike Natale staring at her. He looked as though he knew a secret she was supposed to know or was going to find out. Goose bumps rose on her arms before she broke eye contact.

"Who is staying in cabins 6, 7, and 9? Your cabins also have many original boards. If you run your hands along the walls, you might be able to feel the difference between the newer boards and the originals. The originals are uneven and less perfect by today's definitions. The old boards were hand cut, while many of the new ones were machine cut."

Captain Roberts paused as some of the students ran their hands along the walls behind them. A few "oohs" and "aahhs" brought a smile to his face.

"Impressive, isn't it?" Captain Roberts said with a Cheshire cat grin. "As it should be. The reconstruction took almost eight years. Since then she has sailed every summer with me as her captain. We've had her repaired and renovated four times since we put her back in the water. She measures 108 feet long at the rail, 23 feet wide, and 150 feet long from jibboom end to mainboom end. Both her masts measure 94 feet in height from the water. She carries 6,884 square feet of sail."

The numbers were impressive and staggering. Rebecca would ask again tomorrow and write it all down. She could work this into their first social studies section on the American Revolution. "Excuse me, Captain. What is she made out of?"

Captain Roberts turned to Rebecca. "Her hull is built from over 100,000 feet of native Maine oak. Her spars, or masts, are imported Oregon pine. Her lower masts are 20 inches in diameter as they pass through the deck and each weighs about two and a half tons."

"Whoa! I wouldn't have wanted to have carried those poles," Jason exclaimed.

"Or her lead," said the captain. "She carries 37 tons of lead ballast in her bilges. You can bet that was a lot of lifting."

Rebecca sat enthralled, hanging onto the captain's every word. Some of the kids were engrossed, but most were fading fast. Captain Roberts noticed the increased frequency of yawns. "I think we're all tired. I'll save the rest for another day. Off to bed for all of you."

A few minutes later a chain of cups, washcloths, and toothbrushes snaked through the saloon topside. The kids trickled below deck a few minutes later and made their way to bed. Jonathan Bateman walked by, sulking.

Kevin marched behind him. "Perhaps a night in solitary will cool his temper tomorrow," Kevin noted as he took Jonathan to Cabin 1 as punishment for his attempt to throw Mark overboard during a scuffle this afternoon.

Once all the lights were out, Rebecca closed her cabin door and shut the world away. She sighed as she climbed into bed. "This really has been a perfect day. Thanks, Lord. I'm glad I came after all. You do know best."

She closed her eyes, remembering the sun on her face, the sound of the sails catching the wind, the surge of the ship as she crested and rode the waves. A smile played on her lips as she drifted off....

6

"STOW AWAY!" Rebecca heard from somewhere in her sleep.

When a crewmember shook her awake, Rebecca panicked, fearful one of the kids was in trouble. She leaped up, bumping into a crate and stumbling into the man's arms. She didn't recognize him, which might have concerned her more than his yelling if she hadn't been worried about which child was sick or hurt.

"Stowaway," he yelled as he grabbed her by the arm and dragged her toward the door. Fear jolted Rebecca like a slap on the face. She planted her feet and stared at the oddly dressed man.

He jerked her arm and glared at her. "Walk or you'll be drug."

"Where is Hawk? And who are you?"

"We keep no birds on this boat. Now walk, Madam."

"Very funny. Hawk will not be amused when I report this."

"It is I, Madam, who is reporting you. We do not take kindly to stowaways. Captain Reed will see you hanged in the square if you are a spy for the Regulars."

Rebecca realized with frightening accuracy the man wasn't kidding. In the dim light of his lamp she looked at him and stifled a gasp. Gone were the jeans, T-shirts, and bare feet of the crew she knew.

Holy cow! He looks like he's walked off the page of a history book on Colonial Boston. Rebecca noted his square-toed black shoes, gray cloth pants that looked like a loose-fitting pair of Capris, corded belt, and white buttonless shirt. He had the part down perfectly. Rebecca tried to overcome the sinking feeling in the pit of her stomach by imagining that the man before her was Hawk's idea of a joke to get back at her for the other night.

Rebecca's eyes scanned the room. It looked familiar yet strange. No bunks, lots of crates and barrels. This was *not* her room. It was clearly a storage room, though she had no recollection of any storage area during her tour on Sunday.

That sinking feeling filled her with dread. Her stomach tightened and bile rose in her throat. The room, small and dark and packed floor to ceiling with cargo, reminded her of the dream she'd had the previous night.

"Where am I?" she whispered.

Utter frustration shone in the eyes glaring down at her. "As you well know, Madam, you are aboard the schooner *Shenandoah*. 'Twill be for Captain Reed to discover the reasons for your presence and what shall be done with you."

Rebecca felt dizzy. Something was very wrong. She had to be dreaming, yet everything seemed far too real.

The stranger grabbed her arm. She tried to jerk away, but he held fast.

"You will come with me, Madam," the man said, once again yelling, "Stowaway!"

"No!" Rebecca screamed, yanking away with all her strength and then crashing to the floor as he lost his grip.

He shot his hand out and grabbed a fistful of her brown curls. Rebecca yelled and clawed at his arm as he attempted to tow her across the floor by her hair. She couldn't see the door, but she heard the scuttle of feet rushing in their direction.

"James! Release her."

Rebecca scooted away and turned to see who had come to her rescue. James, with hatred's fire burning in his eyes, blocked her view of the new voice.

"She refused to walk," James spat out in his defense.

"A woman? Who is she?"

"She has not said, Captain." James moved aside to let the second man in.

Rebecca glanced at his face in the light of the flame and trembled. "You!" she gasped before fainting....

*

The sharp pungency of ammonia burned Rebecca's nose and throat. She opened her eyes slowly to see four faces staring down at her. An older man was holding a glass vial that he probably had waved under her nose and was the reason she wanted to gag. She recognized two of the other men from her dream, or what she had thought and hoped was a dream, but she didn't know which one was Ben or which one was Jonah. She needed to sit up. Lying in the bunk, which was definitely not hers, with four worried-looking men staring at her, made Rebecca feel like a bug under a magnifying glass.

She observed their appearances: more Colonial seaman than what she envisioned a terrorist would be. Still, they didn't look like any crew she knew on the *Shenandoah*. She shifted her weight and sat up, tossing aside the coarse blanket someone had been kind enough to place over her.

"Where are her clothes?" Rebecca heard one of the men whisper. "Why does she have lines on her skin?"

Expressions of shock crossed the men's faces. She could have sworn the youngest of them blushed, and all of them looked uncomfortable. They acted stupefied, as though they'd never seen sweats, a tank top, and tan lines before.

"Mayhap this is the sleepwear in her country," said the taller of the two from last night. "She does not appear to be dressed as such to garner companionship."

"Garner compansionship?!" He thinks I might be a call girl! Now I know I'm dreaming!

Rebecca tugged on her shirt, suddenly quite grateful she had thrown on sweats instead of her favorite pajama shorts. Her circumstances no longer felt like a dream, but they had to be. "Where am I?" she asked. "What happened to me?"

"You are on the schooner *Shenandoah*. Adam, our cook and medical man, insisted we lift ye to the cot," said the younger of the two terrorists. "You fainted. Fortunately you were already on the floor when ye swooned, so I doubt you shall be bumped or bruised. Adam gave thee a whiff of smelling salts to bring you round."

Rebecca needed to move. Everything was wrong, and she needed to figure out where she was without arousing suspicion. "Would it be okay if I stood up? I feel much better now."

"By all means, Madam. Let us walk to the saloon where we can talk." The man speaking was very formal, probably the leader of this group. He stepped back and made room for Rebecca to stand.

She smiled at him. "May I have a cup of tea, please?"

Three sets of eyes grew wide. The older man shook his head. "Tea? From whence do you come, Madam? We haven't carried tea onboard since the spring Tea Party. Would you like a mug of coffee?"

She shook her head to the man she assumed was Adam. "No, thank you. I don't believe my stomach is ready for coffee."

"Aye, someone has already warned her about Adam's coffee," joked the youngest in the group. He seemed innocent and kind, yet last night he had spoken of war and bloodshed. Rebecca had no desire to be deceived by boyish charms and good looks.

The leader reached out a hand and touched Rebecca's elbow. Shockwaves spread through her. She wanted to rub her arm. He must have had something in his hand. Rebecca tried to see if he had concealed a buzzer or something. He had to be using something.

Rebecca tilted her head up and stared into the most gorgeous brown eyes she'd ever seen. He looked annoyed, not as though he'd just felt something peculiar or done something funny. He was either a fantastic actor, or she'd imagined that tingling sensation. He urged her forward, giving her elbow a nudge, and led her down past the galley and into the saloon.

She recognized the old stove and felt a momentary sense of relief. They sat on the starboard side, Mr. Electric sitting in the captain's place. Rebecca took a seat on an outside bench, noting there were no swords on the walls. She wondered if they had confiscated them for use as weapons.

Adam brought out a mug steaming with coffee. The aroma was too strong for Rebecca's stomach after the smelling salts and made her a bit queasy. She longed for a cup of chamomile tea, or maybe the ginger-peach would help settle her nerves and her stomach.

While her captor enjoyed half a cup of coffee, Rebecca sized him up. He was over six feet, rather well built, clean shaven, fantastic eyes, not much older than her and, well, pretty darn handsome. He put his mug down on the table. "Madam, perhaps now would be the appropriate time for you to explain your presence here on my ship?"

"Your ship?" Rebecca asked.

Dark eyes with amber flecks locked formally with hers. "Allow me the introductions. I am Captain Benjamin Reed. The young scrapper on my right is my youngest brother, Jonah. The gentleman seated on your right is James Packer, and Adam Greene has seen to your, ah, ailment. Now may we have the pleasure of your given name?"

"Rebecca. Rebecca O'Neill."

"Mrs. O'Neill…"

She shook her head. "No, just Rebecca."

"I am sorry for your loss, Madam. The skirmish with the King's Men has taken too large a toll on many families."

Rebecca cast her eyes down, avoiding the truth and any questions he might have asked. *Better to let him believe I had a husband than to try to explain something I can't explain to myself.*

"How did you happen upon *Shenandoah?*"

Rebecca raised her head. "I don't know. I was sleeping in my bed and the next thing I knew I was in a strange room, and he was yelling at me, calling me a stowaway," she said pointing to James Packer.

"Was your ship attacked?"

"I don't think so, unless you and your crew are terrorists. All I can tell you is that I fell asleep in my bunk, and I woke up in that room."

Captain Reed frowned. "Madam, that is illogical at best. Surely you do not suggest your tale as fact?"

Fury rose inside Rebecca. She hated being called a liar. "But it is the truth. I was sleeping on the *Shen…*ship and then I woke up on your boat. Whether you believe me or not, I have no idea how I got here and, trust me, I wish I could go home this very second. You think I want to be here?"

Jonah leaned over toward his brother. "She talks funny, a bit like Aunt Missy."

Startled, Rebecca leaned forward.

Captain Reed nodded at his brother. "I noticed the same, Jonah."

Rebecca shifted uncomfortably as the two men stared at her. The ship's bell chimed four times, breaking the silence.

"It is late. I suspect no further discussion will yield the truth this evening. Jonah and James, please return to your cabin. Adam and I will see Mrs. O'Neill settled. We will talk in the morning when everyone is rested and has had time to ponder the evening's events."

Captain Reed stood and gently guided Rebecca down the hall. She moved slowly, her brain working overtime. *Think, Becca, think. You know you're on the* Shenandoah. *You've learned enough about the boat in the last two days to recognize the layout. We're walking toward the boys' cabins. So where are the cabins? Where is everyone? Where the heck am I? Better yet,* when *am I?*

Their short walk ended before Rebecca had answered a single question cavorting through her mind. Captain Reed had led her back to the room she had arrived in. She recognized it immediately. *No way. This is Cabin 1! At least, this morning it was. Now, here, wherever here is, this room is not a cabin.*

Rebecca noticed someone had crammed a cot up against the wall near the door. The room was otherwise cluttered with crates and barrels stacked floor to ceiling.

The captain walked toward the cot, shining the light on the small bed. "You should be reasonably comfortable, Mrs. O'Neill. Donald made up a cot for you. Please consider the state you are in and prepare yourself for a lengthy conversation in the morning. You are in grave danger. Reflect on your situation, and we shall discuss what happens next in the morning."

Rebecca was about to speak, but Captain Reed shook his head. "Think, please. There will be a guard at the door throughout the night. Rest well."

Rebecca trembled. "The guard, he will not be James, will he?"

The captain's expression softened. "No, James has retired for the evening."

Rebecca's sigh of relief was audible. "Thank God for small favors."

A flicker of recognition or something like it crossed the captain's face.

"What is it, Captain?"

His eyes seemed to assess more than her outward appearance. "You remind me of someone. I would be remiss to judge you too quickly. Until morning, then." He moved past her toward the door.

Rebecca remembered Jonah's words at the table. "Who?"

He stopped in the doorway and turned back. "Pardon?"

She took a step toward him. "Who do I remind you of?"

"My Aunt Missy."

"Missy?" Rebecca asked with a shaky voice.

He appeared puzzled. "My uncle met her five years ago on the *Shenandoah*. She was in a similar predicament as you find yourself. Unusual, to say the least." Without so much as a good night, the captain closed the door, leaving Rebecca in the dark.

Rebecca told herself over and over that this *had* to be a dream. She knew it wasn't, but it had to be. She sank onto the cot and heard the lock click.

The captain was talking about Melissa Smith. He had to be! Rebecca considered the very real possibility of the captain's Aunt Missy and Melissa Smith being one and the same. She considered the very real possibility that what was happening to her was probably what had happened to Melissa. But Rebecca wondered why Melissa didn't come back. Had she gotten stuck in the eighteenth century?

Rebecca had few doubts now that Melissa had crossed a time barrier. The coincidence was too close to cast aside as unthinkable.

The captain said five years ago. It has to be Melissa. Rebecca wondered if Melissa had stayed in the same cabin. A nervous chuckle escaped Rebecca's lips as she contemplated the young man isolated in Cabin 1 at the moment…well, at one moment in time, at least. She guessed Jonathan Bateman would be scared beyond words if she magically appeared in his room. He might even be horrified enough to behave himself for the rest of the trip.

How ironic that a small room had been used to isolate prisoners, drunken sailors, and obnoxious fifth graders for centuries. Rebecca sobered quickly. None too amusing now that she was one of those prisoners.

Rebecca lay down, her hands shaking and body weak. If only her Gram were there.

"Dear Lord," Rebecca whispered, "please don't leave me here. Could you ask Gram to swoop on down and bring me back to my class trip? I know I complained an awful lot about going on the trip, but I've learned my lesson. I promise I have. I'll be forever grateful to see all those kids tomorrow morning. Amen."

Rebecca listened to the murmurs of the men on deck, unable to make out their words. She felt the gentle rocking of the ship, heard the bells ringing again, and succumbed to exhaustion....

*

Ben paced the floor in his cabin, uneasy questions racing: *Who is this woman? Is she friend or foe? How did she board my ship? And why does she remind me so much of Missy?*

He sat on the edge of his bed and pulled his boots off. He lay down, folding his hands behind his head. The oil lamp's light flickered on the ceiling. He thought of her hazel eyes and the way her hair fell off her shoulders. She was beautiful, stunning—even in the odd garb she wore.

So where are you from, Mrs. Rebecca O'Neill?

He leaned over and turned down the lamp. In the darkness he fought off fatigue and tried to recall his uncle's account of Missy's arrival on the *Shenandoah*. He lost the battle to sleep before he could remember a thing. Any answers would have to wait until morning.

7

A KNOCK ON THE DOOR ROUSED REBECCA. She opened her eyes and noticed her book and flashlight. She bolted up and opened the door. Jessica Andrews was standing there talking about lost toothpaste and wondering if Rebecca had any extra. "Thank You, Lord," Rebecca said aloud.

"Miss O'Neill, are you talking to God about me?" Jessica smirked.

"Yes. No, Jessica. I was just offering thanks for this beautiful morning with all you kids. Now, what did you need?" Rebecca knew she probably sounded a bit too cheery.

"Um, toothpaste. Are you feeling okay, Miss O'Neill? You missed your workout this morning."

Rebecca searched in her bag and extracted a travel-size tube of toothpaste. She handed it to Jessica and patted her on the arm. "I feel great...just needed an extra hour of sleep, I guess. Now put this in your cabin and get up on deck to help with the chores. I'll be up in a few minutes."

"No prob. Thanks, Miss O'Neill."

Rebecca closed her cabin door and slid to the lower bunk. Tears sprang to her eyes. She held her head in her hands and allowed herself a few minutes to recover. "I don't know what is going on, but last night wasn't a dream. I've got to talk to someone. Maybe Mike has done some research, or maybe Captain Roberts knows something."

Morning chores were over before Rebecca had time to talk to Mike. The breakfast bell rang, and everyone headed below deck. Rebecca barely had time to dress and compose herself. She decided to sit at the starboard table hoping Captain Roberts would join the kids for breakfast and she might be able to ask him a few carefully worded questions.

Steaming platters of pancakes and sausages were passed around, the aroma scarcely enticing Rebecca's appetite. She put a pancake on her plate, skipped the sausage, and waited for the fruit bowl to make its rounds. She replayed last night's events over and over in her mind.

"Miss O'Neill, do you want some fruit?" Raz Clewiston nudged Rebecca's arm with the bowl.

"What?"

"I asked if you wanted some fruit. Three times, Miss O'Neill. I think you're in a funk."

"I'm sorry, Raz. Daydreaming, I guess. Thank you."

Rebecca scooped some fruit onto her plate. The few pieces of pineapple and watermelon looked more like garnishes than breakfast.

A shadow moved over Rebecca. "Not too hungry this morning, Miss O'Neill?"

The smile on Mike's face did nothing to hide the edge in his voice. His question was more accusation than interest in her appetite. She hadn't seen him come into the saloon. Now he was hovering over her, apparently waiting for a response. Rebecca shrugged and lifted a piece of pineapple to her lips. She remembered Mike's enthusiasm and insistence the first night up on deck. He had seemed genuinely concerned about Melissa and what had become of her.

But something about the way he was watching her now chilled Rebecca. She decided he would not be the person to talk to, at least not right now. She needed time with Captain Roberts. Too bad Tess wasn't around to answer her questions. Maybe she could risk sneaking a phone call later if the captain was too busy.

Galley Crew 2 handled breakfast duty, while the remaining students prepared their cabins for morning inspection. Rebecca made her bed, then stood in the center of her small cabin. She pivoted slowly, moving her feet an inch at a time. She scanned her eyes over every board, every fixture. She saw nothing out of place, nothing that made her cabin different from the others. "Well, maybe that huge knot in the board between the bunks, but I doubt I would fit through there," she joked without a chuckle.

A knock on the door halted any further investigation.

"Cabin inspection. Are you ready to present?" Hawk announced in a playfully formal voice.

Rebecca opened her door and stood at attention. Hawk smiled, melting the ice chip he'd lodged two nights ago.

"Come in, sir." Rebecca raised her hand to her head in mock salute.

"At ease, Madam." Hawk tossed a quarter in his hand as his eyes roamed the cabin. "Do you think it will bounce, Madam?"

"Bounce?"

"Off your mattress, of course. If the sheets are tight, the quarter should bounce."

"And if it doesn't bounce? What happens to the poor sailor?"

Hawk gave Rebecca a sobering look. "Well, Madam, the poor slob cleans the head for a week."

Rebecca pinched her nose and waved her right hand in front of her face. "Eh gads! I don't believe I could handle that."

Hawk grinned and tossed the quarter off a flick of his thumb and caught it deftly in his right hand. He took a step toward her bunk. "May I?" he asked, holding the quarter directly over her neatly made bed.

"By all means, sir," she said, bowing extravagantly out of his way.

Hawk dropped the quarter and caught it deftly in his right hand as it bounced back. Rebecca felt a ridiculous sense of relief. She giggled, at first just a small bubble escaping her lips. Suddenly all her tension and turmoil turned into the sillies. She giggled uncontrollably, wrapped her arms around her stomach, doubling over at the waist. Hawk eyed her sideways, and she burst into another fit of laughter.

"You are easily amused."

Another round of giggles erupted. "Oh, gosh. Sorry. It's just...I don't know what it is. Thank you, though. I think I needed that."

Hawk raised a brow in mock disdain. "You're welcome, I think. Now if I may continue my inspection?"

Rebecca giggled again. "Please do."

Hawk scrutinized every inch of the cabin. He spent minutes, more than she'd seen him spend yesterday. Rebecca felt he might be stalling more than inspecting. After making a few check marks on his clipboard, he swiveled toward the doorway, then stopped. "I'm sorry about the other night. I shouldn't have yelled."

"I'm sorry, too. You asked me not to talk about Melissa, and I did. My Irish curiosity got the best of me."

Hawk almost smiled, then crossed his arms around the clipboard. "Now that it's out of your system, let's put it behind us."

Rebecca looked away. She had more questions now than ever.

"Rebecca? You will drop it, right?"

She shuffled her feet. "Well, I can't say I'm not curious, Hawk. I would love to know more about the ship and about Melissa."

"Ask me anything you want about the *Shenandoah*, just drop the Melissa questions. Captain Roberts mentioned you are friends with Tess. You should know this is a touchy subject."

"Taboo is more like it."

"Exactly. So stick to the *Shenandoah*. You'll get more information than you could have imagined."

Rebecca's face brightened, and her tension eased away. Maybe she could find out some information without directly talking about Melissa. "I do have a ton of questions. And I'm relieved to know we are on speaking terms again."

Hawk almost laughed. "Do I come off as that much of an ogre?"

Rebecca lifted one shoulder. "Maybe a little."

Hawk drew himself up to full commanding position, a smile playing on his lips. "Good. Perhaps that will keep you all in line."

Rebecca blushed, cursing that ridiculous trait she'd inherited from her mother. She'd never been able to get away with anything because her scarlet cheeks betrayed her.

"I'll take your silence as agreement." Hawk saluted. "Talk to me later. There are some great stories about the ship I would be happy to share."

She returned his salute. "Thanks. I look forward to it."

*

Rebecca was at peace when she went up on deck for the rigging lesson. Josh broke the kids into their work crews. Rebecca went with Crew 1, Sharon with Crew 2, and Kevin with Crew 3. They stood midship with charts in hand.

Josh explained, "The *Shenandoah* has thirty-one points on her basic rigging plan. Most of the rigging is duplicated—outer jib sheet starboard and outer jib sheet portside. With a few exceptions you can learn the location on one side of the boat and know it for both sides."

An hour later Hawk was calling out the names of the rigging pins as the kids raced to identify the pins and earn points for their teams. "Lower brace starboard."

Nick ran toward the stern of the boat and placed his hand atop the first of five belay pins on the last cap rail.

"Yes," Hawk boomed. "Last one: outer jib halyard."

Alexis found the lone freestanding peg on the portside.

"Great job. Let's tally up those points and see which team won a T-shirt."

While Hawk counted the winning points, Rebecca's stomach growled as she watched Brian laying out lunch on the roof of the cabin house. She had barely eaten any breakfast, and now she was starving.

"Crew 4," Hawk announced. Amidst the high-fives and cheers, Brian rang the lunch bell.

Lobster bisque, meatball subs, salad, and a large bowl of fruit all called to Rebecca. She heaped her plate, filled a bowl, and went to sit with Sharon, who had a small portion of salad on her plate and a cardboard cylinder containing some drink in her hand.

"Looks like somebody is hungry," Sharon remarked, patting her taut stomach.

Rebecca ignored the woman's tone. "Famished. How can you resist Dave's lobster bisque?"

"Too many calories and fat grams for me. I brought along these protein shakes expecting the food might not be great."

Rebecca rolled her eyes. "Not great? Are you kidding me? The food is wonderful. I haven't eaten this well since my Gram died."

Sharon waved a finger. "Oh, I didn't mean the food isn't good, just not good for me. You seem to be naturally thin, Rebecca, but I have to work at it. One week of this food and I'd be paying for it for a month."

Rebecca let it go. She took an extra large bite of her meatball sub and nodded, hoping Sharon would drop it. Sharon was too involved in makeup and weight control for Rebecca's taste. Plus, she didn't want any of the girls listening to an extremely thin woman, much thinner than Rebecca, complain about calories. These poor girls were heading into their teenage years and didn't need anyone burdening them down with body image issues. The Good Lord knew magazines, television, and their peers threw enough at them already. Rebecca ate heartily until her plate was clean.

"Who's ready to fly?"

The sun was high in the baby blue sky when Josh announced he was climbing the rigging to hang the rope swing. Sharon volunteered to watch the kids. She had no interest in swinging on the rope. Rebecca and Kevin lined up with the kids. Rebecca couldn't remember the last time she'd jumped off a rope swing. She climbed up onto the railing, grabbed the yellow rope, and jumped. Screaming with delight, she held on until the last possible second. Hitting the water with a great splash, she allowed the coolness to soak into her skin. The kids all jumped and raced back to the boat for another turn. Rebecca opted to float, lying on her back, relishing the salt water caressing her skin.

After half an hour of floating and playing Olympic judge to the students' leaps and dives off the rope, Rebecca climbed up the ladder, grabbed her towel, and found a comfortable spot on deck to warm up in the sun. She closed her eyes, contemplating the good life, which she was surely living at that very moment....

*

"Let me go," Rebecca screamed, certain James Packer had hold of her again.

"Whoa. Relax." Mike stood beside her, and half the kids were staring at them. "The captain has called you twice."

"Sorry, Mike. I must have drifted off."

"Must have been some nightmare, huh?"

Rebecca blushed. "You startled me. I wasn't even dreaming, just lost in thought."

"Care to share any of those thoughts?" Mike sounded sweet, but a chill swept through Rebecca once again. She couldn't put her finger on it, but something about him didn't sit well with her.

"I was thinking this is the life," Rebecca admitted to the half-truth. "Where's the captain?"

"At the helm. Why don't you ask him about Melissa?"

Rebecca stood, picked up her towel, and turned toward the stern. "Melissa who?" she tossed over her shoulder, pretending she had no interest.

Captain Roberts pulled the cover off the wheel, and Hawk called for all hands on deck. The children lined up equally on both sides of the ship. Rebecca stood by Captain Roberts quietly as he gave the orders, and the crew raised the sails. When the foresail was catching wind and the lines were tied, Captain Roberts turned to Rebecca.

"Hurricane Izzy is moving up the East Coast. She's not expected to be here until the weekend. With any luck she'll hit land and die down to a tropical storm. If we get really lucky, she'll hit the Chesapeake area, turn, and head out to sea."

Rebecca gazed up at the beautiful blue sky with only a scattering of puffy white clouds. "Are we in danger? Should we go home?"

The captain placed a hand on the wheel and gazed out at the expansive sea before them. "It is hard to believe on a day like today how the sea can rage and roar and swallow ships whole. Somewhere today she is swelling with waves we don't ever want to see. Not here, though, and probably not this week. Today is Tuesday. We shouldn't see any signs of Izzy until Thursday night, Friday if she slows down, which she should. I just wanted to apprise you of the situation and to confirm you had a call list for the parents in case we need to return a day early."

"Yes, I have the list and I have a cell phone, as do Sharon and Kevin."

"I expected you would. I will keep you posted if anything changes. For now, let's enjoy this fabulous weather and hope for the best."

The conversation was over. Rebecca had a dozen questions on the tip of her tongue, but she knew her time was up. The captain looked miles away, lost in his thoughts. Rebecca stepped up onto the roof, laid her towel down, and stretched out in the sun. She watched the sails fill and billow. She rolled over onto her stomach and picked up her book.

Rebecca heard Captain Roberts bark an order. She glanced up to see Tim and a few of the crew raising another sail.

Captain Roberts grinned, his eyes focusing across the expanse of sea. From the glint in his eyes, Rebecca would swear he was sailing to win the America's Cup. She could tell the ship had picked up speed, not only by the smile on the captain's face, but also by the feel of the boat rising and falling over the waves. "How fast are we moving, Captain?"

"About eight knots now. The wind is perfect today. We're going to have her at full sail shortly and should reach twelve knots or better."

The crew moved fluidly, hoisting the three smaller sails, then tying off lines until the *Shenandoah* was moving across the water in all her regal splendor.

"Oh, Da." Rebecca sighed.

Captain Roberts approached Rebecca and she stood. "She does take your breath away. I never tire of sailing her. Plenty of days I wish I could take her out and sail until the winds stop."

"My dad would have given just about anything to go with you. You know he loved this boat. She was his favorite ship in the harbor, probably on the planet."

Captain Roberts patted Rebecca's shoulder. "I wish I had taken him sailing. I saw him many mornings heading out with Paddy in the *Siobhan*. Never had a chance to say more than 'Good morning' or to ask about a catch on those days I saw them coming in."

Rebecca grinned. "He told me stories of the *Shenandoah*, of the battles she fought, the secret missions she sailed, and of her great speed and stealth."

Captain Roberts nodded. "Many of the battles she fought in were more folktale than fact, I believe. She was only set with eight cannons, enough to defend but hardly adequate to wage war. Her greatest accomplishments were the missions she completed carrying much needed supplies."

Rebecca got up and walked to the rail to stand beside the captain. "My father told me she was captured once during the Revolution."

Captain Roberts gripped the wheel, a faraway expression settling in his eyes. "Your father was a true Irishman, loved a good tale. No one knows for certain if the *Shenandoah* was captured, though it makes for a good story. It is rumored she was. The ship's logs from the summer of 1775 through 1776 were either lost or destroyed. In General Washington's notes there is mention a schooner was captured on June 28, 1776 by the British ship *Greyhound*, and then retaken by an American sloop. The names of both American ships are unknown. Many believe it was the *Shenandoah*. I'd like to think so."

Rebecca took a deep breath, wanting yet not wanting the answer to the question on the tip of her tongue. "Do you know who the captain was then?"

"Now that I can tell you. I have a list of all her captains from the day she first sailed. A fellow named Benjamin Reed was at the helm in 1775."

"Perfect," Rebecca exclaimed while placing both hands on the rooftop to steady herself.

Captain Roberts reached out a hand to help her. "Are you okay? Not getting seasick on me, are you?"

Rebecca waved off his hand and tried to quiet the pounding of her heart, certain Captain Roberts could hear the racing thumps. She pasted a smile on her face and met his gaze. "I'm fine, really. Benjamin Reed, huh? I think I read about him. Wasn't his brother on the boat, too?"

The captain relaxed his stance. "Well done, Rebecca. You've done your research."

"I wouldn't say I did any research, Captain. I came across the information accidently one night."

"There were three Reed brothers who fought in the War: Benjamin and Jonah, who both sailed on the *Shenandoah*, and Magnus, who was killed at Bunker Hill."

Rebecca sank back against the rail. "Oh, no! Are you sure? I don't remember a third brother. I only met Benjamin and Jonah."

Captain Roberts went still and stared at Rebecca as if she had two heads. "Met?"

Great, Becca, explain that one, she thought. "Oh, I didn't mean here or in town. I Googled the *Shenandoah*'s history on my computer. I don't remember anything about a dead brother, though."

Captain Roberts' face relaxed, the sharp creases releasing into sun-baked wrinkles.

In for a penny, in for a pound, thought Rebecca. "Do you know how long Benjamin Reed was Captain of the *Shenandoah?*"

"Land ho. Nashawena Island," Tim called out.

The quiet ship instantly became a flurry of activity. Captain Roberts called out commands. Tim hollered for the kids who had gone below to come up on deck. The crew lowered the smaller sails; then Hawk ordered the kids to form equal lines on each side of the fore boom.

"Quiet!" Hawk yelled as the crew prepared to lower the sail so the kids could fold, or flake as sailors said, the canvas neatly on top of the boom. "There is no talking during flaking time. Flaking time is quiet time, everybody's favorite time."

The kids groaned. Hawk scowled. The crew began lowering the foresail. Hawk instructed the kids on starboard side to push the sail over the boom, then step back as the kids on port side folded the sail over to them and continued until the sail was neatly flaked atop the boom. The exercise was repeated with the mainsail.

"Work crews, report for duty." Hawk ordered the students into their five work groups and paired them off with a crew member. He had promised they would learn Flemish coils and the moment had arrived. The lengths of rope used to hoist and lower the sails lay on deck like sunning snakes, a totally unacceptable condition on the neat and tidy *Shenandoah*.

The students quickly learned to roll the ropes into huge coils, beginning with a large outer loop and slowly twirling the rope tightly along the inside until the lines formed a tight coil resembling one of those giant lollipops with the ridges and strips of color.

A half hour later Kevin walked over to Rebecca. "The boys are asking to swim. Do you think there is time before dinner?"

She glanced about. "Probably. Why don't you ask Hawk?"

A mass disrobing let Rebecca know Hawk had said yes. She wanted to swim, too, but if Captain Roberts were free, she would rather find out more about Benjamin Reed. She searched the deck and didn't see him. He'd probably gone into his quarters to rest before dinner.

Rebecca shed her shorts and shirt, climbed up onto the cap rail, and dove in.

"That was only a six, Miss O'Neill."

"Oh, really, Casey? Let's see what you've got."

"Diving contest," Casey announced.

Everyone in the water raced to the ladder.

Sharon, dressed in khaki shorts and a peach-colored Ralph Lauren polo, was elected judge. Pretty dives, goofy dives, artistic dives, and the ever-popular cannonball were all judged until Brian called for Galley Crew 5 to set up for dinner. Rebecca made a beeline to her cabin. She knew most of the kids would merely slip on shorts and a T-shirt and eat in their swimsuits. She, however, wanted dry clothes and a towel to dry her hair.

*

When Captain Roberts took his seat at the head of starboard table, heaping platters of chicken and vegetables and potatoes were passed around. Rebecca ate heartily, eager to discover what the topic would be during dessert.

Two trays of apple crisp were brought out. Captain Roberts leaned back and settled in for his nightly talk. "Does everyone know that Hurricane Izzy is traveling up the East Coast?"

A mixture of head nods and shakes let the captain know he had the kids' attention. He explained the conditions of the sea during a hurricane, the movement of a hurricane, and the dangers of being caught in one, and he told a short story about a time the *Shenandoah* had to be towed into a nearby harbor when a nasty storm threatened a school trip. Rebecca might have been interested if she hadn't been wishing for more history on the ship and a chance to ask about Benjamin Reed. When the captain was done, the group of yawning kids got ready for bed.

Once the kids were bunked down, it was time to find Hawk. Rebecca went up on deck to brush her teeth and wet her hair down so she could put some conditioner in it to help untangle some of the knots brought on by a day of standing in the wind. Before she went back down, she casually asked where the first mate was. Discovering he'd gone to bed, she returned to her cabin muttering to herself. "I might as well go to sleep, too. I won't be getting any answers tonight."

The cool crisp evening air of August was the perfect weather for sleeping on a ship. Rebecca pulled on her sweatpants and a T-shirt. Her pulse quickened as she worked the conditioner into her hair and then brushed the tangles out of her curly mess. Surely she would stay in her own bunk tonight. But just in case, Rebecca figured it couldn't hurt to do something to ensure she remained in the twenty-first century and out of the stockades.

Rebecca rummaged through her duffle bag until she found a cloth belt. Acknowledging that she might be going to extremes, Rebecca still thought tying herself to the bedrail might not be a bad idea.

She picked up her flashlight, as well, and crawled up into her bunk. Strapping her right wrist to the sturdy wood frame of the bunk rail, she lay down on her back. After switching on her flashlight, she took a deep breath and closed her eyes.

The noise in her head kept her awake. She started twitching her left toes back and forth, nervous energy getting the best of her. Rebecca refused to open her eyes, stubbornly willing herself to run through the alphabet backwards. "Z, Y, X, W, V, U, T, S..." Somewhere in the midst of her fourth trip through the alphabet, Rebecca gave herself up to sleep.

8

BANG...BANG...BANG...

Rebecca rolled over onto her left side and opened her eyes to total darkness. *Bang...clang. It's just the stove, Becca. Go back to sleep.*

Rebecca rolled back onto her right side. Plumping the lumpy pillow under her head, she tucked her right hand under her chin. Her body went rigid. She lifted her right hand slowly, hoping the belt would still be attached.

"No," she whimpered, sitting up quickly. "Maybe it's in the bed somewhere."

Rebecca patted the blanket frantically in search of her belt and flashlight, dreading the truth she already knew. "So much for tying myself down," she shouted into the dark. "This is not funny, God. I want to go home. Now! Before James Packer decides to have me keelhauled."

Silence engulfed the room. She wondered who was up and about on the ship. She knew Adam was awake as the stove was lit, which also meant it was around 5:00 a.m. She considered her circumstances. How much time did she have before someone came to get her? And what were they going to do with her today?

She crept slowly to the door and wiggled the handle. Still locked. "Goodie for you! Last night your locked door didn't stop me from going home," Rebecca yelled as she slammed her fist into her left hand. She stomped back to her cot mindless of the near-dark room and the obstacles of crates and barrels. She dropped down with a thud. "Argh!"

Her mind raced over the last twenty-four hours. She woke in the middle of the night in 1775, was taken prisoner as a stowaway, questioned, locked in this room, then woke up again with her kids on the *Shenandoah*, spent the day with the kids free and relaxed, then went to bed all in the twenty-first century and now woke up again in 1775. Add into that her no-longer-a-dream episode on Sunday night, and she'd now awakened in the night for the three evenings in a row on the original *Shenandoah*.

Nothing made any sense. She couldn't figure out how she was moving through time, never mind how to get home. Her stomach flipped. Her heart ached. She'd known loneliness since her grandmother's death, but never so poignantly as now. Her empty little house on Skiff Avenue sounded pretty fantastic at the moment.

Rebecca dropped to her knees. "Lord, help. I don't know how I got here in this time. I want to trust You, but I'm scared, and I really want to go home. I know You work all things out for my good, but if they throw me overboard and I drown, I don't see how that will be for my good. Please, please, please help me. Amen."

"Praying always helps to ease my mind."

"Ahhh!" Rebecca spun around on her knees and looked up into the face of Benjamin Reed. "What are you doing here? Haven't you heard of knocking?"

"My apologies, Madam, I did not mean to startle you. And I did knock. I will, however, remind you that you are a prisoner on my ship, and I am not required to knock."

Rebecca got to her feet, brushing the dust and dirt off her knees. "I am well aware you consider me your prisoner, Captain Reed. I would hope, however, that you and your crew would treat a lady with a modicum of respect."

The captain lowered his eyes to the floor. "Again, Mrs. O'Neill, I apologize for interrupting your prayer."

Rebecca noticed a softening in his voice. "Do you pray, Captain Reed?"

He appeared surprised. "Of course, Mrs. O'Neill."

Relief washed over Rebecca like a salve on her battered nerves. Surely God had sent the captain to help her. She offered a silent, heartfelt, "Thank You, Lord," before stepping closer to Benjamin Reed. She needed his friendship, at the very least his compassion. Would he listen to her story? Could she even explain her story? Maybe it would be better to talk about something easy, Rebecca mused.

"When I was a child, I used to pray with my Gram. The night she died I was holding her hand, asking the Lord to give her peace and bring her home. She squeezed my hand and told me to always keep the lines of communication open with God. I haven't been as faithful in my prayer life as I promised her."

Captain Reed hung the lamp he was carrying on a hook by the door, then faced Rebecca. "The Most High knows your heart, Mrs. O'Neill. My father preaches on the Holy Spirit, on His intervention on our behalf, especially when we neglect to pray or are at a loss for words."

"My Gram used to say the same thing."

The captain nodded. "She sounds like a fine woman."

Rebecca took a step closer, noting the kindness in his eyes, the way they filled with love when he spoke of his family. *He must be a good man. Someone to help me, not harm me.* She wanted to know more about him, to figure out if he could be trusted to help get her home. "So your parents are still alive?"

The captain smiled and then examined Rebecca's face. "Yes, they are. You mentioned yesterday you were alone. Is this to say your parents have passed, as well as your husband and grandmother?"

Loneliness swamped Rebecca, and tears threatened. She wanted a hug. She needed to be strong. "Please, just Rebecca," she said through a constricting throat. "You're lucky to have your parents, Captain Reed. My father died in an accident when I was eleven. My mom died two years later, I'm convinced, of a broken heart. She cried herself to sleep almost every night. It was the saddest sound I've ever heard."

And the reason I vowed never to lose my heart to any man.

A few tears rolled down Rebecca's cheeks. She brushed them aside, embarrassed and determined not to appear weak.

The captain reached out and squeezed her hand, turning it over gently and placing his handkerchief in her right hand. She felt those tingles again, the ones she'd felt the first time he'd touched her. She wondered if maybe it had anything to do with her time traveling. Perhaps her body wasn't quite her own or maybe human contact wasn't allowed for some reason. Rebecca couldn't figure it out, but something was different when he touched her.

"Captain!" James Packer barked as he entered the cabin.

Benjamin Reed moved away from Rebecca as if she had been branded with a scarlet A. "Good morning, James. I was talking to Mrs. O'Neill."

Rebecca cringed when James flashed a menacing grin. "Are we taking the prisoner to Boston today, Captain?"

Captain Reed sighed. "Yes, James, we will sail toward Boston today."

Packer sneered. "Good. I'm in the mood for a hanging."

Rebecca gasped. "What?"

The captain stepped between James and Rebecca. "James, you will refrain from such talk in front of Mrs. O'Neill. We have yet to prove she is a spy. She will not be condemned on my ship without due cause."

Packer grumbled under his breath. The captain took a step in his direction. "Have you something to say, James?"

Rebecca glimpsed around the captain's shoulder and saw James open his mouth to speak and then shut it quickly. "Nay, Captain. The truth will out. I can wait."

Ben's jaw stiffened. "Good. As you pass the galley please ask Adam to

50

bring us a couple of mugs of coffee."

Packer glared at Rebecca, then shook his head in disgust. "Whatever you say, Ben, I mean, Captain."

Captain Reed turned his attention back to Rebecca and the muscles in his jaw relaxed. "I apologize for James. He lost his best friend in the battle at Lexington. He hates anything and anyone for the King."

"I'm not British, Captain."

His tall frame stiffened. He ran a hand through his dark auburn hair. Brown eyes met hazel. "We are all British, Mrs. O'Neill. The only question is to whom are you loyal."

Rebecca stood tall and met his gaze. "I'm an American. I swear to you. My family emigrated from Ireland before I was born."

When the captain raised an eyebrow, she knew immediately that she had said something wrong.

"An American? I haven't heard anyone speak that particular phrase before. Where did you say you were from?"

Careful, Becca. Slow down and watch what you say or you will be hanging in Boston. Don't say "Vineyard Haven," since the town doesn't exist until 1871. "I'm from Holmes Hole on the Island of Martha's Vineyard."

Rebecca's heart stopped when the captain scowled. She had said something wrong again. Maybe talking hadn't been such a good idea. Just as she was about to sit down and give up on conversation, Adam knocked on the open door holding two steaming mugs in his left hand.

"Good morning, Captain, Mrs. O'Neill. Will you be moving to the saloon?"

Captain Reed placed his hand just above Rebecca's elbow, guiding her toward the door. "Yes, Adam. Thank you."

The captain allowed Rebecca to slide onto the bench first before taking his seat at the head of the table. "How long have you lived on Martha's Vineyard, Mrs. O'Neill?"

"My whole life, Captain. I was born there."

"I see. Can you tell me how or where you boarded my ship? We didn't anchor near the Island. Did you get on in Old Dartmouth?" the captain asked, leaning forward, his eyes searching hers.

"Old Dartmouth?"

"Ah, yes, I believe you call it Bedford Village."

Oh, he means New Bedford, Rebecca thought. She knew it would probably be safest to say she had boarded in New Bedford, but she couldn't bring herself to form the words. "No, Captain, I was not in Bedford Village, at least I don't think so."

"You don't think so, Madam?" Now the captain was shaking his head. "Madam, I cannot impart to you enough the danger you are in at this moment. Your tale will be told, and it is better here than in Boston."

Rebecca brought her left hand to her forehead and rubbed her fingers across her brow. "You don't understand, Captain. Heck, I don't understand. I honestly don't know how I got here. I know I sound crazy. This is as unbelievable to me as it is to you. The last thing I remember was falling asleep on the boat."

"You were on a ship? Excellent. What ship were you on?"

Oh great. There is no way I can tell him I was on the Shenandoah. *Forgive me, Da.* "The *Siobhan*."

"I am not familiar with her. Where does she sail from?"

"The Vineyard, Captain."

"Where was she heading?"

She shrugged. "I don't know. I don't believe Captain Roberts had a set course."

"Hmmm, I am not familiar with Captain Roberts. It would be most helpful, Mrs. O'Neill, if we could return you to your ship."

Rebecca didn't know whether she felt like crying or laughing. It didn't matter either way, as both would be inappropriate at the moment. "I wish I could, too," she said staring into her coffee.

"Excuse me, Captain," Adam interrupted. "Will Mrs. O'Neill be joining us for breakfast in the saloon?"

Captain Reed frowned. "I think it would be best if Mrs. O'Neill eats in her cabin."

"Very well," the old man said, shaking his head as he walked away.

"Excuse me, Mrs. O'Neill, I lost track of the time. I must go up on deck before breakfast. Let me escort you back to your cabin."

Rebecca flinched as he stood and motioned for her to stand. "I promise not to be a problem. Please don't lock me in."

The captain's face softened. He looked at her hard, just as her Gram had done whenever Rebecca asked to stay out late with her friends and had to promise a dozen times to keep out of mischief, especially if Tess was with her. "Your word, Mrs. O'Neill, and the door will remain unlocked."

Forgetting herself and the formalities of the eighteenth century, Rebecca jumped up and hugged him. "Oh, thank you, Ben. I promise to remain in the room. You won't hear a peep from me."

"Captain?" Adam entered the saloon and took in the strange scene.

Rebecca dropped her arms and stepped back. The captain was clearly embarrassed and appeared equally shocked.

"What is it, Adam?" he asked while regaining his composure.

The cook chortled. "Jonah called down from the deck. They are looking for you."

"Adam, please take Mrs. O'Neill back to her cabin. Bring her a wash bowl, soap, and a towel for her ablutions before breakfast."

"Yes, Captain."

The captain walked away without looking back. Adam stepped in front of her and asked her to follow him down the hall to the last cabin. She watched him walk, wondering if he was in his fifties or sixties. His hair was gray, but his stride was strong, giving little clue to his age. "How long have you worked onboard the *Shenandoah*, Adam?"

"I came aboard with Captain Reed, Mrs. O'Neill."

"Please, Adam, call me Rebecca."

"No, Ma'am, the captain would have my hide if I did."

Rebecca winced and slowed her pace to a crawl. Adam had to be at least twice her age. If the captain would beat an old man, as she knew they had centuries ago, would he beat a woman? Adam turned around and Rebecca realized her feet were barely moving.

"Are you feeling unwell?"

"Would he really beat you, Adam?"

Adam chuckled. "No, Ma'am. I am sorry if I scared you. The captain wouldn't hit me, and I know for a fact his mother didn't raise him to hit a woman. The thought would never cross his mind."

Rebecca breathed an audible sigh of relief and began walking at a normal pace again. When they reached her cabin, Adam went to get her supplies. He returned within minutes and left Rebecca to clean up before breakfast. She washed her hands and face and wished for a brush or a comb. A mirror and toothbrush would be great, too, though she knew they were likely out of the question for prisoners. In the absence of the little necessities she kept in her backpack, she ran her fingers through her hair, then sat down on the cot, staring at the open door, and waited for someone to bring her breakfast.

9

No one else mentioned a hanging. Rebecca could hear the men talking while eating their breakfasts, so perhaps the rest of the crew didn't share James Packer's instant loathing and prejudice. The cabin was hot and muggy, which did little to improve her appetite. She picked at the biscuits and ham Adam had brought her. Forty-five minutes later a young man knocked on her door, introduced himself as Samuel Marsh, and collected her plate and mug. Shortly after he left, the captain returned, holding a fancy dress and what looked to be one of his shirts.

He stood in the doorway, neither in nor out of the cabin. For a man in charge of a ship full of rugged men, he looked rather uncomfortable and unsure of himself as he shifted his weight from one foot to the other. Rebecca couldn't imagine what was bothering him. She gave up waiting for him to say what was on his mind.

"You don't happen to have a fan, do you, Captain?"

"Nay, I do not. It is stifling below. I thought we could continue our conversation on deck, where the air is slightly cooler."

Rebecca stared at the clothes, waiting for him to offer them to her or say something about them. "Are you getting ready to sail?"

"There is little chance we shall sail this morning. The wind is nowhere to be had, and the air is heavy. If I did not know better I would say 'twas the middle of August." The captain transferred the clothes to his right hand, pulled a bandana of sorts from his pocket, and wiped his brow. He held the dress out to her. "I thought you might appreciate a dress."

Rebecca assessed the pale green gown without touching it. The buttons and lacing alone were enough to terrify her, never mind the rich fabric. The dress, which was surely silk, must have cost a fortune. Seconds passed before the captain cleared his throat. "Whatever you're thinking, Mrs. O'Neill, I assure you this dress is new. My aunt made it for my sister, Lucy, and gave it to me to bring home to her. Lucy will understand if you wear it now."

Rebecca stuttered, "I can't..."

The captain stepped closer, bringing the dress into the room with him. "I beg your pardon?"

Rebecca wanted to back away, but there was nowhere to go. How could she explain to the captain she had no idea how to get into it, never mind lace it up? "Captain, if you wouldn't mind, could I borrow the shirt instead? I fear a ship is no place for so fine a dress."

"Jonah was right," the captain said, shaking his head in obvious disbelief. "He suspected you might prefer my shirt, though how he knew I do not know." He passed her the clothes and took a step back. "I shall leave you both items. Dress as you see fit. I will wait outside your door until you are ready."

Rebecca laid the dress gently on the cot and slipped the white linen shirt over her head. "Ready," she announced before the captain had time to close the door. She lifted her hair from underneath the collar and let it fall softly around her shoulders. She watched the captain's eyes change, but she couldn't read his expression.

"You put my sisters to shame, Mrs. O'Neill. They spend hours getting ready for the day."

"I'm sure you are exaggerating, Captain. And I didn't exactly 'get ready for the day.' Trust me; it would have taken me hours to get into that garment, too."

Captain Reed laughed. Rebecca liked his smile, the way his brown eyes sparkled and reflected his pleasure. "I shall never understand women. You complain about the very clothes you insist upon having."

"It's a mystery, Captain, and I fear I am sworn to secrecy."

Another smile tugged at her heart. "Point taken, Mrs. O'Neill. Now, before you change your mind and decide to wear Lucy's finery, let us proceed up the companionway. Stay close to me and do not wander if I am in conversation with another. The crew is restless to be underway, and James is now in a foul temper. I do not envy another round with him this morning."

"Thank you, Captain."

As he moved aside to let her pass, Rebecca's heart fluttered. She was nervous about James Packer, for certain, but she didn't think it was nerves that had her pulse racing. And one thing, perhaps the only thing she was sure of lately, was that Captain Benjamin Reed was not and could not be a man to fall for. She hurried ahead of him so he would not be able to take her arm. She scurried up the ladder, determined to put all thoughts of Ben Reed out of her mind.

Once she was on deck, Rebecca's eyes adjusted to the bright morning sun. Not a cloud was in the sky. The morning was indeed hot and humid. Rebecca could only guess what the temperature would be this afternoon if it already felt like 85 degrees with 100 percent humidity. She brushed her hands over the long white sleeves, grateful for the protection from the sun.

The ship's deck was still damp from the scrubbing before breakfast. Rebecca walked carefully in her bare feet toward the stern. The captain motioned for her to sit atop the main cabin house. Her sweatpants were cotton, but still too warm for the muggy day. She wished like crazy that she had worn shorts to bed the night before.

No sooner had she sat down than James Packer stormed over. Rebecca shifted her legs to stand. "Be still, Mrs. O'Neill. I will speak with James."

James halted to the left of the helm. The captain stood his ground. Rebecca held her breath.

"Shouldn't the prisoner be locked below, Captain?"

Ben gripped the wheel. Rebecca wondered if James noticed the captain's fingers were turning white. "James, Mrs. O'Neill has yet to be proven guilty. I will remind you that on my ship a man, or woman, is innocent until proven guilty. I take full responsibility for Mrs. O'Neill. Is that clear, James?"

"Aye, Captain, I hear you," James said with a sneer.

Rebecca scooted farther away from James. The captain stepped between them. "James, we go back a long way. Don't let hatred for one poison you toward all. Mrs. O'Neill has done you no harm."

"How can you trust her, Ben? I know a Cockney accent when I hear one."

Rebecca knew full well James was insinuating she was a whore or of lower class, as the Cockneys were referred to in the 1770s. She opened her mouth to protest, took one look at the captain, and clamped it shut. "I will not debate her innocence with you. We will anchor soon enough, and the matter will be out of our hands. Your accusations shall rest until then, James."

"Fine, Ben, but you mark my words; when she is discovered to be a spy, I hope it is before this ship is taken hostage and our cargo confiscated." James spun on his heel and marched away.

Rebecca released a long exhale, unaware she had been holding her breath again. She twisted her fingers together, chin to her chest. "I am sorry to be so much trouble."

The captain stared at her. "I am inclined to believe you, Mrs. O'Neill. Jonah likes you for reasons I cannot explain, and Adam has also taken a shine to you. I trust Jonah and Adam, but I also have a crew and ship to care for. If you prove me wrong, James will be the least of your concerns."

At his implied threat, her hackles went up. "I am not a liar, Captain Reed," Rebecca snapped. She clenched her teeth, swallowing the stream of words she wanted to scream at James and the captain. "I may not be able to explain my presence on your ship to your satisfaction, but I am not one to fabricate the truth."

Rebecca watched the captain's shoulders drop.

"I have put some faith in your word, Madam, but I also have a duty to my men and my country. As such I ask for your understanding, as well as for irreproachable behavior."

Rebecca held his gaze, realizing for the first time the weight he must be under. His ship was loaded with much-needed gunpowder, rice, and supplies, and now he had a stranger on board that at least one member of the crew thought to be a spy for the British. He had every right to be cross with her, to question her every word and action, yet he was patient and kind. Her heart went out to him. He could be no more than thirty and bearing incredible responsibilities.

Without a thought to propriety, Rebecca squeezed his left hand. "I hope I can prove I'm not a spy or your enemy, Captain."

"Thank you, Mrs. O'Neill. That is all I could ask," he said, placing his right hand over hers, enclosing her left hand between his two.

Electricity ran through Rebecca's fingers, up her arms, and down her spine. Bewildered yet again, she shot a glance upward and saw her own surprise mirrored back at her. She blushed and tried to ease her hand from his. For a moment he seemed reluctant to let go, then he dropped her hand as William Barton, the first mate, approached.

"Excuse me, Captain. May I have a word with you below?"

He didn't move at first—pausing, it seemed, for the connection between them to fade or pass. The first mate altered his stance, waiting for a response. Rebecca stepped aside and the captain finally turned toward William. "Aye, William. I believe we are of the same mind. While we wait for a chance along, the crew could begin cleaning the bunks and storage area."

"That was my thinking, Sir."

The captain scanned the ship. "Jonah?" he called out. His brother's curly brown head lifted on the companionway. "Jonah, please join Mrs. O'Neill on deck while I go below."

Jonah popped up and walked over. "It would be my pleasure. Perhaps I could interest you in a game of cards?"

Rebecca's eyes twinkled. Cards were a favorite pastime and something she did well. "That would be great, Jonah. What games do you play?"

"Are you familiar with piquet?"

A sweet smile belied the card-shark-killer-instinct Rebecca concealed behind a poker face. "Rather well, actually. It was my grandmother's favorite card game."

She liked Jonah, an affable young man. Friendly and outgoing, he appeared to love life and held no prejudice against her. *But all's fair in love and war and cards, and you're going down.*

Rebecca sat down demurely while secretly contemplating her first moves. Jonah shuffled the cards and dealt the first hand. The captain left them to their game.

When he returned a couple hours later, Jonah had been thoroughly beaten, and Adam was whistling chanties in the galley while preparing lunch. The midday meal was served on deck. Jonah brought Rebecca a plate. "If you have not tired of my company, may I join you for dinner, Mrs. O'Neill?"

"I would love your company, Jonah. Please have a seat."

Jonah looked at his brother, who nodded his approval. He leaned in, glanced around to be sure no one else could hear him, and whispered loud enough so the captain would hear, "Tired of Ben's company would be more like it. He can be quite the bore. The young ladies at home fell hard and fast until they discovered how dull he was. I am, I'll have you know, the catch in our family." Jonah winked.

Rebecca giggled. "I am sure you have to beat them off with a stick, Jonah."

The captain snorted.

"Ben has always been one to talk ye to death about ships and yards and latitudes. Lucy told me he used to drive Mother crazy with his questions. By the time I came along, I think Mother was questioned out. I believe she taught me to sing to save herself."

Rebecca couldn't help herself; she glanced at the captain and started to giggle again. The two brothers were having fun, and she loved it. She'd never had siblings, and she'd always imagined how much fun it would be to have someone to tease and joke with. Jonah was the perfect brother, whether the captain agreed at the moment or not.

"Hasn't stopped you from babbling on, though," the captain quipped as he walked by Jonah and Rebecca to get some lunch.

Jonah sat with Rebecca for a while. They shared stories of their childhoods, Rebecca always mindful of what she was saying.

By midafternoon she was hot and tired. She was trying to sleep in the shade of the sailcloth tied between the masts when the captain startled her.

"You were guarded talking to Jonah earlier."

You bet I was, Rebecca thought. *Now I have a headache from thinking over every single word before I spoke one out of place. I'm exhausted. And here we go again.* She sat up slowly. "I didn't want to say the wrong thing."

He arched a brow. "What would be the wrong thing, Mrs. O'Neill?"

Gee, thought Rebecca, *let's start with my favorite television shows, computers, cell phones, cars, my boyfriend who isn't really my boyfriend, men walking on the moon and flying into outer space. Take your pick.* "I don't know, Captain, but I didn't want to say too much about Ireland, just in case." Rebecca knew the words sounded flat even before the captain lifted a brow.

"I have an idea, Captain," Rebecca interjected before he could comment. "Why don't you ask me what it is you would like to know? Perhaps that would be easier?"

His open-mouthed expression let her know she'd caught him off guard. Rebecca allowed herself a moment of satisfaction.

"As you wish, Madam." He stood with his legs slightly wider than shoulder length with his arms crossed. In that moment he looked every bit the captain, and Rebecca hoped she was ready for him. "Where do the Island residents stand? Are they for the King or the colony?"

Finally! An easy question I can pull from a history test, thought Rebecca. "They are fairly cautious, Captain, though most favor the colony. There was a meeting in June, and almost all of the young and able men signed up to serve. There were Vineyarders serving at Bunker Hill, and I believe in Lexington, too." Rebecca paused to see if the captain was interested or if she had said something to abate his curiosity. He motioned with his right hand for her to continue.

"The Island is in a precarious position, exposed as she is with no defenses save the men, women, and children who live there. The British continue to come and purchase goods as well as cattle and sheep. The Patriots joke about selling to the British and giving the money to the Colonials to fight for freedom."

He nodded, clearly believing she was telling him the information from a present-day experience. "I heard something similar in Old Dartmouth. I believe the King's Men will find a united front in New England."

Adam appeared through the galley's hatch. "Are you talking war with a lady, Captain?"

"No, Adam, I am asking about life on the Island."

Adam gave the captain a hard, fatherly look and frowned. Rebecca liked the old man immensely. There was knowledge in his years. He said little, yet spoke volumes. "Sounded like talk of war to me. Why not ask Mrs. O'Neill to play a game of piquet? She seemed quite capable with Jonah. She may be good enough to play you."

The captain matched his stare. "She is not here to be entertained, Adam."

"Quite right, Captain. But as she is here, no harm in passing the time of day. We shan't be sailing today." Adam placed a deck of cards in front of Rebecca. "I brought these for ye just in case."

Rebecca picked up the cards and began to shuffle. She gave the captain a smug grin, then asked sweetly, "Do you know how to play piquet, Captain?"

"Aye, Mrs. O'Neill, I am well acquainted with the game."

"If you've nothing better to do, perhaps we could play while you question me? I promise not to beat you too soundly."

Rebecca hadn't noticed Jonah's approach. "Ye aren't afraid of a challenge are you, big brother?" Rebecca sensed Jonah was pushing a button beneath his grin.

Captain Reed scanned the deck of the boat. "Have you nothing better to do with yourself, Jonah? A line to coil, a sail to mend?"

Jonah ran his hand along the rail pretending to inspect for dust. "Nay, brother, I do not. Shall I help Mrs. O'Neill or will it be thee needing my advice?"

"Go polish some brass."

Rebecca laughed as Jonah's slight frame scooted beyond the captain's reach. "I shall return to check on you, Mrs. O'Neill, though I trust you can handle yourself."

Rebecca picked up the deck of cards and pulled out the twenty lower ones. "Shall I deal first, Captain?" she asked while expertly shuffling the remaining thirty-two cards.

"Indeed, Mrs. O'Neill. Ladies first."

The captain lowered his six-foot frame to the roof deck and sat, an inch or two closer than necessary, facing Rebecca.

Rebecca arched the cards in a perfect shuffle and listened to the rhythmical sound as they fell into place. She gave the captain a Cheshire grin.

"Have you played often, Mrs. O'Neill?"

"Piquet was a family favorite. When I was a child, my grandmother would remove the twos through the sixes and pass them to me so I could build a card house. I wanted to learn the game and was relentless in my begging. In her later years we played almost daily."

"This would explain Jonah's present enjoyment."

Rebecca shrugged nonchalantly and dealt them each twelve cards. She placed the remaining eight facedown between them and divided them, the talon, into piles of five and three. Rebecca expected a steady stream of questions during the game but found there was little conversation. The captain focused on the cards, speaking only to make a declaration or tally points. He dealt the fourth game, ahead in the count two games to one.

Rebecca immediately lowered her hand to the deck calling, *"Carte blanche."* The captain reached across to fan her cards and brushed his fingers over hers. Goosebumps moved up her arm like ripples on the water. Her body gave a slight shiver. She needed air. She caught the amused look on the captain's face as she was about to snatch her hand back. Her emotions reeled. He'd done it on purpose. He'd wanted to touch her, to see her reaction.

Of all the... Rebecca couldn't finish the thought. She didn't want to think about her reaction or his desire to tease and touch her. *Just focus on the game, Becca, and keep your hands out of reach.*

She put on her best poker face and asked politely, "Looking for face cards, Captain?"

He stared into her eyes. "Aye, Madam. One should never underestimate one's opponent."

She swallowed the lump in her throat. "No, Captain, one should not. It is your move, Sir."

Unspoken words hung in the hot, humid air. Rebecca forced her mind to ignore the tingling in her hand and to concentrate on the game. She held onto her anger to regain her focus. Keeping her eyes on the cards and her mind on the score, she notched a win, tying the score two games to two. "Shall we play another hand, Captain? Best three out of five?"

"Are you baiting me, Mrs. O'Neill?"

I most certainly am, Rebecca thought, before replying. "Nay, Captain, merely enjoying my victory."

He laughed, and Rebecca felt her foolish stomach flip. His eyes danced. "I would hate to deny you a simple pleasure, Mrs. O'Neill, but if we play again, victory shall be mine."

Rebecca had had enough of his one-sided flirting. She crossed her right leg over her left knee, leaned over, and whispered, "That remains to be seen, Captain. I believe it is my deal."

Silence engulfed them throughout the first five matches—each intent on besting the other, speaking only to play, lest one gave away a secret. Neither noticed the audience they had drawn. Adam and Jonah were watching, as were three or four of the crew. When Rebecca called out the winning hand, a cheer went up, startling them both.

"Well done, Mrs. O'Neill. I do not believe I have seen our captain beaten at cards in quite some time. I believe you are a perfect match."

Rebecca ignored the implication. "The captain is a worthy adversary, Adam."

"'Twould appear so, Mrs. O'Neill."

Jonah was grinning at the captain, who looked less than pleased with Adam's remarks. "How long before supper, Adam?" the captain asked in a flat voice.

Rebecca stifled a giggle when Adam rolled his eyes. "Would an hour suit you, Captain?"

With a nod, Captain Reed turned and strode toward his cabin. Rebecca sat on the roof deck of the galley close to Adam, enjoying the time to think and relax. The day was still a scorcher. She would love to jump overboard and go for a swim, but she knew that was out of the question. James Packer would accuse her of jumping ship, while she'd be at loss to explain to the captain that women in the twenty-first century swam on a regular basis in bathing suits that resembled ladies' undergarments. She settled, instead, for a bit of shade under the boom and the peaceful sound of Adam's whistling.

Adam eventually asked her to help put the plates and mugs and platters of food on the cabin roof for dinner so the crew could eat on deck in the cooler evening air. The conversation over supper ranged from war to families at home to the next sail. Their talk gave way to song with Jonah leading them through lyrics and chanties Rebecca had never heard before. The time passed quickly.

The sky began to glow with oranges and pinks. The sea was as smooth as glass. The men grew quiet. Everyone watched in peaceful admiration as the sky changed in broad brushstrokes before them. Rebecca sighed as the sun dipped below the horizon. The captain announced that anyone who wanted to sleep on deck in the hopes of catching a breeze was welcome to do so.

"May I, Captain?" Rebecca said.

Jonah glanced at his brother, who said nothing. "She can rest by me, Ben. I am not on watch tonight."

"No, Jonah. You sleep atop the cabin house. Mrs. O'Neill may sleep in front of my quarters. I will sleep beside the wheel box. Please go below and bring up a blanket for her to rest upon."

Jonah returned with blankets and pillows. He passed them to Rebecca, holding onto the pile as he offered his services. "If Ben snores, wake me. I shall kick him for you."

Rebecca feigned shock and took the linens. "Thank you, Jonah. I'll do my best to live with it if he does."

Rebecca stretched out on her blanket, heard the ship's bell chime four times, and gazed at the stars. At ten o'clock at night the air was finally cooling, and the sky sparkled. She picked out Cygnus, Scorpio, and her favorite, Cassiopeia. With the captain to her left, Jonah above on her right, and the stars overhead, Rebecca settled securely into her makeshift bed and drifted off to sleep.

*

Ben tossed and turned. The woman was getting under his skin. He could smell her, hear her breathing. How was it she slept so soundly? He wanted to inch closer and watch her sleep. She had been enchanting this afternoon. Her pure joy after beating him at cards made him want to gather her into his arms and kiss her until he took her breath away.

"Aarghh!" Ben rolled away and stared at the sides of the boat, angry with himself for feeling anything for her. He had no business touching her during the game. No business being attracted to her at all.

She's a stowaway, for pity's sake. Ah, but the look on her face! The fire in her eyes! I could have, if only.

He flipped onto his stomach, resting his head on his arms, and turned yet again to stare at the sleeping beauty all too close, yet completely out of reach. He longed to run his fingers through her long brown hair. "If only," he whispered before closing his eyes....

*

An unusual ache in his shoulder and the scent of flowers woke him in the early morning hours. He felt her presence even before he opened his eyes. Sometime, somehow, in the middle of the night they had rolled together with only the wheelbase separating them from the waist down. She rested her head on his shoulder as though she belonged there. He inhaled the scent of her hair, an intoxicating mix of florals. His hands twitched with desire. *Dear Lord, save me from myself.*

He could move, should move, but he didn't want to wake her, didn't want to shift her at all. Fact was, he liked her there. The nearness of her filled him with a longing he hadn't experienced before. He lay there for nearly an hour listening to her breathe, trying to make out the features of her face in the dim, early morning light.

A strong breeze sent a shiver through her and had her reaching for a cover. She searched with her right hand, still sleeping, still unaware where she was. Unknowingly, she ran her hand over his shirt, down his chest. He sucked in his breath, tensing every muscle in his body.

He felt her stiffen, then watched her eyes open slowly. He tried not to chuckle at her shocked expression, which immediately turned to anger.

"What are you doing?" she hissed, her indignant tone unmistakable even at hushed levels.

"I would think that was obvious, Madam. I have been waiting for you to awaken, so I may have the use of my shoulder back."

He was certain she was blushing. She opened her mouth, then hesitated. He couldn't help but smile.

"I…well…I must have rolled over in my sleep."

"'Twould appear so. Were you comfortable?" he asked with laughter in his voice. He knew he was baiting her, but he was enjoying himself far too much to stop. He watched her ponder his question. A furrow appeared in her brow, a spark flashed in her eyes.

"You are a little lumpy."

"L-lumpy?" he stammered. "I have never been called *lumpy* in my life."

He could have sworn she grinned before laying her head back on his shoulder. When she ran her fingers over his white linen shirt, across his chest, and down his stomach, it was all he could to do to remain still. Every fiber in his being screamed. The woman could not know what she was doing to him.

Then she frowned, yes, frowned at him before replying, "Yup, definitely lumpy."

She withdrew her hand and attempted to roll away. He captured her wrist and grinned at her sharp intake of breath. He wanted to kiss her soundly. Neither moved. He couldn't tell whether his heart had stopped or was racing so fast he couldn't distinguish a beat. He turned slightly onto his right side, drawing her closer, taking in the beauty of her face as the first rays of sunlight danced over her skin. Her eyes widened. He sensed she might feel like a mouse trapped by the big, bad cat ready to devour her with more than his brown eyes.

A loud "Ahem" startled them both. Ben released his grip and sat up.

Jonah was smirking. "Sorry to interrupt, but it is after five, and the crew is starting to move about. I thought you should know." Jonah shifted his gaze to Rebecca and flashed a charming, albeit smug smile. "How are you this fine morning, Mrs. O'Neill?"

She didn't reply. Ben watched the heat sear her cheeks once again. Jonah left without a word to begin his morning chores. Rebecca scrambled to her feet. When her back was turned, Ben ran a hand over his chest. *Did she really think he was lumpy?* He stood. It was going to be a long day.

10

GOOD MORNING? JONAH HAD SAID, "GOOD MORNING." The sun was rising, and she was definitely still in 1775. Rebecca kept her back to Ben and waited for him to go down to his cabin. Yesterday had become today, and Rebecca was still in the past. She hadn't gone home during the night. Actually, she'd awakened beside Ben...well, sort of, kind of, *on* Ben.

Too many emotions swirled. Stuck in 1775. The feel of her hand on Ben's chest. Someone back home discovering she was gone. Ben's hand on her wrist. A trial. *Her* trial as a stowaway...or worse. Too much to think about. All she could do was mutter silently, *No, no, no!*

She started wringing her hands. Beads of sweat formed at her brow and her upper lip. *What if I'm stuck here? What am I supposed to do now? I could use a little help here, God.* Rebecca moaned louder than she intended. She picked up her blankets and started pacing back and forth as she folded them.

Adam walked over. "Go easy, Mrs. O'Neill. You will wear a hole in the deck if you continue. Jonah told me what happened. The captain is an honorable man. You have nothing to fear."

Rebecca, totally confused, stared at Adam. What was he talking about? She started to cry and buried her face in the blankets. "Oh, Adam, I just want to go home."

"Please do not weep so, Mrs. O'Neill. Benjamin meant you no harm."

Between sobs, a fog lifted, and Rebecca blushed. Adam was referring to Ben's near kiss, which she most definitely did not want to think about. "Adam, I need to go home. I don't belong here. And I'm scared. I don't know what is going to happen. My life has always been so normal and predictable. Now I'm on a boat with no recollection of how I got here, I'm accused of being a stowaway, I'm about to stand trial, and I was, well...there's Ben."

Adam didn't miss a beat. "What troubles you most, Mrs. O'Neill?"

Rebecca's head snapped up. "Huh?"

"As I see it, you are no spy and will not be convicted as such. Benjamin will see to your safe return to Martha's Vineyard. If the first two problems are eliminated, you are only left with, excuse me for speaking so directly to a lady, your moment with Benjamin this morning."

The heat flamed on her cheeks as she scanned the deck to see who was within earshot of their conversation. Everyone looked busy scrubbing, polishing, and sponging off the morning damp. No one was paying them any heed. She shifted her focus back to Adam and put her hands on her hips. "I only met the captain three days ago. I barely know the man. Surely you aren't suggesting I am attracted to him and that is what's bothering me?"

"I do not know what time has to do with attraction."

Rebecca looked to the heavens. *Little do you know. If I drift off to the twenty-first century tonight, it would definitely be a relationship killer. And who said I want a relationship with Benjamin Reed? Now what do I say?*

When Rebecca failed to reply verbally, Adam merely grinned and walked back to the galley.

Rebecca went back to pacing. "I am not attracted to Benjamin Reed," she muttered to herself. "I will not *be* attracted to Benjamin Reed. I am going to find a way home and will not need to think about him, his brown eyes with flecks of golden sunlight or his gorgeous smile ever again!"

"I heard that," Jonah whispered, startling Rebecca.

"No you didn't, Jonah. And don't you dare repeat a word of what I just did not say!" She wished she could kick herself. *Is this day going to get any better? The last thing I need is for Jonah to tell his brother what I'm thinking when I don't even want to be thinking it in the first place!*

The younger sibling appeared amused at her embarrassment. "Your secret is safe with me, Mrs. O'Neill. Ben's ego is healthy enough. I preferred your remarks this morning. I think I am going to start calling him *Lumpy.*"

They both laughed.

"You're surely everything a little brother should be." She let her smirk tell them both that, if she'd ever had a sibling, she would have picked Jonah.

"Truer words have not been spoken."

Rebecca and Jonah spun to find the captain standing behind them. Rebecca wondered how much he'd heard. From his impassive expression, she suspected he hadn't caught more than the tail end of their conversation.

"I have asked Samuel to bring you a basin of water and soap to the cabin below. I thought you might like to wash before breakfast."

Rebecca nodded. "Thank you, Captain. That would be wonderful."

"Jonah will escort you below."

Her temper sparked. "I can find my own way."

"I do not doubt your abilities, Madam. I simply meant to have you accompanied lest you run into unwanted individuals."

Rebecca's face softened. "Gotcha."

Jonah gave her a quizzical look. "You Vineyarders have a strange way of speaking on occasion."

She gulped. "Why do you say that?"

"My Aunt Missy often says the oddest expressions, too."

Rebecca held her breath, uncertain what to say. "Do I look like your Aunt Missy?"

"Hardly. You share a heritage, is what I meant. Missy is also originally from Martha's Vineyard."

Rebecca knew who Missy had to be. She wondered what else Jonah knew. "When did she move to Boston?"

"She does not live in Boston. My uncle met her five years ago aboard…"

The captain laid a hand on Jonah's shoulder. "You can discuss Missy later, Jonah. I'm sure Mrs. O'Neill would like some time to wash prior to breakfast and you should be helping with the morning chores."

"Aye, aye, Captain," Jonah said with a mock salute. The love and affection between the brothers was obvious. Rebecca shuddered when she remembered Captain Roberts' comments about the third brother dying at Bunker Hill. They couldn't know. Neither one had mentioned nor said anything about their brother dying in battle. She forgot about Melissa as she brooded over how sad Jonah and Ben would be later today or tomorrow when they anchored. She hoped Captain Roberts was wrong.

Jonah walked her to the cabin where Samuel had left the basin, soap, and a towel. "I shall leave you now," he said, closing the door without locking it.

Rebecca sat on the cot and mulled over what the day could bring. Her Gram had always told her to leave the worrying to God, but she had never been successful in those efforts. She washed her face and body as best she could. The cool water on her skin centered her thoughts and kept her in the present. The winds were already picking up. Undoubtedly they would sail after breakfast. *Okay,* she thought, *now would be the perfect time to disappear to the twenty-first century. But how?*

She set the basin with the dirty water over by the door and laid the towel and soap beside it. Rebecca returned to the cot and stared into space. She leaned back and rested her head against the wall. "If only I was Dorothy and could click my ruby slippers and go back to Kansas," she said to the barrels of rice. "Or maybe Scotty could beam me up to the *USS Enterprise* and then transport me home to Skiff Avenue."

Shifting to get more comfortable, Rebecca brought her hands behind her head. Feeling the unevenness of the boards against the back of her hands, she pivoted and found herself staring at a huge knot in a board. "No way! It can't be." Rebecca ran her hand over the knot. "It looks exactly like the one in my cabin between the bunks."

Rebecca stood and examined the walls. The location would be a perfect match with the boards on her walls. What had Captain Roberts said about the remodeling? He had ordered each board to be numbered and put back in the exact same location from where it had come. "That's it! The boards! They are the same ones in Cabin 8. Mike Natale was right. It is the cabin!"

Rebecca gave the knot a high-five. "I figured it out. The cabin is the clue or the time machine or the...I don't know what. Either way, that's why I didn't leave last night. I slept on deck. I wasn't in the cabin to go home. There's nothing to worry about. I will sleep in the cabin tonight and be home tomorrow morning."

Rebecca danced around the room until a knock on the door curtailed her excitement. "Breakfast, Mrs. O'Neill."

So much for a celebration party, I'm banished to the cabin again! "Come in," she called.

Samuel Marsh walked in, carrying a steaming plate of eggs and biscuits. "Special treat today, Mrs. O'Neill. Adam is using up the fresh goods; scrambled eggs for everyone. I also brought you a piece of ham with your biscuit."

"Thank you, Samuel. It all smells delicious."

Rebecca's stomach growled, and she ate her breakfast much too quickly. Her exhilaration was barely containable. How she wished she could tell someone about her discovery. She tapped her feet, drummed her fingers, and kept glancing at the open door, hoping Jonah or the captain would step in. Any conversation would be better than just sitting.

Time dragged on until Captain Reed finally appeared. "Did you enjoy your meal, Mrs. O'Neill?"

He was back to being formal. Rebecca needed a friend, not a warden. But she wasn't going to beg. She could be as distant as he was. "Very much. Thank you."

He glanced down the corridor. "We are going to hoist anchor shortly. The winds are in our favor, and we should reach our destination by midafternoon. I would like you on deck with me. I trust you will be able to sit and be quiet and remain out of the crew's way. Today is a work day, and there will be no card playing. Do you understand?"

Like a schoolgirl in the throes of her first crush, Rebecca's heart leapt. He wanted her with him. She felt giddy, all thoughts of remaining distant cast to the first breeze and forgotten. She answered with an enthusiastic, "Yes!"

He cocked his head at her overly buoyant response. "I want you up on deck to scout for any ships that might be your *Siobhan.* If by any chance we meet her, we'll ask to come alongside and confirm you belong on board. It would be best if we spy them before we anchor this afternoon."

Rebecca hung her head. "We won't see them, Captain."

"How can you be so certain, Mrs. O'Neill? If you have told the truth, there is a chance that we might see your ship."

Rebecca cringed. She hadn't lied, but she hadn't exactly told the truth. Either way, she knew with absolute certainty she had no hope of being rescued. "I know Captain Roberts will not be anywhere near Boston. He hardly ever sails up the coast, especially this summer."

"Aye, I can understand why most ships are avoiding the harbor. It has been nothing but trouble since the King's Men claimed Boston. General Washington has arrived, but word is he has not made an attempt to regain the harbor. I doubt he will anytime soon—would be foolish to even try."

Rebecca tossed the information around in her head. She wanted to ask about Washington and the War, but she also desperately wanted to be allowed out of the cabin. It took her only a moment to weigh her options. History could wait. "May I still go up on deck, Captain?"

He gave Rebecca the same cold, hard stare he had given her the day before. She knew now this was more effect than threat. In a childlike voice she half-jokingly pleaded, "I was on my best behavior yesterday."

The captain's face softened, a smile almost cracking through the stare. "So you were. If I have your word that you will continue to behave, then you may accompany me to the deck."

"I promise. I have no desire to jump overboard or cause a scene."

"One should hope not."

Rebecca followed the captain to the helm. His mood had changed since their...what to call it?...*incident* this morning. He was somber and edgy. He barely looked at her, never mind spoke to her. While she didn't want to flirt with him, he could at least acknowledge her presence and talk with her.

A dozen men, give or take, were on deck.

"Aweigh anchor," the captain called. Rebecca watched from a distance as four men, two on each side of the windlass, pushed up and down in a seesaw motion, hauling the iron off the ocean floor. When the anchor was secure, the captain called to the first mate, William Barton, "Raise the foresail."

The crew moved quickly and athletically, raising the sail and tying off the ropes to the belay pins. Rebecca marveled at the precision and teamwork of the crew. They were like a well-oiled machine. It was very different from watching the children learning to hoist the sails two days ago. There was no giggling, no goofing off. These men were working, and their conversation was a mix of sea chanties and friendly banter. Jonah sounded even better than he had the night before. He sang louder and with a deeper, richer voice.

Rebecca turned back to the captain. "Your brother has an amazing voice."

"Aye, he does. Takes after my mother. Though she'd never admit to it, I believe Jonah is her favorite. The two of them can sing from sun-up till sundown. It is rather remarkable to listen to their voices blend and complement one another."

"And you, Captain, can you sing?"

He grinned at her. "My talents, musical or otherwise, do not reside in my singing voice."

"You can say that again," Jonah chimed in as he moved to lay the lines of the mainsail. "Mother taught four of us to sing, but no one ever encouraged Ben to join in."

The captain glared at Jonah in mock anger, then watched as Jonah and the crew raised the mainsail and tied off the lines. As Jonah finished his knot, the captain threatened, "I am, however, very skilled at ordering insubordinate crew members to polish brass and clean the head."

"Being the elder suits you, Brother. You boss people around extremely well." Barb tossed, Jonah darted toward the bow to help hoist the fore staysail, the inner jib, and the outer jib.

The captain kept an eye on the men, occasionally calling out directions. The wind filled the sails, and the ship surged through the water. They would be in Boston in a matter of hours. Thinking of Boston reminded Rebecca of Captain Roberts' comments about Bunker Hill. She wondered when Ben had last seen his family.

"How long have you been away from home?"

Ben exhaled. "Almost three months. After Lexington, General Putnam spoke to my father, my uncle, and myself about a run down to the Carolinas. The Patriots were short on supplies and gunpowder. My uncle had retired from sailing. He gave the *Shenandoah* to me last year. I knew what needed to be done. I volunteered to go."

Rebecca's mind kept coming back to the Battle of Bunker Hill. She frowned. "How many brothers and sisters do you have?"

"I have one brother between Jonah and myself and two sisters, Lucy, whom I have mentioned, and Abigail. Jonah is the youngest."

"Oh. Why isn't your other brother sailing with you and Jonah?"

Ben laughed. "Magnus? He hates the sea. Turns green as a cabbage leaf just looking at a boat. He tried sailing with me a couple of times last summer. He gave it up after his third attempt. He joined the militia with our father."

Rebecca spoke through the lump in her throat. "Have you had any letters from your family?"

"Letters? On a ship? No, we have had little word of things at home. It will be good to sit down with the family and hear about the events that have transpired since we departed. We have picked up pieces of news when we put into ports. In Old Dartmouth I discovered the harbor is fully controlled by the King's Men, including Boston Harbor Light. We will need to unload our cargo near Quincy. I will decide then whether to sail on to Boston. My purpose is to serve my country. I will go where I am needed. I don't know, however, what I will do with you."

Only half listening, Rebecca missed the last sentence. She remembered her history well. If the lighthouse had yet to be burned and Washington was in Boston, then this must be early to mid-July. Life in and around Boston was still fairly comfortable. The harsh realities of war were to come. Not to mention the disease that would spread through the city in August and September.

A hand on Rebecca's shoulder startled her out of her reverie. "You look pensive. I did not mean to frighten you, Mrs. O'Neill. I will not let you go without a fair trial."

Rebecca jumped up. "What?"

The captain stepped back. "When I said I would not let you go without a fair trial, I meant it. Once we anchor and reach land, we will have to send for a magistrate. I will keep you on the ship and ask for him to come to us. It is the best I can do."

Rebecca paled and swayed, thinking aloud, "What will happen to me if I don't make it back to the *Shenandoah?*"

The captain steadied her with one hand. "You had best sit down." He helped her sit atop the cabin roof. "You are on the *Shenandoah*, remember?"

His words sounded like a bad joke. Of course she remembered! What she didn't know was if she could make it home to her *Shenandoah* before he turned her in. "Yes, um, I meant the *Siobhan.*"

"I assumed you meant as much. I do not want to alarm you. I do not know what will happen. I have never had a stowaway onboard, never mind a woman stowaway. My uncle thought he had a stowaway once, but he discovered the person actually belonged with him. In your case I presume they will send a rider to Falmouth or a ship to Martha's Vineyard and inquire about you."

The captain took small strides, pacing in front of Rebecca. "I suspect my father will make his way to the ship once he hears we have anchored. He is always a good man to have around in a crisis and your story will interest him."

"This is a crisis for me, isn't it?"

"Aye, it could well be. Your story has not changed in the last few days, you have not faltered, but I am not the one who will judge you. You claim no knowledge of how you arrived on the *Shenandoah* as she carries precious gunpowder to the Colonialists. We are at war, though it is unofficial as yet, and you appear to be a potential threat."

Rebecca stared up at Captain Reed, at Ben, the man she woke beside this morning. "If you were the one to judge me, would you find me guilty?"

He stopped pacing and searched her eyes. With his right hand he gently moved stray strands of her hair behind her left ear. "Everything in me tells me you are an innocent. If the decision were mine, I would personally sail you to Martha's Vineyard and deliver you home."

Rebecca felt an irrepressible desire to sink into his arms and let his strength protect her. She gazed into his eyes, seeking answers to questions she couldn't yet put words to. His eyes searched hers, too. Her breath caught in her throat. "Thank you, Ben."

He started to say something, then stammered and took a few steps back. "I need to talk with the crew," he said rigidly. "The closer we sail to Boston, the more dangerous our circumstances. I cannot have you near. Would you like to go below to the cabin, or would you prefer to remain on deck?"

Rebecca flinched at his cold tone. She needed his warmth and strength. She wouldn't admit it to Ben or anyone, but she was scared. She didn't want to be alone or where James Packer could find her. If she were truly honest with herself, she'd be forced to admit that she didn't want to be away from Ben. She desired to have Ben in sight. "I would like to stay on deck, please."

"Very well. Have a seat by the galley. Adam will keep an eye on you. I will trust you to remain there. Is this understood?"

Rebecca willed her voice to ice, hoping she could somehow sound as indifferent as he had. "Yes, Captain, understood."

He called for William to take the wheel and walked her down to the roof of the galley, checking the rigging along the starboard side as they went. Adam was slicing onions with a sack of potatoes waiting to be peeled. He waved up to her.

Rebecca was grateful for a friendly face. "I would help you if I could."

"I would appreciate your help."

Rebecca looked from the captain to Adam and back again. Crossing her fingers behind her back, Rebecca told another half-truth. "I love to cook, Captain."

"She would not be in the way, and I could use the help," Adam called up.

The captain rolled his eyes. "You have managed to cook for two months without any help, Adam."

"True, but I have never had so beautiful an assistant to share my kitchen with." Adam winked at Rebecca.

The captain shook his head in defeat. "Fine, fine. You may assist Adam. Now if I may get back to work…"

Rebecca locked her eyes on Ben and took all the joy out of her voice. "Don't worry, Captain. I'll just peel and slice and leave the cooking to Adam so I don't ruin your dinner."

Adam laughed. The captain merely uttered a curt "good" and strode toward the bow.

"Does he have a sense of humor?" she asked Adam.

"Aye, Mrs. O'Neill, he does. He has a job to do, though. These last miles will be the most treacherous we've traveled. And I gather his mind is a bit preoccupied with other matters complicating an already difficult journey."

"Oh, Adam, please don't go there again. There is nothing between the captain and me. He can barely manage to be civil. You saw how he treated me. I can't stand the man."

"If you say so."

Rebecca placed her hands on her hips. "I do!"

"Then we'd best get to work. I'll share some stories with you if you would not be too bored."

Rebecca dramatically brought the back of her right hand to her forehead. "I could probably suffer through a few."

"I thought so." Adam passed Rebecca a knife and moved a couple inches to the left so she stood beside the burlap sack of potatoes. She peeled and listened while Adam regaled her with stories of the captain and his siblings. Tales of Ben kept her spirit light as she nicked her thumb over and over again with the knife. Adam graciously withheld any comments on her peeling abilities or her obvious enjoyment of Ben's past. She refrained from complaining about the old-fashioned potato peeler.

11

"CAPTAIN! SHIP APPROACHING ON THE STARBOARD SIDE," James Packer bellowed, hustling toward the helm to hand the captain the spyglass.

Rebecca stood.

"Sit down, Madam," the captain snapped at her. Rebecca crouched down, trying to look as though she was seated, yet still attempting to observe the boat heading toward them.

A small ship loomed in the distance. Rebecca knew from her history books how British patrols had sailed the waters around Boston searching for smugglers and Patriots. From this distance, Captain Reed had no way of knowing if the ship was friend or foe. He and Adam had warned her before lunch of the dangers as they approached Boston. She hadn't given it much thought as this was July 1775 and the War hadn't gone full scale yet.

The men on the deck were signaling one another. The ship was drawing closer, probably less than two miles away. Rebecca forgot herself and stood again. She walked over toward the rail, trying to see the ship.

"Madam! I told you to sit *down,*" Captain Reed barked. "If they believe we have women and children on board this ship, they will think we are unprepared to defend ourselves."

Rebecca moved quickly to the cabin house roof and sat down. "I'm sorry. I wanted to see if I could tell what flag they were flying."

The captain ignored her, asked William to take the wheel, and continued moving toward midship until he reached Jonah. He peered through the spyglass, lowered it, and shook his head. "Trouble, I fear. Jonah, go below and gather the men. Tell everyone to ready, with the utmost discretion, for an attack."

Rebecca's mind was racing. *Think, Becca, think.* She couldn't remember any recorded naval battles south of Boston Harbor in July. How she wished for her library or the Internet now. Her father had loved American history, especially the Revolutionary War. He'd told her stories, embellished and factual, about the battle between Britain, Ireland's bitter adversary, and the States whenever he had Rebecca's ear. On the boat, walking to the beach, playing in the yard, sitting on the dock, there wasn't a place or time Rebecca couldn't remember her father sharing his love of history with her.

It was his passion that had spawned her own love of history and the main reason she chose to become a social studies teacher. As she wracked her brain, not a single battle or struggle came to mind. But another thought did.

Rebecca stood once again. "Captain, wait."

He pivoted and glowered at her. He marched the short distance to her with menacing strides. "Mrs. O'Neill, I will not have you endanger my crew or my mission. You are going below deck, *now!*" He grabbed her by the upper arm and pulled her toward him. Those on deck, including James Packer, were watching and stepped closer.

"I have an idea if you would only listen," Rebecca shouted across the inches between them. He glared at her. She rushed on. "I could pretend to be your wife. Don't bring the crew up. Make it look like we're merely sailing, coming back from a visit to my family. You said they wouldn't think you could defend yourself with women on board. Let them think that."

No one said a word. Seconds seemed like hours.

Adam spoke. "It could work, Captain. Who would believe a woman made the trip south to purchase gunpowder?"

"It's a trap, Captain," James called out. "Most likely the ship from whence she came. They have probably been shadowing us since Old Dartmouth."

Rebecca whirled to face James. She slammed her hands onto her hips and stared directly into his eyes. "It's not my ship, Mr. Packer. I haven't a clue who they are."

Packer pointed a finger at her and jabbed the air repeatedly as he fumed, "She's lying."

"I am not!" Rebecca stomped her foot on the deck.

The captain eyed Rebecca. She felt the heat of his stare going right through her. He shook his head. She wilted. *He really doesn't believe me.* He took hold of her arm again, and Rebecca bolted ahead, furious to be locked in the cabin again. She jerked to a halt when she reached the length of the captain's extended arm. He wasn't moving. She turned and he nodded.

"Your idea has merit."

"No! It's a trap, I say," James screamed to everyone within earshot.

The captain swiveled to face Rebecca's nemesis. "James, if you continue shouting, it shall be you who gives us away. Mrs. O'Neill's idea may very well work." The captain dismissed James and turned to Adam. "Notify all the crew quickly without drawing attention. They are probably watching us through the glass."

Adam headed toward the bow. The captain motioned for Jonah to join them while he addressed Rebecca. "You will need to change into Lucy's green gown quickly. No captain or crew would believe a married woman was dressed as a sailor. I apologize, for Jonah must help you prepare. Time is of the essence."

A tinge of pink spread over her cheeks. "I can dress myself, Captain."

"Not fast enough, I'm afraid. Please don't argue, Mrs. O'Neill. If your ruse is to work, you must look the part."

"You're right, of course, it's just…"

Rebecca could have sworn the captain blushed, too. "I understand, Mrs. O'Neill. Jonah will wait outside while you assemble the dress. You may leave your clothes on as undergarments. Now please, make haste."

The captain motioned his brother closer. "Jonah, take Mrs. O'Neill below. She needs to dress quickly. Lace her with speed."

Jonah looked flustered. "I don't know how, Ben. My hands will be useless."

The captain glanced at the approaching boat. "Lord, give me patience! Pray tell, Jonah, how ye missed a plea from Lucy or Abigail to fasten them in?"

Jonah started to say something, but the captain waved him off. "Not now. Go below and bring the dress to my cabin. Meet us there. I shall assist Mrs. O'Neill…William, alert me when the ship is nearing."

The captain and Rebecca hurried below. Rebecca's heart was racing. Why had she opened her mouth? What if her plan didn't work? If they were caught now, it would be all her fault.

In minutes, Jonah brought the dress wrapped in a sheet.

"Thank you, Jonah," Rebecca said.

"You are quite welcome. If I may make a suggestion?"

"Of course. What is it?"

"Your lovely ring would suit perfectly if you placed it on your left hand."

Rebecca looked down at her grandmother's ring. She'd forgotten she had it on. She moved the ring to her left hand. "You're right, Jonah. Thanks again."

"I am happy to assist, *Mrs. Reed.*"

Rebecca blushed from head to toe as Jonah departed quickly under his brother's scowl.

The captain unrolled the dress from the sheet while Rebecca took off the borrowed shirt. Her back to the captain, she started to pull down her sweats.

"Mrs. O'Neill!"

Rebecca spun around. "What?"

"Leave…your…clothes…on, please."

Rebecca thought he sounded as though he were begging. A part of her was pleased, very pleased indeed that he showed some attraction to her. Her practical side kept to the business at hand. "The blue will show through the dress, Captain."

His face reddened. "Yes, clearly. Simply leave the pants on while you dress. You may remove them once the dress is in place."

In a different time and place, Rebecca might have been amused at the way Ben stumbled over the last sentence before averting his eyes, and she might have teased him further. But she was too nervous to analyze and act on his obvious discomfort. She picked up the dress and focused her attention on the ever-present danger at hand.

Lifting the dress over her head, she pulled it down over her form. After moving her tank top straps under the sleeve caps and edging her shirt below the bust line, she tugged her sweat pants off from under the dress. *Lord, please let this work.*

She turned to face the captain. "Ready. How do I look?"

When she heard his sharp intake of breath, her fears evaporated like drops of water on hot pavement in the summer sun. His eyes roamed over her body. She fought the impulse to cover herself. She suddenly felt naked under what felt like two hundred pounds of cloth. She raised her head and met his gaze. Her heart plunged to her stomach. He was devouring her with his eyes.

"The dress does not do you justice, Mrs. O'Neill."

"Mrs. Reed," Rebecca corrected, hoping desperately to divert his attention from the dress.

"I stand corrected, Mrs. Reed. Now turn about so I may fasten the laces."

Rebecca felt Ben's hands moving up her spine, his knuckles resting on her back as he stretched and pulled the laces together. *Why in the blazes does the barest touch, through cloth nonetheless, send my heart racing?*

Rebecca lost all focus when Ben's fingers reached the top of the dress and brushed across the base of her neck. Before she had time to recover, Ben drew his thumb over her skin along the edge of the dress. She struggled to catch her breath.

"Relax, Mrs. Reed." His words caressed her skin. "Lift your hair so I may tie these off."

He is torturing me and surely knows. If I live through this day, I'm going to kill him. Rebecca's silent vow brought a small amount of satisfaction.

Ben spent an eternity tying the bow, and then lazily, ever so softly, dragged a finger up her neck to the base of her hairline. Rebecca sucked in her breath and dropped her hair. She thought she heard him stifle a chuckle. He leaned closer and whispered, "You have beautiful hair. I can't get the smell of it out of my mind."

As he eased back, he ran his fingers through her hair and turned her around to face him. Rebecca was certain every emotion she felt would be reflected in her eyes.

"Ben?" she asked softly.

He grazed his thumb over her cheek, never taking his eyes off of hers. There was such tenderness in his touch.

Rebecca wanted. She didn't know what she wanted. Something. Something to...to what? Ben took her left hand, running his fingers over hers and turning her grandmother's ring around her finger. She thought of her parents and her grandparents, how happy their marriages had been, and wondered for a moment if she could be as happy with Ben. Her eyes misted, and she brushed away a tear with her right hand.

Ben practically threw her hand from his. "I'm sorry." He moved swiftly away from her. "I did not think."

Rebecca had no clue what he was talking about, but a chill whipped through the cabin as Ben changed once again into her warden/captain. She held back the sobs pressing to be released. She searched his eyes and saw remorse and, maybe, shame. What had happened?

He straightened under her gaze and extended his hand formally to her. "We'd best make haste, Mrs. O'Neill. The ship will be upon us shortly. Gather your hair and tie your bonnet on quickly."

Ben climbed the three steps of the ladder, resting his right foot on the deck and his left foot on the third step, and then turned to offer Rebecca his hand after she finished tying her bonnet. Unaccustomed to the weight and length of the dress, she tripped on the dress and stumbled on the second step. Ben caught her about the waist and lifted her up. He lowered her gently to the deck. His hands were like firebrands on her hips. Her body became liquid heat. Her legs gave way as soon as her toes touched the floor. He drew her to him and held her steady.

"Thank you, Captain," she said, her breath shallow, her eyes glued to the deck. She didn't dare look up. She couldn't deal with the fire burning within, or Ben's coldness.

"My wife should call me Ben. 'Thank you, Ben.' Surely you called your husband by his given name."

Rebecca faltered. Was that his problem? Was that why his mood changed down in the cabin? Was he angry about a husband she'd never had? "I tried to tell you..."

Ben put a finger to her lips. "For the moment, let us pretend that you are mine and mine alone."

Under the icy surface, Rebecca saw heat in Ben's eyes. *Yes!* she thought in response to his suggestion, but more so to a feeling she suspected he might share. During her moment of joy, Ben's finger had stayed upon her lips. She became aware of the soft pressure and longed for his lips to claim hers. The heat inside her reached her cheeks.

"You shall be most believable, Rebecca. The blush on your cheeks will evidence well a new bride's blossoming."

She brought both hands up to her face. "I am glad my humiliation will serve you."

Ben laughed. "I do not wish to humiliate you. I am truly enjoying your company."

Rebecca stared, uncertain whether he was mocking her again or telling the truth. Her nerves were worn thin without him adding to her dilemma. She was about to tell him so when William called.

"Captain, the ship is requesting to come alongside."

"Bring them on, William. Mrs. Reed is ready." Ben offered her his right elbow. He placed his left hand over hers, gave her an encouraging squeeze, and walked them midship to greet the approaching vessel.

Rebecca gulped when she noticed the British flag.

"Poise, Mrs. Reed." He studied her face. Rebecca knew she must look nervous. "Smile, Rebecca. Do not be afraid. I will not leave your side."

Rebecca exhaled and did as he asked. "As you wish," she said with a smile.

He touched the tip of her nose. Then, surprising them both, he kissed her on the forehead before turning to greet the enemy ship.

"Good day, gentlemen. Captain Benjamin Reed at Her Majesty's service."

"Good day, Captain Reed. Captain Richard Blake at your service." Both men bowed. "A beautiful vessel, Captain."

"Thank you, Captain Blake. My uncle had her built seven years ago. She's mine now, and I'm fortunate to have married a lass who enjoys a day of sailing."

"Fortunate you are, Captain Reed. Where are you bound?"

"Home. We are returning from a visit to my bride's family."

Ben wrapped his right arm around Rebecca's shoulder. He must have felt her tension, for he pulled her close and offered her the support of his strength. She exhaled slowly and sighed into the comfort of his embrace. Ben smiled down at her and the fading pink across her cheeks deepened once again to a bright red.

Captain Blake chuckled. "Where are you from, Mrs. Reed?"

Ben tightened his hold, giving her shoulder a few little squeezes as if speaking in Morse code, and addressed Captain Blake. "She is your countryman of sorts, Captain. My wife is originally from Ireland."

"Are ya from Ireland, Captain Blake?" Rebecca turned on an accent so thick she hardly recognized her own voice.

"I am not, Mrs. Reed. I hail from Cornwall."

Rebecca disliked the man instantly. His snobby tone turned her off, though she feigned extreme interest in each word he spoke.

"Perhaps ya've visited the green isle?" she asked, smiling innocently.

"I am afraid not, Mrs. Reed. How is it you came to be on this side of the Atlantic?"

"Me Da brought us over when I was just a wee lass. Me Uncle Paddy wrote to say he bought a boat and needed Da's help to bring in the fish. Me mum was none too pleased, mind ya, but she packed us up and here we be."

"Where is here, Mrs. Reed?"

Rebecca knew he was asking more than current location. She felt Ben squeeze her again, and she spoke confidently. "Why, Martha's Vineyard, Captain Blake. 'Tis a lovely place, 'tis."

Ben stepped forward toward the rail before Captain Blake could ask another question. "Captain, we are headed home and would like to be there before evening meal. My parents are awaiting us today. Are you headed for Boston? Would you care to sail with us?"

Rebecca did everything she could not to register shock on her face. Ben was practically inviting them to watch his crew unload the gunpowder. What was he thinking? She reached for his hand, seeking assurance. He took the opportunity to draw her close again. She was certain she was blushing from head to toe.

Ben pushed on. "My bride would like to be home and settled before dark. I believe you can understand? We would welcome you for a visit on the morrow."

She turned quickly to stare at him, mouth open, and heard Captain Blake laugh. "I recollect my younger years quite well, Captain Reed. I believe your bride would prefer to be home alone. Thank you for your offer. I regret we are headed south to New York and must decline."

Ben bowed to the Captain. "A safe journey to you, then, Captain Blake."

"And to you, Captain Reed. Best wishes, Mrs. Reed."

Rebecca raised her hand and waved. Turning up her Irish accent to full force, she conveyed an Irish blessing in Gaelic her Gram had taught her years ago.

Captain Blake smiled stiffly. Rebecca was sure he had no clue what she'd said. He nodded formally to Ben. "We shall grant you the first move, Captain Reed."

"By your leave, Captain Blake." Ben bowed, then turned to face Rebecca.

She smiled and winked. He drew her into his embrace, his arms encircling her waist. He placed his right forefinger gently under her chin and tilted her eyes up to meet his. His smile warmed Rebecca. He bent close to her ear. "You were brilliant, Mrs. Reed! Pray tell, though, what did you say to Captain Blake?" Ben straightened to look at her.

Rebecca smiled, quite proud of herself. She leaned in closer and whispered, "It is an Irish blessing, wishing good luck and a safe journey. The literal translation is: 'May the road rise with you.'"

Ben's eyes held her tight, flecks of gold reflecting the afternoon sun. His arms hugged her so close, Rebecca thought he could surely feel her heart beating like that of a racehorse during the last furlong. Rebecca wondered if this was for show or if Ben wanted to kiss her as badly as she wanted him to kiss her. He wasn't moving…at all.

William broke the spell. "Captain, shall we tack away from the ship?"

Rebecca stepped back first. Ben released her gaze with obvious reluctance. "Aye, William. Let's go home."

The ships continued side by side as Ben gave the orders to tack left. The crew moved with haste, as much in obedience to Ben's commands as in their desire to put as much distance between themselves and the British as quickly as possible. Soon the *Shenandoah* was once again sailing toward home. *Ben's home,* Rebecca reminded herself.

As the British ship diminished in size, Adam walked over to Rebecca. "You were fabulous, Mrs. Reed. Well done, indeed."

"Just Rebecca, Adam," she said, shifting her grandmother's ring to her right hand.

Adam put his hand on hers. "Best leave it where it is till we drop anchor. I believe you are Mrs. Reed for a few more hours at least. You fill the role well. Benjamin must be happy with his decision."

Rebecca reddened for what felt like the millionth time that day. Adam's remarks had hit home. She liked the idea of being Mrs. Reed more than she cared to admit to anybody, especially herself. Ben's arm around her shoulder had felt like an extension of her, only better, like it was made to be there, like she was created to fit perfectly against him.

Jonah meandered over, gloating like a cat who'd cornered a fat mouse. "You did great, Mrs. Reed. I think you are a natural."

"Please, Jonah, I don't think I can stand to blush another time today."

He gave her an exaggerated bow. "A gentleman never wishes to embarrass a lady."

Rebecca put on her stern teacher face. "Ha! You meant to do exactly that, Jonah Reed. Now go polish some brass."

As Jonah turned to depart, head down in mock shame, he imparted loudly to Adam, "She's even beginning to sound like Ben."

"Aye, she is, lad." Adam chuckled in reply. He knew better than to glance in Rebecca's direction. He made an about-face and headed back to the galley without another word.

12

I WONDER WHAT JAILS LOOK LIKE IN 1775? Rebecca watched as they drew closer to land. An hour ago she had been so grateful when the British ship had sailed away and left them alone, unharmed and cargo intact. Now her relief wasn't so palpable. In a few hours she could be in prison, and would be if James Packer had his way. She sat on the roof close to the galley, her hands tucked underneath her legs. Ben had promised he would keep her on the ship, but what was going to happen when the magistrate came to get her?

She jumped up and paced back and forth in front of the galley. Would she be able to convince the magistrate she wasn't a spy? Would Ben help her? She shuffled over to the roof and plopped with a sigh.

"I didn't ask for this, God. Why did you bring me here? I am not asking why me, just why here? What am I supposed to learn or do?" Rebecca tilted her eyes up, hoping by some miraculous occurrence a skywriter would be doing loop-de-loops and spelling out the answers to her questions. She'd never been very good at reading or seeing signs. A direct answer, an explicit sheet of directions, or a clear, concise sign were what she appreciated.

Staring at the empty sky, no help in sight, she leaped up and started pacing again. She glanced back at the heavens—still nothing—so plopped back down on the roof. "I was perfectly happy on the Vineyard."

Pointing her right index finger to the sky Rebecca stood once again. "Okay, so not perfectly happy, but I was happy. "

She strode four steps forward, turned around, took three steps back, and stopped. She hung her head and kicked her right foot back and forth. Well, maybe *happy* wasn't the right word, but she was content and knew what to expect and what to do and when to do it. There were few surprises, and she had liked it that way.

She kicked an imaginary rock, hard and far. Staring into the sun, she dared it to kick the rock back. "Now I'm lost, and I need a miracle."

"Hold fast, Mrs. O'Neill."

Rebecca swung around and looked down into the galley to see Adam smiling up at her. "I didn't know anyone could hear me."

"The Good Lord surely heard ye. Have faith, Mrs. O'Neill. He knows what He's doing."

"You sound like my grandmother, Adam."

"Good advice is good advice. I appreciate ye might be nervous, given your situation, but you must trust even when you cannot see. I cannot speak for Benjamin, yet I am certain he shall not be letting you go to a magistrate or anywhere else where he is not."

Rebecca dropped her chin to her chest. What Adam was suggesting was impossible. Ben couldn't know where she was from, and he couldn't go where she was going. And that was the killer. She thought she wanted him too and thinking that made her heart hurt so she'd determined it would be best not to think about being with Ben at all. Easier not to wish for what could never be.

"Adam, I keep telling you there is nothing between us."

The way Adam surveyed her let Rebecca know she was lying only to herself if she was trying to pawn that idea off. "Aye, ye do. However, I am not blind, *Mrs. Reed*, and I know what I see."

Rebecca flashed him a piqued look. "You see too much, Adam. Did you ever think it might all be your imagination?"

"Nay, I cannot say I have. People's actions define them. A look here, a touch there. The clues are there if one has eyes to see, and my eyesight is excellent."

Rebecca knew it was pointless to argue. Adam knew the truth as well as she did: She had fallen for Captain Benjamin Reed.

She closed her eyes. No point in telling Adam that Ben was technically two hundred years older than her and destined to break her heart or she his, which was all the more reason to pretend she didn't have feelings for him. A warm breeze caressed her skin. She opened her eyes and glanced down into the galley.

Adam smiled warmly. "All will be well, Mrs. O'Neill. The Good Lord works things out in His own time. Have faith." He winked and went back to preparing supper, probably the last the crew would eat onboard for some time.

Rebecca sat back down and turned toward the helm to watch Ben as he watched the sails and the crew. She knew it was beyond foolish, yet there she sat, absorbing every move he made: how he often talked with his hands, the ripple of muscles in his forearm as he turned the wheel, his shoulder-length hair blowing in the wind, enticing her fingers to run through it .

She memorized every nuance: his fingers tapping on the wheel, the sun warming his already golden skin, and the smile he flashed her way when he caught her looking at him. Rebecca burned the images into her mind like photos onto a CD to replay over and over. Just in case.

All too soon the ship was pulling into a small harbor. The crew once again became a blur of activity. Rebecca heard the commands and willed her nerves to steel. Every sail lowered, every rope coiled, every inch of the chain dropped brought her closer to a fate she was unprepared to face. She wanted to move closer to Ben, but she knew he expected her to stay near Adam.

Jonah walked by, whistling. He paused. "Do not fret so, Mrs. O'Neill. There is little danger here. The King's Men shall not bother us tonight."

Rebecca struggled to focus on what Jonah was saying. Were they staying on the boat tonight? Who was staying? It was still early, with a good deal of daylight left. Surely the crew was eager to be home to wives and family. "Are you sleeping on the boat tonight, Jonah?"

"Aye, Mrs. O'Neill, there is still work to be done."

"Work?"

"Our cargo is best unloaded when the King's Men sleep."

"Oh, of course." Rebecca remembered the gunpowder they carried along with the barrels of rice. "How will you get it ashore?"

Jonah looked past Rebecca. "I shall defer your question to the captain. I had best be about my tasks."

Rebecca spun to face Ben. She extended her hands to hold his, to find reassurance he would be safe, then quickly withdrew them. "Will you be in danger?"

Ben must have seen the worry in her eyes and heard every ounce of concern in her voice. His tone and words were soothing and comforting. "You need not worry, Rebecca. The harbor is a Patriot port. We will be safe."

Rebecca ran her fingers through her hair, holding onto a section with her left hand. She played with the ringlet, twisting the loose curl around her index finger, letting it fall and then wrapping it again while she remembered her conversation with Captain Roberts. He would have mentioned if Ben or Jonah had been killed or wounded. He clearly said one of the three brothers had died during the War. She relaxed, knowing more than Ben could, knowing he and Jonah would be safe tonight and throughout the War.

"What will happen now, Ben?"

"I will send word to my father we have arrived. He will gather the necessary men to help tonight."

Rebecca's eyes lit up. "I can help, too."

Ben put both hands firmly on her shoulders, his eyes both pleading and demanding. "No! You will remain in your cabin. Under no circumstances are you to appear on deck. If you will not give me your word, I will be forced to lock you in for your own good. No one must see you, Rebecca."

Miffed at his initial remark, Rebecca had been working up a tsunami of defiance, which dissipated into a light breeze when Ben brought the point home. He was right; no one must see her. Her presence would raise too many questions and could give James Packer the opportunity he'd been waiting for. She wouldn't endanger Ben or the crew or risk complicating their mission by doing anything foolish, even if her intentions had been to help. Ben was right.

Rebecca nodded. "I understand, Ben. I will remain in my room without lock and key. I give you my word."

His face instantly relaxed. He released her shoulders and turned toward his right, laying both hands on the rail. His eyes scanned the docks and the town and the hills beyond. "There is much to be done this night, Rebecca. The cause is great. What we do here could change the course of history. War is inevitable, if it has not already been declared. We must stand for liberty or submit to absolute despotism."

Rebecca wanted to hold him. She wanted to encourage him. She wanted to tell him that everything would be okay, that the Colonists would be successful, and victory and freedom would be theirs after a few hard years of war. But she couldn't say a thing about the future, so she remained silent.

"Please excuse me now as I see to the departure of William and Matthew. Stay with Adam. I will speak with you after supper."

Rebecca moved back over to the galley and sat within eyesight of Adam. She needed something to do, something to keep her mind from wondering what was going to happen to her tomorrow. She felt total ease about Ben and Jonah. Surely Captain Roberts, or even her Da and the dozens of stories he'd shared, would have told her of any great battle, capture, or event involving the *Shenandoah*. She trusted the night would go as planned and the morning would come. Her fear was what the morning would bring. She realized with disgust she was chewing on her fingernail. "Ugh! I gave this up years ago!"

"Cast your cares to the Lord, Mrs. O'Neill," Adam said quietly. "The captain shall be fine."

Without thinking Rebecca confidently replied, "Oh, I'm not worried about Ben. I know he'll be fine. You and Jonah, too."

"I'm glad to hear your faith is strong. Why the furrowed brow, then?"

Rebecca rubbed where she'd chewed her nail. "I was thinking about the magistrate and James Packer."

"Ye might be borrowing trouble before it arrives. Benjamin will see to your cares."

Rebecca laced her fingers together and flexed her hands back and forth. "I hope so, Adam. I don't think I can leave this boat."

The movement of the yawl being lowered interrupted their conversation.

Rebecca watched as the crew manned the ropes, and Ben called out commands. In short order the yawl was in the water and being rowed to shore. No one approached the boat as William and Matthew reached the beach and pulled her up onto the sand.

Rebecca kept her focus on the small figures in the distance. William eventually spoke with some men working further down on the larger dock. She noticed Ben was also keeping close track of the two men. Otherwise the crew meandered about, pretending nothing out of the ordinary was happening. Rebecca decided she could try to do the same.

She crawled up onto the roof and leaned against a brace under the boom. Closing her eyes, she pictured Ben before her. She replayed every precious moment between them, her heart racing as she realized how deeply she cared for him. She couldn't explain it to herself, hadn't a clue how these feelings had developed so quickly, yet couldn't deny she felt them. Rebecca lost herself in fact and fantasy, letting the world slip away.

Jonah's voice brought her back around. "Did ye rest well, Mrs. Reed?"

His teasing told Rebecca she had been out longer than she thought. She stretched and noticed the tension in her neck was gone. She felt better, peaceful. "I believe I did."

"Ben has asked me to escort you down to your cabin before the crew goes below for supper."

Rebecca cringed momentarily, then remembered her promise to Ben and plastered on a smile. "Thank you, Jonah. Lead the way."

The room was empty, except for a couple of crates and the cot. She paused before entering.

"We moved the barrels while you rested. Ben thought it best."

Jonah left her with the door open, promising to return shortly with her meal. He returned sooner than she'd expected, though not with her supper. He carried a leather-bound book in his right hand. "Adam felt ye might be comforted with the Good Book."

Rebecca smiled, gratitude filling her heart. She had found an easy friendship with Adam and Jonah in a place and time when she needed it most. And she sensed they both felt protective of her, a feeling she hadn't known in a long, long time. "Thank you, Jonah, and please thank Adam for me. My heart could use an infusion of faith."

Jonah shook his head.

"What?" Rebecca couldn't imagine what she had said wrong that time.

"You sound like Missy again with those fancy words."

Rebecca winked. "Great minds think alike."

Jonah nodded and left. Rebecca moved a crate close to the open door to have more light for reading. She opened the King James Bible to the Twenty-third Psalm and read the words her grandmother recited daily.

"The Lord is my Shepherd; I shall not want. He maketh me to lie down in green pastures: he leadeth me beside the still waters. He restoreth my soul: he leadeth me in the paths of righteousness for his name's sake. Yea, though I walk through the valley of the shadow of death, I will fear no evil: for thou art with me; thy rod and thy staff they comfort me. Thou preparest a table before me in the presence of mine enemies: thou anointest my head with oil; my cup runneth over. Surely goodness and mercy shall follow me all the days of my life: and I will dwell in the house of the Lord for ever."

As Rebecca read the verses a second time, slowly, word by word, peace settled over and around her. She could almost hear her grandmother speaking the words as she made breakfast. Rebecca sensed she would travel to the twenty-first century tonight. She knew it was safer, yet a part of her ached. She wanted to stay. She wanted to go. With no explanation other than her own intuition, she knew she had to leave tonight. Her departure didn't even feel like a choice.

A knock on her door simplified her thoughts. "Supper, Mrs. O'Neill."

"Come in. What has Adam made for us tonight?"

"Fish stew," Jonah said as he passed her the bowl. "I am sorry you are not able to join us at the table."

Rebecca smiled warmly. "Ben has his reasons, and he's right. I will miss your conversational skills, though."

He blushed ever so slightly before turning to leave. "I shall leave you to your meal."

"Thanks, Jonah."

Rebecca nibbled on the food, hungry yet preoccupied. She could hear snatches of conversation in the saloon. The men were obviously excited about the evening's activities. Rebecca finished her stew and set the bowl outside the door for Samuel or Jonah to take down to the galley.

She sat on the cot and picked up the Bible. The light was fading fast, and reading was no longer an option. She wished for a pen and paper and the chance to scribble down her thoughts, maybe even write a letter to Ben. She knew in her gut she would rejoin her class trip when she fell asleep. If she didn't return to 1775 again, she had so much she wanted to tell Ben.

As if he read her mind, Ben appeared in her doorway. "I have come to bid you good night and to remind you again to stay in the cabin with the door closed. If the unloading wakes you, do not arise. If you hear…whatever you might hear, stay put."

Ben looked serious and solemn and worried. Yes, definitely worried. He gazed at her questioningly. "Please, Rebecca?"

Realizing he'd been waiting for a reply, she walked toward him. "Yes, Ben, I will do as you ask. I know tonight will be a success, and you will be safe. I will stay here and leave the work to you and the crew. I promise."

Ben smiled for a moment, then cocked his head to the right and frowned. "Adam shared with me your concern for the morrow. I cannot dispel all your fears, but I do promise to help you in whatever way I can."

Rebecca breathed a mixture of relief and longing. She wanted to say thank you, she wanted to ask him how he would help her, she wanted to melt into his arms, she wanted to stay forever, she wanted to go back and be safe. Instead, she smiled and dropped her eyes to the floor, trying not to show or express her fears and confusion.

They stood just inside her cabin, neither moving, neither wanting to say good night. Rebecca gathered her hair and turned around. "Can you help me with the laces, Ben?"

Silence engulfed them. Rebecca waited. Finally, after what seemed like years, Ben's fingers brushed over her skin as he untied and loosened the laces. She held the bodice of the dress close to her chest as the sleeves fell off her shoulders. Ben slid his hands across her bare shoulders and gently pulled the sleeves back up. Rebecca's flesh burned where his fingers touched her skin. Heat crept up her neck and climbed to her face. An involuntary moan escaped her lips.

Suddenly his fingers were gone. Rebecca turned quickly to see if someone had come upon them. She saw only Ben and the fire burning equally hot in his eyes. She didn't know whether to step back and avoid getting burned or to rush forward and be consumed by the rising flames.

Ben took a step forward, then backed up and swiftly stepped outside the cabin. He shook his head, denying the need for both of them. "Go to sleep, Rebecca."

She didn't want to move, didn't want to leave him, didn't want to say good night, didn't want to risk no more tomorrows. She placed her right hand on the doorframe and leaned into it for support. "Ben, if I'm not here tomorrow, I want you to know the last two days were some of the best of my life."

Rebecca quickly closed the door, not daring to see Ben's reaction to her confession. She collapsed against the door and listened for the sound of his footsteps. She held her breath. Seconds passed and no sound came. She felt more than heard his hand press against the door. She waited for his footfall and heard instead, "For me also, Rebecca."

Her heart leapt. She exhaled and placed a hand over her mouth to contain the joy bubbling up inside her. She tiptoed to the cot, mindful of the dim light, and stared at her sweatpants neatly folded and situated atop her pillow. Jonah must have brought them down from Ben's cabin. Thinking of the cabin reminded her of the look on his face when she'd turned about in the gown, the feel of his hands on her skin and the desire in her heart.

Rebecca changed out of the dress and donned her sweat pants, sure she was leaving and certain she wanted to stay. "I shall not want. I shall not want," Rebecca prayed as she lay on the cot. "He makes me to lie down in green pastures...I will fear no evil."

*

Ben waited to move until he thought she was settled. "Keep her safe, Lord," he murmured. "Watch over us all tonight, but please protect Rebecca from any who would see her harmed. Help me to ensure her safety. Help me to comfort her. And please, Lord, help me to understand the feelings in my heart."

13

REBECCA HEARD THE CLANGING. *It's just the stove, Becca, go back to sleep.* In a heartbeat Rebecca sat up. She surveyed the cabin and knew instantly she was reunited with her class trip. She flopped back onto her bunk, hugged her pillow to her chest, and sobbed.

She knew she should be happy she was home. She knew she should be grateful she was safe. She knew she was born in the twenty-first century and therefore belonged there. If only she could convince her heart to listen to her head. She wanted to see Ben. She needed assurance he was safe, that everyone survived last night's escapade. How many hours until she could go back? Would she go back? How was she supposed to focus on the children when all she wanted was to see Ben's face?

Rebecca let the tears flow. She had never considered herself one given to tears. Her Gram could cry at the drop of a hat. Her mom never stopped crying after her dad died. Until the summer cruise, the tears had skipped a generation.

"Fine moment to be making up for lost time," Rebecca sobbed into her pillow.

As the gray of twilight gave way to the morning's colors of dawn, Rebecca realized she needed to get herself together and prepare to face the kids and the crew. She dried her eyes, found a box of tissues, and blew her nose. Grabbing her exercise mat, she decided a gazillion sit-ups, some push-ups, and a lot of stretching might lift her mood and energize her for the day.

She changed into a T-shirt and a school sweatshirt before heading upstairs. Heading to the rail, she gazed out over the water. "I stood with Ben in this same spot only yesterday," she quietly told herself. She wiped the small tears from her eyes. "Don't start again, Becca."

Rebecca walked forward to the ship's bell. Different. She walked midship to the galley. Different. She walked aft to the yawl. Different.

"Okay, Lord, it's all different. No Ben, no Jonah, no Ben, no Adam, no British, no hanging and, did I mention, no Ben." She shuffled back to their spot on the rail. Rebecca carefully placed her right hand on the spot where Ben had held the rail yesterday. She imagined the feel of his hand, felt of the warmth of the wood, and breathed in the ocean air.

She cast her eyes to the heavens. "I shall not want, I shall not want. Not today at least. Tonight will be a different story, Lord. Sorry about that, but You know I'm thinking it, so I might as well say it. Please send me back tonight. This is not a want, it is a need, Lord. I need to see Ben, I need to know he's okay, and I need to explain to him who I am…and why I'll disappear for good one day soon."

Movement at the bow caught Rebecca's attention. Tim was up and waved. She waved back, wishing it was Jonah. *Stop it, Becca. Stop it right now!* she scolded herself. *Get to work and get your head in the here and now.*

Rebecca unrolled the mat and dropped to her hands and knees. She began her workout and rushed into the harder exercises. Her breathing quickened, and her heart rate elevated. She started to feel better. She brought her hands to the edge of her mat and extended her legs. She hated push-ups but knew they were a necessity regardless of her mood. Twenty-five of them would do her some good and be a great finish to her workout.

"Do you do this every day?" Hawk asked.

Rebecca laughed as she exhaled. "Only if I'm breathing."

"I thought as much. One of the girls said you coached track."

Rebecca completed her last two push-ups, walked her hands back toward her feet until her heels were flat on the floor, and held the Downward Dog pose. "I coached the last two years. I had Kayla's older sister, Lily, on my team. Lily will be an eighth grader this year and a formidable sprinter for anyone to battle. I hope Kayla will try out. I've seen her run on the playground for the entire recess and she has the stamina to do distance."

Rebecca exhaled and drew in another deep breath.

Hawk's feet remained in view, upside down and not going away. "Sounds like you enjoy coaching more than chaperoning."

Rebecca released her breath gradually, walked her hands back to her feet, and rolled up slowly, vertebrae by vertebrae. She met Hawk's smile with one equally bright. "Funny thing about this boat, Hawk, I came on dragging my heels and wishing I could stay home. Now I don't want to leave. I can't explain it to you, but I need to be here as I've never needed anything else."

Hawk looked surprised, then grinned. "I know what you mean. I spend the rest of the year waiting for the season to start again." His gaze roamed over the boat like a lover watching the woman of his dreams. "I would love to convince Captain Roberts to take her down to the Caribbean for the winter months. We could do kids' cruises there, too, or adult cruises like he used to do. I think the best option would be to hire her out for private weeklong charters. We'd be in winter vacation paradise, lots of wealthy people who might love to have their own sailboat for a week. So far he's not the least bit interested."

Rebecca shook her head. She knew Captain Roberts would never leave his family or the Island. "Good luck with that idea. The captain will never sail so far from home. I know he talks about sailing till the wind runs out, but I think he'd be circling the Island the whole time. Not to mention Katherine would have much to say about him being gone for so long."

He chuckled without enthusiasm. "Tell me about it. Last summer the captain listened to my idea, then told me to talk to Katherine at the end of the summer. I thought he was giving it some serious thought. Little did I know he was setting me up for the ultimate 'no.'" The disappointment in Hawk's voice was unmistakable.

Rebecca placed a hand on his shoulder. "What happened?"

Hawk grimaced. "Katherine told me in no uncertain terms, 'Never, I repeat, never will the man I love be so far from home.'" He glanced around the boat, his eyes settling on the ship's bell behind Rebecca. "Katherine insisted five days a week, ten weeks out of the year was more than she wanted as it was. I'm going to pitch the idea again, this time with me taking the boat and Captain Roberts staying home."

Rebecca stepped back and ran her eyes in mock shock up and down Hawk's ridiculously fit frame. "You're really cruising for a bruising, Bud. You honestly think he'll let this ship out of his sight?"

Hawk's eyes filled with dreams and hope. They glazed over and Rebecca knew he was sailing over crystal blue waters on another continent. He sighed. "It's my dream job, Rebecca. I have to try."

Dreams. Rebecca knew about dreams. Her nights had been consumed by a very real dream, a dream she didn't want to let go of. Her heart swelled with compassion. She recognized the emotions his eyes conveyed. Her dream was even more impossible than Hawk's, yet she wanted it as much as he wanted his. "I understand, Hawk, I really do. Ask Captain Roberts, and if that doesn't work, find another way or another boat. Don't give up."

Hawk tilted his head and stared at her. "I barely know you, Rebecca, but I know you're different. There is something about you now, maybe even in you, that wasn't there a few days ago. I can't put my finger on it, but I think this trip has been good for you."

"Could be her evening activities."

Rebecca and Hawk spun to find Mike Natale standing directly behind them. Neither had heard or seen him approach.

"What are you saying, Mike?" Hawk snapped.

Mike sneered. "Let's ask Rebecca, shall we?"

Two sets of eyes bored through her. Her mind raced. Her body went rigid. Could Mike possibly know the truth? Had he sneaked into her cabin at night and found her bunk empty? She eased her breathing and relaxed her muscles, steadying her nerves. "Ask me what?"

"Been to Boston lately?"

Rebecca wanted to laugh. The tension eased out of her body in one long breath. She could tell the truth. "Sure. I went up twice this summer to catch a Sox game. Why?"

Hawk chuckled.

Mike asked sarcastically, "Did you sleep in your bed last night?"

All amusement drained from Hawk's face. Rebecca sucked in her breath. "What are you implying, Mike?" Hawk growled between clenched teeth.

Mike didn't answer. He glared at Rebecca like a cobra hypnotizing his prey. She felt the venom as surely as if she'd been bitten by a poisonous snake. He took a step in her direction, pointed a finger in her face, and accused, "I don't believe you were in your bunk last night, Miss O'Neill."

Hawk lunged forward. Rebecca reached out a hand to stop him. He brushed her hand off. Rebecca grabbed his arm. "Don't, Hawk. Please."

Rebecca looked between the two men, both ready to pummel one another in sheer acts of male stupidity. She had to say something to break the tension, even if that something wasn't totally honest. "Mike, I didn't leave my cabin until this morning when the stove woke me. I certainly wasn't in anyone's bed, if that's what you're insinuating."

Mike's mouth twisted into a frown. "I wasn't suggesting you were sleeping with anyone onboard. I believe you weren't here at all. I believe you were with Melissa. Isn't that right, Miss O'Neill?"

Hawk stormed two steps closer to Mike, unadulterated anger steaming from every pore. Mike scurried a few steps back.

Hawk stood toe to toe with the husky freshman. "Drop it, Mike! You've pulled that line on every person who's stayed in Cabin 8 this summer. We have one more trip to make this summer. If you want to keep your job and earn the end-of-the-season bonus Captain Roberts is famous for, you'd best keep your mouth shut and leave Rebecca alone. I've had it with your time-travel theories." Hawk walked over to Rebecca.

Mike didn't move, simply stared at her. "You didn't answer my question."

Hawk started for Mike, but Rebecca held up her hand again. In a clear, soft-spoken voice, Rebecca replied, "Mike, I haven't visited Melissa, seen Melissa, or been visited by her."

Rebecca held Mike's gaze, knowing she had spoken the truth, the truth about Melissa at least. She felt a small amount of guilt for she knew Mike was partly right in his thinking, but she knew now was neither the time nor the place, nor was Mike the person to share her experiences with. For reasons she couldn't fathom, she saw malice flash in his eyes before a blank stare met her gaze. "I don't believe you," he said with less force.

Rebecca stepped in front of Hawk, who appeared ready to throttle Mike. "I don't know what else to tell you, Mike. What can I say or do to prove to you I have not seen Melissa?"

Rebecca watched the anger in Mike's face evaporate. She didn't know whether it was what she said or her tone, but Mike seemed to crumple before her.

"Nothing." Mike hung his head. "Maybe you are another dead end."

Rebecca's shoulders slumped. The truth was too complicated here. She wanted to escape to her cabin, out of the line of fire and away from questions she couldn't fully answer.

Hawk stepped in and saved her. "I need to turn the generator on. Rebecca, you need to get the kids on deck. Mike, you have chores to do. This conversation is over. I don't want to hear another word about it. Is that clear?"

Mike puffed up in defiance, met Rebecca's kind eyes, and deflated like a sad blowfish. "Clear," he said as he turned to walk toward the bow.

Rebecca felt like crying. She'd needed peace this morning, not another battle. She forced a smile. "Thanks, Hawk. I'll go round up the kids."

"No worries. Sorry about all that. Mike has been a problem all summer. I should have fired him weeks ago. I hope he lets it go for the rest of the trip. He's a strong sailor and good worker when he's not focused on Melissa Smith. I just don't get why he cares. It's not like they were related or anything."

Rebecca frowned. "There is more to his story, Hawk. He's angry and scared and disappointed all at the same time. Did you notice how he almost crumpled when I said I hadn't seen Melissa? It is as though he wants or even needs to find her."

Hawk placed a hand on Rebecca's shoulder. "You are a kind woman, Rebecca. I can hear your sympathy and compassion, which I applaud." Hawk stepped back into a wide stance and crossed his arms. "Just don't get sucked into whatever is going on with Mike. I want this issue dropped before Captain Roberts catches wind of it, okay?"

Rebecca couldn't look Hawk in the eyes. She mumbled an "I'll try" and hurried away before he could stop her.

14

REBECCA PUT ONE FOOT ON THE COMPANIONWAY STAIRS just as the generator kicked on. She jumped back as the first head barreled up the stairs. "Deck wash," Hawk yelled.

"Look out, Miss O'Neill. I'm getting a broom today or else," Raz said as he raced past her. The stampede continued as boys and girls tried to edge each other out of line in their rush to pick the equipment of their choice.

"Slow down before somebody falls down," Rebecca said to the group pushing at the bottom of the stairs. Starr, wiry and quick, slipped by Alexis and Ashley as they squabbled over who was next in line. Starr giggled, hopped onto the third step, and began scurrying up.

"Hey," Alexis hollered. Starr, almost to the top, laughed and turned back to stick her tongue out at her two friends. Rebecca saw it before Starr felt it. Her right thumb on her nose, fingers wiggling, Starr brought her left leg up and missed the step, smacking the top of her foot on the seventh step. Starr instinctively reached for her foot, only did so with her left hand. Rebecca watched in horror as Starr tumbled backward, landing with a ghastly thud. The girls screamed. Rebecca yelled for someone to find Hawk as she bolted down the stairs.

"Don't touch her!" Rebecca said.

"She's not breathing," Alexis shrieked.

Rebecca felt for a pulse. Strong and steady. "Thank You, Lord."

In seconds Hawk was by her side. "She fell backwards off the stairs. She hasn't moved or made a sound, but she has a strong pulse. Do you think we should move her?"

Hawk shook his head. "We've got a backboard stored in a closet past the galley. I'll go get it. She looks fine, but we don't want to risk any spinal or internal injuries. Stay here. I'm going to get Dave, too. He's an EMT. This is his area of expertise, not mine."

Rebecca noticed the kids had gathered around. Many were crying, and every one of them looked frightened. "Nick, please go wake up Mrs. Butler. Everyone else listen to me. Starr is going to be fine. Her pulse is strong. She probably just hit her head hard enough to knock her out for a few minutes. We're going to put her on the backboard and check her out. I wouldn't be surprised if she woke up any second now."

Rebecca willed Starr to move, but the petite brunette remained far too still. Rebecca knew of only one answer. She held Starr's hand and bowed her head. "Lord, Starr needs Your healing touch. Please surround her with Your love, hold her gently in the palm of Your hands, and breathe wellness into her." Rebecca continued to hold Starr's hand.

Alexis started to cry. "It's all my fault."

Rebecca glanced over her shoulder at the tall blonde with wavy hair and tear-stained cheeks. "Oh, sweetie, it's not your fault. Everyone was goofing off, including Starr. She was racing up those steps and whacked her foot. You had nothing to do with her fall."

Rebecca reached back with her free hand and gave Alexis a reassuring squeeze. "I don't want you to blame yourself for another second."

A soft moan brought all eyes back to Starr.

"She's waking up!" Ashley announced in her usual loud, confident voice.

Starr began with a whispering moan and built to an ear-piercing scream. Rebecca gripped her hand, moved into Starr's line of sight, and spoke firmly. "Starr, look at me. I need you to stop screaming and tell me what hurts."

Starr whimpered. "Everything. Everything hurts." She started to cry again. Rebecca felt her tears were more shock than pain. "It's going to be okay, honey. Take a deep breath. Help is on the way."

Hawk and Dave worked their way through the kids with the backboard. "Well, young lady, I'm glad you're awake." Hawk said as he leaned down and gently brushed the tears from her face.

Hawk's presence seemed to bring Starr around. She gave him a weak smile, which he returned like only a knight in shining armor could. Dave squatted beside her, too. He leaned close and whispered into Rebecca's ear, "We need to examine her. Can you talk her through it for me?"

Rebecca nodded, then spoke to the young damsel in distress gazing into Hawk's blue eyes. "Starr, honey, we need to move you onto the backboard and check you out. Dave is an EMT and wants to make sure you're all right. Okay?"

Starr sniffled and moved her head up and down in weak consent.

"There's a girl," Dave said. "Now we know your head and neck still work. Did you feel any pain when you moved your head?"

"No, not moving, but my head really, really hurts. I feel like someone is squeezing my brain and banging on my bones or something."

"Tell me about it, tell me about the squeezing sensation," Dave said. He looked into Starr's eyes and picked up her hands as he waited for her reply.

Starr watched Dave moving her hands. "It just hurts. You know, like all over, inside and out. Not like a headache. Worse."

Dave held up one hand with three fingers raised. "How many fingers am I holding up?"

"Three."

"Do they look fuzzy or blurry?"

"Nope. They look like your fingers. You have a big burn on your first finger."

Rebecca and Dave chuckled. "Old Bessie got me yesterday," he said.

Starr followed Dave's instructions, placed her palms flat against his palms, and pushed down as hard as she could. "Does that hurt?"

"No."

"Good. Now, can you lift your right arm?"

Starr moved every limb Dave asked her to. She felt no pain in moving. Rebecca began to breathe easier. She noticed the kids were now talking amongst themselves. A good sign they were relaxing, too.

Dave moved to Starr's head. "Okay, Starr, you're doing great. I want to feel your head and see if you've got a big bump somewhere. It might hurt when I touch you. I'm sorry."

Hawk stepped away as Dave went behind Starr.

Rebecca stood beside him. "What do you think?"

Hawk kept his eyes on Dave as he answered. "I think she's fine, though she may have a concussion. We should probably bring her home, but let's wait to see what Dave says."

"Owww!!" Starr yelped.

"Sorry, Starr. You have quite a lump on your head. I'm going to get some ice for you to lay on to help keep the swelling down. Hawk and Josh will carry you back to your cabin. Don't try running up those stairs again while I'm gone." Dave winked and stood.

"I promise," Starr mumbled, new tears welling in her eyes. "Am I going to die?"

"No," Dave and Rebecca answered in unison.

"You're going to be fine, Starr. You've got a big bump and some bruises, but you'll be in school next week. You do need to go see a doctor, though, so he can give you the okay to run around and swim this weekend."

Rebecca patted Starr's hand. When Dave stood and walked over to Hawk, Rebecca asked Kayla, Starr's best friend, to come sit beside her.

Dave stepped over to Rebecca and Hawk. He was all business. "Good news and bad news. I don't think anything is broken. She's likely to have a few ugly bruises, but that should be the extent of her lower body injuries." Then he lowered his voice. "But the bump on her head is pretty nasty and swelling quickly. I think we need to get her to the hospital just to be safe."

"I'll go speak to Captain Roberts. The Coast Guard can pick her up and get her to the hospital faster than we can," Hawk said.

Dave moved his head in agreement and turned to Rebecca. "I'm going to get an ice pack. Don't leave her. Try to keep her talking. If she needs to vomit, turn her head."

Rebecca flinched. This was worse than she thought.

Dave put a hand on her arm. "I don't think we have to worry. I'm telling you as a precaution."

Rebecca visibly relaxed. Hawk whistled to get everyone's attention. Heads poked over the hatch and those in the galley stepped closer. "Starr is feeling much better, so we're taking her down to her cabin for some rest. Breakfast is going to be a few minutes late, but morning chores have been cancelled. Why don't you all go back to your cabins and prepare for inspection."

Kayla raised her hand. "Can I sit with Starr in her cabin?"

"Me, too," Ashley said.

Josh and Hawk carried Starr on the backboard down to her cabin. Hawk shrugged at Rebecca as he walked by. "Probably no harm if they take turns."

Rebecca called for quiet. "Okay, kids. Here's the deal." The group settled. Rebecca walked a few steps closer to the saloon and directly under the hatch so everyone could hear her. "Starr is going to the doctor's in a little while. Until then, she needs to rest, but we also need to keep an eye on her while we wait for the Coast Guard to arrive. Kayla, you can sit with her for the first ten minutes, then Ashley, then Alexis, and then whoever else would like."

Rebecca searched the faces until she saw Sharon. "Mrs. Butler will make a list. Anyone who would like to sit with Starr, sign up. Mrs. Butler will let you know what time your shift is." Sharon gave Rebecca a weak smile and walked to the galley with all the girls hot on her heels. Rebecca sped to Starr's cabin.

Dave was in the room placing the ice pack under her head when Rebecca arrived. Starr winced. "I'm sorry, Starr. I know it's cold and probably hurts a lot, but we need to keep the swelling down. I've got to go make some breakfast for your friends, but you call me if you need anything, anything at all. Okay?"

Starr smiled weakly.

Rebecca thanked Dave and sat beside Starr. "Your friends are really worried about you. Do you feel up to a visitor every few minutes?"

Starr grabbed Rebecca's hand. "Can I call my daddy?" Tears formed in her soft brown eyes.

Rebecca heard the fear and longing in her voice. "Of course, sweetie. When Kayla gets here, I'll send her down to my cabin for my phone."

Kayla arrived a few minutes later. Rebecca told her where to find the cell phone. Rebecca spoke to Mr. Gates first and explained the situation. She assured him she would call back as soon as she knew more about the plans to transport Starr.

Starr hugged the phone and asked her dad to meet her the second she arrived. Rebecca could tell by Starr's smile that he promised to be there.

Twenty minutes later Hawk came in with the news. "A special boat is coming to take you to your dad. It will be here in about fifteen minutes. Miss O'Neill will go with you." Hawk paused and eyed Rebecca. He mouthed "okay?"

Rebecca nodded.

"I'll pack your gear and stay with you and Alexis while Miss O'Neill runs back to her cabin to get ready."

Rebecca dashed to her cabin, changed her clothes, grabbed her backpack, and went in search of Sharon and Kevin. She found everyone in the saloon eating scrambled eggs and toast and explained what was going on. Kevin assured her they'd be fine. Rebecca grabbed two pieces of toast and an apple.

The Coast Guard arrived and transferred Starr into an emergency bed onboard. A paramedic was examining her before they pulled away. Rebecca watched the *Shenandoah* shrink before her eyes. A wave of panic seized her heart, and Rebecca clutched her hands to her chest. "Oh, no! What have I done?"

"Are you okay, Miss?" the paramedic asked, rushing over. Rebecca felt like she was going to faint. She'd left the boat. She'd walked off the *Shenandoah* and hadn't even thought about Ben!

"Miss?" said a loud voice.

Rebecca looked up. "Ben?"

"Richard, Miss. Are you okay?" His expression let Rebecca know she'd better get it together quickly, or she'd be the next patient.

"I forgot to call Starr's dad before we left. Where will we dock, and what time will we get there?"

"We are coming into Vineyard Haven. We'll be there in about twenty minutes."

Rebecca rummaged through her bag for her cell. She had to take care of Starr; she wanted to take care of Starr; she needed to get back to Ben. She called Mr. Gates and let him know they were on their way. The boat moved over the calm sea with great speed but little bounce. Starr rested comfortably, although she wasn't too happy when they hooked her up to the IV.

Rebecca wandered over and sat next to Starr. Their hands met and Starr grabbed on. "I hope my dad is there."

"He will be. I just talked with him."

Starr closed her eyes. "I hope he's not mad at me."

"Mad? Of course he isn't mad. I'd bet on it. He's probably very worried, though."

Starr squeezed Rebecca's hand tighter. She opened her eyes slightly. "You told us not to run. Hawk told us not to goof off. I was teasing Alexis and Ashley when I fell."

Rebecca could see the worry and guilt written all over the tanned olive skin on Starr's pretty young face. Her brown eyes shifted anxiously.

Rebecca eased a finger under Starr's chin and tipped her head up slowly. "Kids will be kids. I don't blame you; I bet your dad won't blame you either. Accidents happen. Some lessons we learn a little more painfully than others. I bet you'll remember this one." Rebecca leaned down and gave Starr a kiss on the check. "No more talk of blame. Let's think about the ice cream and presents you'll probably get."

Starr's eyes brightened. "You think?"

Rebecca laughed. "I would bet on the ice cream, and I'm pretty sure a present or two will find you."

"I'm sorry, Miss O'Neill. I'm ruining your trip, too."

A lump formed in Rebecca's throat. She had no idea how true Starr's words may be. When she made it back to the *Shenandoah*, would the spell be broken? Did her leaving the ship mean she'd never see Ben again? She shouldn't think about Ben, not now with Starr lying here hooked up to an IV, but she couldn't help herself. Her heart ached with fear and longing. Would she ever see Ben again? Rebecca lifted her face into the breeze, felt the wind raise her hair and the sun warm her face. Everything *had* to be okay—it just had to be.

Rebecca rubbed Starr's arm and forced a smile. "Hey, don't tell anyone, but I'm going home and sneak in a shower."

Starr giggled. "Bet Mrs. Butler wished she was taking me home."

Rebecca laughed, then caught herself. "Mrs. Butler's not so bad." Starr made a face. "Okay, you're probably right about her wanting a shower."

Starr chuckled. "Are we almost there?"

Rebecca sighed, all too aware that where Starr wanted to be was in the opposite direction of where she wanted to be. Rebecca glanced toward the shoreline. "Almost, sweetie. We are going by West Chop right now. I can see the harbor. The *Island Home* is docked. We'll probably pull in alongside her."

"Daddy doesn't like the new boat. He says the *Islander* was a classic, and there will never be another like her. I like the new ferry. She's huge, with televisions, games and the Internet, not to mention the big snack bar with the hot pretzels."

Rebecca felt a twinge of nostalgia. "I agree with your dad. The new ferry is nice and can handle more cars and people, but the *Islander* was special. I have so many memories of riding to the mainland with my parents. When I was your age it was a big treat to ride the *Islander.*"

"I love going to America. We only go a few times a year."

Rebecca heard the wistfulness in Starr's tone. She remembered begging her parents to go to the mainland, or America, as Islanders call the rest of the continental United States. Rebecca wondered if she could give it up—life as she knew it with phones and indoor plumbing and freedom. The twisting knot in her stomach forced her to ponder whether she'd even have a chance now to make that decision.

Rebecca would have lost herself in images of Ben if the captain of the Coast Guard vessel hadn't announced their docking. Starr tried to sit up. "Just lay still, Starr. A few more minutes and we'll be off the boat."

Starr looked anxious. "Can you see my dad?"

"Would he be the handsome man waving enthusiastically and holding a stuffed blue dolphin?"

Starr giggled. "That's Daddy. Maybe he's not so mad if he brought Bernie."

Rebecca cocked her head. "Who's Bernie?"

Starr blushed. "Oh, he's my dolphin. Don't tell anybody, but I sleep with him."

"Your secret's safe with me if you don't tell anyone I'm going home for a long shower."

The two shook hands just as Brant Gates boarded the boat.

"Daddy!" Starr yelled.

Brant ran over to his daughter, love filling his eyes and concealing whatever worry Rebecca knew he must be feeling. "Well now, Princess Starr, you can't be too hurt if your lungs are still working that well."

"My head hurts, Daddy, but I don't feel too bad. Can we just go home?"

Mr. Gates turned to the paramedic, who shook his head. "She really should go to the hospital, sir. She has a nasty bump on the back of her head. Better safe than sorry. The ambulance is ready whenever you are."

Mr. Gates stroked Starr's check and squeezed her hand. "Time to go, Starr-Starr. The sooner we go, the sooner we can go home. And maybe, if you're really good, we'll stop off for some ice cream."

They disembarked from the boat, and Mr. Gates thanked Rebecca at least a half dozen times before he climbed into the ambulance. Rebecca kissed Starr on the cheek as they lifted her up and promised to check in on her later.

"Are you going back to the *Shenandoah*, Miss O'Neill?"

Rebecca winked. "Right after that shower. I'll tell all your friends how brave you are and how much better you're feeling."

"Thanks, Miss O'Neill. You're my favorite teacher already."

"And you're my new favorite star."

"Don't forget to call me later," Starr said right before they closed the ambulance doors.

"I promise."

Rebecca watched the ambulance pull away, said a prayer for Starr, and headed toward Skiff Avenue. A shower would be good, as would some time alone. She looked at the boats in the lagoon and immediately thought of Ben. "Who are you, Benjamin Reed?" Rebecca said aloud. She noticed the free WiFi sign in the coffee shop as she walked by. "I can Google Ben and the *Shenandoah* and try to find out more information."

Her heart racing, Rebecca started to jog the half mile home.

15

REBECCA REACHED HER HOUSE IN LESS THAN FIVE MINUTES. She ran around to the back and pulled the key off the wall in the outdoor shower. She chuckled, thinking about how many off-Islanders were amazed at the easygoing lifestyle on the Vineyard. Many houses were never locked, cars were left with keys in them, and friends and neighbors always knew where the extra keys were stored (hidden not entering into anyone's vocabulary).

Rebecca stepped into the front hall, slipped off her Birks, and took a deep breath. She waited for the usual feeling of peace to settle over her as the walls of her childhood home welcomed her back. Nothing happened. She stood for a minute longer, momentarily discombobulated by the foreign feeling, then walked down the hall to her bedroom.

After her Gram died, Rebecca had moved downstairs into the master bedroom her grandmother had occupied after her parents' deaths. Rebecca loved the spacious room with the big bay window overlooking her grandmother's flowerbeds. One rainy week early in the summer she'd stripped the wallpaper off the walls, sanded everything down and then painted the room a soft yellow to match a great pair of floral curtains she'd found in town. Rebecca had splurged a little on a new duvet and sheets, but the finished product was so worth it. Sitting on the bed, she finally began to feel at home.

She spied her computer lying on the desk and itched to find out more about Ben. "First things first, Becca," she mimicked her grandmother. "You need a hot shower, fresh clothes, and then the computer."

Rebecca pulled her sweatshirt off and dropped onto the duvet, staring at the ceiling and thinking about Ben. The bed felt so good. Before she knew it, Rebecca was fast asleep....

*

A ringing woke her nearly two hours later. Rebecca reached over to hit the snooze button, only to discover it was almost noon and her alarm was not going off. She leaped out of bed and dashed for her purse.

"One missed call," her phone read. Rebecca stomped her foot and hit redial. "Please, God, don't let me have missed my boat."

"Summer Sails Tall Ship office, may I help you?"

"Hi, Vera, it's Rebecca O'Neill. Sorry I missed your call."

"That's okay, dear. I thought you might be in the shower or running errands."

Rebecca looked in the hall mirror at her disheveled appearance. "Not yet, though I was heading that way."

Rebecca heard Vera cluck her tongue. "You'd better hurry, then. The boat will be here by one. You are going back today, right?"

Rebecca's eyes widen. *"Yes!* I have to. Please don't let them leave without me. I'll be there in thirty minutes." Rebecca hung up and hustled to the bathroom. She would have preferred the luxury of her outdoor shower. Feeling the sun on her skin and looking up at the sky while the shower washed her clean was pure paradise. Today Rebecca didn't want to waste the five minutes walking to and from the house. She showered quickly, barely able to enjoy the hot water and her mango-citrus body soap. She slathered on her favorite lotion, applied some sunscreen, and threw on clean clothes.

Rebecca glanced at the computer, mad at herself for falling asleep and wasting precious time she could have used researching the past and learning more about Captain Reed and his part in the Revolutionary War. "Sorry, Ben, there's no time now. I have to get back to you."

Rebecca felt compelled to take her photo albums, her mother's silver hairbrush, her grandmother's knitting needles and her father's pipe, but she knew it was pointless. If she could go back to Ben, the present had to stay in the future. Rebecca tapped her hand on the doorframe, wiped a tear from her eye, and headed down the hall, wondering what the future held, if she would ever come back to her little house, if she wanted to come back?

She slipped on her Birks, opened and closed the front door, walked the key around to the outdoor shower, and headed for the dock. She waved to Mrs. Bangs on the way; she considered checking her mail but opted to wait. The only news she wanted revolved around Ben, and he wouldn't be sending her a letter. She reached the office at a quarter to one. Vera looked displeased when she entered. Rebecca held her breath.

"Bad news, Rebecca. Tim took the yawl to shore with the dogs first before coming to fetch you and he ran out of gas. Someone forgot to check the tank on Sunday. Hawk called to say they are rowing some gas over to Tim from Menemsha, and then they hoped to sail this way and pick you up. Looks like it will be a couple of hours after all. Sorry you rushed down here."

Pain registered quickly. Rebecca glanced down to find her knuckles white as snow and her fingers clenched around the back of the chair. She shook her hand out, trying to shake off a feeling of dread. "But they are coming, right?"

Vera examined Rebecca with a grandmother's concern. "Relax, honey, those kids are in good hands. If you don't make it back today, everyone will be fine."

The words were not soothing. Rebecca gripped the back of the Queen Anne chair, nearly tipping it over. "I *have* to get back. I can't stay here. Someone has to come for me before dark."

Vera stood and stepped around her desk. She put her hands gently on Rebecca's shoulders. "Now, honey, you'd better sit down before you fall down. You don't look so good. Too much stress and worry." The office manager felt Rebecca's forehead. "Well, you're not running a fever. Let me get you a glass of water."

As Vera walked away, panic rose inside Rebecca. She covered her eyes with her hands. Questions pummeled her overwrought mind. *What if? What if I don't get back to the* Shenandoah *tonight? What if I never see Ben again?*

A glass was placed in her right hand. "Sip this a little. Maybe you got a touch of heat stroke riding over on the boat this morning and then running around to get back here?" Vera sounded doubtful and eyed Rebecca closely until she drank some water.

The water tasted stale. Rebecca put the glass down on the desk. She didn't feel the least bit better, but she smiled for appearance's sake. "Did Hawk happen to mention what time they would be here?"

"No, honey, he didn't. He said they were hoping the winds would stay steady, and they could be underway as soon as the yawl and the rowboat were back and secured. Why don't you head back home, and I'll call you when I hear something?"

Rebecca jerked her head up and searched for her cell phone. "Can I call Hawk? I really need to talk to him. I must explain to him that I *have* to be on the *Shenandoah* tonight."

"Of course you can call him, Rebecca, but first why don't you tell me what is really worrying you? I've seen a lot of chaperones in my years and not one has ever been this upset about leaving a group of kids who are well attended."

Rebecca opened her mouth and then snapped it shut. She desperately wanted to talk with someone, to pour out her heart, but she knew she would sound crazy, which could easily land her in the psych ward instead of back on the *Shenandoah*.

She cast her eyes to the floor, hating to lie. "I'm in charge of those kids.

Starr fell this morning, and I can't let anything happen to anyone else. Sharon is a fine person, but she's not loving the trip. Kevin is great with the kids, but there are too many for him to keep an eye on alone. I simply have to get back there. Maybe the Coast Guard could take me back out?"

Vera frowned. The idea obviously didn't please her. "You'll have to wait on Hawk. We can't ask the Coast Guard to play taxi service. Let's give it a couple of hours and see what happens. Why don't you go get some lunch and relax?"

Rebecca didn't want to leave the office. She wanted to sit right there and wait for Hawk's call. But she sensed Vera was telling her politely to leave. She stood and picked up her backpack. "Please call me as soon as Hawk calls you. I will keep my cell on at all times. Maybe I'll stop by in an hour and check in."

Vera walked Rebecca to the door and patted her on the shoulder as Rebecca stepped out into the hot August sun. "No need to stop back, honey. I promise to call. Now go relax. Maybe a walk on the beach would do you some good."

She couldn't do anything but agree. "The beach does sound good. I'll stay nearby in case you call."

Rebecca walked by the bakery on the corner and up past Beetlebung, her favorite coffee shop with the great soups and salads. She wasn't hungry; she didn't want anything to drink. She just wanted to get back to the *Shenandoah*. She reached Main Street and stopped, uncertain where she was going.

Cars and pedestrians were everywhere. She needed quiet. "Susan's!" she shouted. A few people walking nearby stopped and stared. Rebecca turned right and headed up Main Street. She walked the mile down to the town beach, kicked off her Birks when she hit the sand, and then snaked her way along the shore's edge, momentarily trespassing on a few private beaches before she reached Susan's property.

Rebecca had been to Susan's many times. They had grown up together and now both worked at Holmes Hole Elementary School. Susan taught eighth grade, God bless her. Susan's family had owned the house for centuries, literally, and now she was living here with her husband and their two little girls, Vicky and Vanessa. Rebecca knew they were camping in the Berkshires this week, so she would have peace and quiet—and cell phone reception— while she waited for Vera to call.

Beach chairs and lounge chairs were placed strategically along the shore. Rebecca plunked down in a blue chair, extracted her sunglasses and cell phone out of her purse, and dialed Mr. Gates' number. He answered on the second ring. "Hello?"

"Hello, Mr. Gates, it's Rebecca O'Neill. How's Starr doing?"

"Hi there, Ms. O'Neill. Wonderful news. Starr only has a slight concussion. They released her about an hour ago, and we're sitting here in Ocean Park having an ice cream right now."

Rebecca offered silent praise. "That is great news. Does Starr have a free hand to talk for a second?"

Mr. Gates laughed. "She must, because she's grabbing the phone out of my hands."

Rebecca chuckled.

"Hi, Miss O'Neill. Are you back on the boat? Did you tell everyone how brave I was? Did Hawk ask how I was doing? Can I talk to Kayla?"

Rebecca's emotions flipped from sadness to joy hearing Starr's exuberant questions. "I'm still waiting for my ride, Starr. I'll be sure to tell everyone not only how brave you are, but more importantly, that you are on your way to a full recovery. They'll all be so happy to hear that. Hawk has checked in and I know he'll be thrilled, too. I know you want to tell Kayla all about your day, but you'll have to wait until she gets home. How's that ice cream?"

Starr giggled. "Yummy. You were right. I got ice cream and a present. Daddy bought me a little stuffed dolphin in the store next to the ice cream shop. I can clip him to my school bag and always remember our trip. I named him Hawk."

Rebecca heard the tender crush in Starr's voice. She'd have to tell Hawk he'd won another heart, as she was sure he'd done all summer. "I'm so happy for you, Starr. Now stay home and relax for a few days. I'll…um…see you next week."

"Thanks, Miss O'Neill. Have fun on the boat. Don't get sunburned," Starr joked. Her witty sense of humor had returned.

"And no jumping off any ladders for you."

They both laughed and hung up.

Rebecca called the sailing office to say Starr was fine, though what she really wanted to know was if Hawk had called. Vera insisted he hadn't, but said she would let him know Starr was fine when he did.

Rebecca left the cell phone in her lap. She took in her surroundings—not a soul in sight. She leaned back and closed her eyes. The sun warmed her skin, and she appreciated the cool ocean breezes.

"Lord, I am so grateful Starr is okay. I really have no right to ask for anything more today. *But,* I need to see Ben. Please help me get back to the *Shenandoah* tonight. Something doesn't feel right. I know I'm anxious and Gram would tell me to 'stop borrowing trouble,' but I'm nervous about getting back. Please."

Rebecca focused on her breathing, listening to the intake and release of air. She tried to capture her thoughts and center herself in the moment in the chair on the beach. Stillness settled around her. Rebecca felt her toes relax, then her feet and then her legs. She was relaxing her hands when a gull drifted overhead and squawked, startling Rebecca from her reverie.

She flipped her cell phone open. No calls. "Okay, relaxation is not happening. I should have known this was a waste of time. What was I thinking? I could have been home Googling Ben."

Rebecca checked the clock on her phone. It was already 1:35. She couldn't think about the wasted time. She just needed to go home and make up for lost time.

Rebecca stopped off at the post office to pick up her mail on the way home. Just bills, not that she expected a card or note from Ben, but who knew these days? She opened the phone. Still no calls. She checked the answering machine as soon as she walked in the door. No calls. She turned on her computer and went into the kitchen to get a glass of water, an apple, and a granola bar.

She sunk into her favorite chair, clicked onto the Internet, and Googled "*Shenandoah*, Benjamin Reed." Thousands of matches came up. Most of the matches were for the current *Shenandoah*. Lots of Benjamin Reeds, but none of them her Ben.

Rebecca tried Benjamin Reed 1775 and received thirty-five thousand matches. She'd never get through them all before she had to leave—at least she hoped she'd be leaving soon. She clicked on the first one and kept going. About a hundred hits in, Rebecca rubbed her eyes and checked the time. Almost 4 p.m., time to check in.

"Tall Ships Office, can I help you?"

"Hi, Vera, it's Rebecca. Any news from Hawk?" There was a long pause, which brought Rebecca to her feet. She started pacing in front of her computer. "Hello?"

"Honey, I didn't want to upset you, so I've put the call off for a bit. Hawk called about an hour ago to say there was too little wind and the *Shenandoah* wouldn't be sailing today. He doesn't want to risk sending the yawl with so little gas. He said to tell you everyone is fine, and they will definitely pick you up tomorrow. I told him Starr was doing well and resting at home."

Rebecca's whole body shook. She couldn't form any words.

"Rebecca? Are you still there? Dang cell phones." The phone went dead, then started ringing less than thirty seconds later.

Rebecca stared at her cell. Maybe she had imagined the first call? "Hello. Vera? Any news from Hawk?" Rebecca stood stock still, holding her breath and wishing for the impossible to be true.

"Oh, honey, I guess you didn't hear the last phone call. Hawk did call and said they will pick you up tomorrow, probably around noon. The wind is supposed to be fairly strong tomorrow morning."

"No," Rebecca whispered, a lump forming in her throat.

"Did you say something, Rebecca?"

Rebecca tried to clear her throat, but a weak cough barely made her voice audible. "Is there any other way to get out to the boat tonight? I will pay somebody. I have to be there. Please."

"Gosh, Rebecca, I can't think of anyone to take you out there now. Not too many of the local guys with motorboats are even in the harbor right now. By the time they get back, it would be too late to take you out. Don't worry about those kids, honey. Everyone will be fine tonight."

Rebecca wanted to scream, "It's not the kids!" but held her tongue. Realizing the futility of the conversation, Rebecca said good-bye and collapsed on her bed as the tears flowed. *Why, Lord, why?*

She cried for Ben, she cried for herself, she cried for her parents, and she cried for her grandmother. Rebecca cried until there were no tears left to cry.

Exhaustion and despair weighted her body. Sleep finally took over. The glow of the computer cast its twenty-first century light on Rebecca as she slept through the night.

16

EARLY MORNING LIGHT LIT THE BEDROOM. Rebecca rolled over onto her stomach and hugged the pillow. Memories of waking on Ben's shoulder and his smug expression filled her mind and she snuggled deeper into the pillow. Sighing contentedly, Rebecca replayed every word, every image, every moment with Ben she could remember. She simply *had* to see him again, which was a first. She'd never felt that way before about any man.

Come hell or high water, she was getting back to the *Shenandoah* that day, even if she had to build an ark to get there.

Her intentions determined, Rebecca got out of bed and changed into workout clothes. It was only five-thirty, and she had plenty of time to go for a walk, do some yoga on the beach, and maybe kayak around Lagoon Pond. Vera wouldn't be in until ten, which gave Rebecca almost five hours to fill. Better to keep busy and enjoy her morning then worry about what she felt for Ben, if she'd see him again, how the kids were faring and when she'd get back to the *Shenandoah*.

She walked the mile or so to Eastville Beach, stopping frequently along the way to smell the beach roses. The pink, white, and red flowers emitted an intoxicating fragrance Rebecca had loved since childhood. She cherished the half-dozen bushes her grandmother had planted in their yard on her sixth birthday. From those bushes they had made rosehip tea, sugared flower petals, and numerous floral arrangements. Rebecca picked a pink blossom, breathed in the scent, and wondered if Ben had ever smelled a beach rose. Ben again? She shook her head and kept walking.

When she reached the beach, Rebecca dropped her mat, fished a plastic baggie out of her yoga tote, and headed to the shoreline. She combed the beach, down to the jetty and back, searching for sea glass. She paused to watch the sun break the surface of the ocean like a dolphin jumping high in extremely slow motion. The sky glistened with streaks of oranges, pinks, and blues. It was a beautiful day.

After a successful hunt, which included three decent-sized pieces of blue, numerous whites, browns, and greens, and one unique piece of yellow sea glass, Rebecca unrolled her mat and began a series of breathing exercises before her workout.

An hour later, with sweat dripping from her pores, Rebecca shook the sand off her mat, rolled it up, and headed for the water. She walked in up to her knees and splashed the sand off her legs and arms. She loved a salt-water mini-bath after a workout on the beach. The cool water cleansed her body and her mind. Now happy and peaceful, she picked up her mat and headed for home.

A steady stream of traffic, bikes, and people crowded into Rebecca's personal space as she walked back to her house. She decided an hour spent kayaking would do her more good than pacing the floors at home or tootling around her tourist-infested town.

The kayak she shared with a fellow teacher was stored on a rack with her neighbors' kayaks by the old wooden dock at the bottom of the hill just before Rebecca's street. She left her tote on the ground, hoisted the kayak off the rack, and carried it down to the water. Rebecca put on her life vest, took off her sandals, and pushed the kayak into the lagoon. She rowed around the marsh grass, startling a few ducks and fish, then headed toward the inlet and the open sea.

Rebecca returned home around eight-thirty. She checked her cell phone and answering machine for messages before heading to the outdoor shower. She turned on the hot water, stripped down, and stepped into the spray. "Ahh, this is the good life! Sun shining, hot water streaming down, and the scent of mango and roses in the great outdoors."

Like many Islanders, she had grown up showering outside, and not only when they returned from the beach covered in sand. Before the LaBelles built next door, Rebecca's family only had a privacy wall blocking the view from the road. Now the shower was fully enclosed with plants growing outside and in. From April till November, there was nothing better than an outdoor shower, especially after the week she'd had so far.

Rebecca lingered a little longer than usual, shaving her legs and buffing her feet while she deep-conditioned her hair. She hadn't had a good shower since Sunday afternoon, though it felt much longer than four days. "Today might be Thursday, but I feel as though I've been traveling for years!"

She rinsed her hair, tried to push the encroaching visions of Ben aside, then wrapped up in her fluffy pink towel.

Still thinking about Ben, she toweled off quickly and hurried inside. Her message light was blinking. Rebecca's heart skipped, and she dove for the play button. "Good morning, Rebecca. It's Vera. Hawk called me at home and asked me to call you. They've raised the sails and are headed this way. Perhaps you could be at the office within the hour. I will go in a bit early and meet you there."

Rebecca picked up the phone, pushed the missed calls button, found Vera's number, and punched redial. Vera picked up on the second ring. "Hi, Vera, it's Rebecca."

"Good morning, Rebecca. Did you get my message?"

"Yes, thanks. I'll be there in thirty minutes. Has Hawk called again?"

"No, he hasn't, though I suspect he'll call shortly to give me an update. It's a great day for sailing, so I gather they'll make good time. See you shortly?"

Rebecca wanted to do cartwheels. "Yes! That's great. I'll be there in a bit. Thanks, Vera."

"You're welcome. Bye now."

Rebecca hung up the phone and dashed into the closet. She pulled on a pair of jean shorts and a "Yoga On The Rock" T-shirt. She made a bowl of Irish oatmeal, added raisins, dried cranberries, and pecans, and poured a glass of water. Rebecca ate quickly, tidied up after breakfast, stocked her backpack with nuts and dried fruit, and slipped on her sandals.

She walked through the living room and halted as she passed her father's bookshelf. Dozens of books on sailing, boats, and the sea, as well as history, lined the shelves. She opened the front door and turned back. A wave of nostalgia washed over her. "You're a great house. Thanks."

Rebecca prayed on the walk down to the sail office. She prayed all the kids would be in one piece. She prayed Sharon hadn't driven Kevin crazy. She prayed the boat would be anchoring when she arrived at the office. But she prayed most reverently that she would travel back in time at least once more to see Ben.

Since she'd gotten out of bed, Rebecca had tried to avoid thinking about Ben. Now her heart wouldn't let her stop. She considered whether her overnight here would affect her time in 1775. What if Ben went down to find her in the morning and she wasn't there? How would she explain her absence to him?

Rebecca hoped last night would vanish in time as her extra night with Ben had on Tuesday. She wondered how it was possible to stay with Ben and only have nighttime hours pass here in the twenty-first century. If she could stay in 1775 for two days with everyone unaware she was gone, surely Ben would be oblivious to her extra time here in her modern-day life. "Please let it be so, Lord," she whispered.

The traffic at five corners was a pedestrian nightmare. The ferry was unloading another hundred or so cars of day-trippers and other forms of tourists, while Islanders and summer residents were starting their days at full speed. Rebecca snapped to attention at the sound of the first horn. Lost in her reverie, she nearly crossed the street before the taxi van driver blasted his horn and saved her life. She jumped back to the curb, let the van pass, and waited for the little Smart car to stop.

"Gosh, wouldn't Ben be amazed at what life has become? Probably better I'm traveling back in time than him coming forward. The shock alone might kill him even before he got run over." Rebecca chuckled and picked up her pace. As she came around the row of buildings leading to the Tall Ship office, Rebecca peered out to sea. She saw the sails instantly.

A jolt of excitement rushed through her. She'd be back on board before lunch. Who would have ever thought she had once dreaded the class trip? Rebecca laughed to herself.

Vera met her outside. "The skiff is ready to take you out if you're ready."

Rebecca smiled so broadly her face hurt. "Ready!"

The women walked from the office to the outer point on the dock. Vera glanced sideways. "I have never, in all my years, seen a chaperone as eager to get onboard as you are, Rebecca. May I ask why?"

Yikes. How can I answer that question honestly? "I can't explain it to myself, never mind anyone else. Honestly, I went kicking and screaming on Sunday. Then something happened, and I, well, I just love that boat."

Vera grinned that I-Know-Your-Secret grin Rebecca had seen on her grandmother's face many times when she had, in fact, had a secret. Now Vera wore it and offered her guess. "Would that 'something' be Hawk?"

Puzzled, Rebecca said, "No, nothing to do with Hawk. He's a nice guy and all...."

Vera gave her a grandmotherly smile. "Guess I read that one wrong. Yesterday I could have sworn you were in love when you were so desperate to get back to the ship."

Rebecca stared straight ahead. In love? Is that what she felt? She'd never been in love, at least not as an adult, and she had nothing to gauge these emotions by. She had thought herself in love with Billy Calhoun during the summer of her junior year in high school, but her emotions cooled and soon faded after his departure on Labor Day. In college she was too busy studying, working, and missing home to invest any energy into serious dating. Lately she'd been going out with Jeff, but she knew in her heart she had no lasting feelings for him beyond friendship.

Ben was...what? Surely God wouldn't have her fall in love with someone two hundred or so years older than her? There had to be a guy in the twenty-first century, right? Even as the thought passed through Rebecca's musings, her heart expanded and contracted as an image of Ben smiling at her across his cabin came to mind. She sighed audibly.

Vera patted her arm. "Don't fret, honey. You'll meet someone when you least expect it."

Rebecca didn't know whether to laugh or cry. If Vera only knew she was heading toward the most least-expected romance she could never have imagined in her life....

They reached the end of the dock, where a young man waited in a small motorboat. "Jeremy will take you out. Will save time to have him bring you instead of Hawk sending the yawl from the ship. Enjoy the rest of your trip, Rebecca."

"Thanks. Have a great day."

Rebecca climbed into the skiff and tried to contain her delight as the *Shenandoah* drew closer. Kayla spotted her first and began waving. Soon the kids were screaming her name. She waved back and thanked her lucky stars everyone appeared to be fine.

Rebecca barely set foot on deck before the questions started.

"How is Starr? Hawk said she went home last night. Is that true?" Ashley said.

Raz elbowed Nick. "Have any ice cream or fudge without us, Miss O'Neill?"

"Can we call Starr?" Kayla asked, her big blue eyes begging to talk with her friend.

"What was the Coast Guard boat like? Is it a hospital?" Nick said.

Alexis crept forward through the throng of students. "Is Starr really okay, Miss O'Neill? She doesn't have any broken bones or brain damage or something, does she?"

Rebecca hugged Alexis. The poor girl was still blaming herself. "Listen, everyone." Rebecca's voice was lost in the melee.

A shrill whistle pierced through the noise. The kids fell silent as Hawk walked over to Rebecca. "Welcome back, Miss O'Neill. How was your day off?"

Rebecca smiled at Hawk, trying not to blush as she thought of Vera's questions and implications. "Hi, Hawk. Thanks for bringing the troops to attention."

Rebecca made eye contact with as many children as she could, then brought her focus back to Alexis. "Now that we have some quiet, let me tell you all about Starr. She was very, very brave. And she is doing great. She only spent a little time at the hospital and then was sent home with instructions to take it easy for a few days. When I talked to her in the afternoon, she was at Ocean Park having an ice cream with her dad."

A loud round of clapping and cheers erupted. Hawk called for all hands on deck and the kids prepared to hoist the lowered sails and set off for another day of adventure.

*

The day flew by. Rebecca relished their afternoon swim. Everyone feasted on a delicious turkey dinner with apple pie for dessert.

By the time Hawk called lights out, every man, woman, boy, and girl was exhausted. The kids went off to bed quietly after washing up.

When all was silent below, Rebecca went up on deck to find Hawk. "I wanted to thank you for yesterday, for getting Starr taken care of so quickly and keeping the kids under control. Kevin told me Sharon wasn't much help."

Hawk put down the rag he was using to polish one of the brass night lamps. "You're welcome. The kids were somewhat mellowed after Starr left and pretty easy to handle. Kevin did well. He's a great guy. I think Sharon is out of her element."

Rebecca grinned at Hawk. "I should tell you that you made quite an impression on Starr. I think you might just be her first major crush." She giggled as Hawk blushed.

"You mock me?" Hawk adopted his traditional commanding stance, legs braced and arms crossed.

Trying to contain her laughter, Rebecca replied with all the seriousness she could muster between chuckles, "No, hardly. Just surprised someone of your rather stern demeanor blushed so easily."

Hawk dropped his hands and took a step toward Rebecca. Leaning closer, he whispered his secret. "It's all a front. I'm actually a big softie."

Rebecca winked. "In that case you won't mind that Starr named her new stuffed dolphin Hawk and plans to clip the little guy to her school bag so she can always remember you." Rebecca stepped back and watched Hawk's expression go from playful to reflective. She gave him five guy points even before he spoke.

"Wow, that's really sweet. All the kids are special, even the ones you want to keelhaul, but every trip there are one or two who tug at your heart a little extra. Usually the galley boy gets the lion's share of fans since he interacts with the kids the most, but the rest of us manage to get a few crumbs now and then."

He wasn't joking, and Rebecca appreciated this newly exposed side of Hawk. She realized why Tess had fallen for him two years ago. Perhaps in another time and place Vera would have hit the nail on the head. Then again, in another time and place Tess and Hawk would have dated—at least Tess would have given it her best shot. But right now Rebecca wanted desperately to say good night and head down to her bunk. She hoped beyond hope that she would wake up and find herself in Ben's company.

Rebecca yawned and Hawk nodded. "Long couple of days. Why don't you grab some shut-eye? The kids will be well rested and ready to go come morning. I wouldn't want the teacher to be dragging."

Rebecca rolled her eyes. "Spare me. Come dawn, I'll be up and stretching. See you in the morning. If you're game, grab a towel and do some push-ups and sit-ups with me. Then we'll see who's tired."

Hawk laughed. "I just might do that one day. I'll wait till you're in top form, though, and you've had a good night's rest. Sleep well, Rebecca."

Rebecca waved as she started down the companionway. She closed the door to her cabin, changed quickly into her sweatpants and a tank top, then stretched out on her bunk. She closed her eyes and pictured Ben's face.

Dear Lord, please.

17

REBECCA HEARD THE STOVE AND ROLLED OVER. Accustomed now to the sound, she didn't give the first bang much thought. Slowly, then with an increasing pulse, Rebecca realized where she might be. Without opening her eyes, she offered up a heartfelt prayer. "Lord, please, oh please, oh please, let me be with Ben."

Gradually, as though she might be able to change reality or blink away a situation she didn't like, Rebecca opened her eyes. She was on the cot. "Yes!" she whooped, jumping out of bed faster than a hummingbird flaps his wings.

"Thank You, thank You, thank You!" Rebecca sang the words as she spun in a tight circle, careful not to bump any of the barrels. She was midway through her fourth spin when she realized there were none. It took her a few seconds to remember that the crew had moved them before she went to the cabin last night. She moved slowly in the dimly lit space. If the supplies were still gone, then the night must have been successful.

"They did it," Rebecca whispered. She inched to the bed and perched on the edge. Her eyes glanced at the door. She listened carefully. The stove was lit, which had to be a good sign. Ben and the crew had to be be okay. They must have gotten all the gunpowder and supplies ashore safely. So where was Ben? When would he come to check on her? Dear God, she hoped he had not already knocked on her door and found her gone. She wasn't ready to explain her absence. She didn't even know if she could explain it, at least not in a way that Ben wouldn't think she was an alien or a witch.

Rebecca ruffled up the bed to make it appear as though she had slept in it. She sat counting the seconds to when Ben might be at her door and then realized that Ben would have expected her to rise and make the bed. On a ship as well run as the *Shenandoah* he wouldn't be surprised to find her bed made; he would probably be disappointed to find it unmade.

Shaking her head at her own silliness, she began smoothing out the sheets and felt a lump toward the end of the cot. "My dress!" She gingerly picked up the fine green fabric and held it to her. She closed her eyes and saw Ben's face when she'd first put it on. She sighed and hugged the dress tighter.

She knew she should get dressed. Ben would expect her to be clothed in something other than her sweats. She was fairly certain his sisters hadn't walked around in their pajamas all morning. They probably ate breakfast in their pretty dresses.

Rebecca did the best she could to assemble and tighten the laces. She would ask Ben to pull them tighter and re-tie them when he finally showed up. She sat back down, fluffed the dress about a dozen times and then started a nervous, fidgety tap with her feet as she continued to stare at the door. She guessed it probably wasn't locked.

Even as she rose and reached for the door handle, Rebecca knew she shouldn't leave the cabin. She had promised Ben that, no matter what she heard or didn't hear, she wouldn't leave her room. "Darn it," she exclaimed as she stomped her foot. She was about to sulk back to her bed when she heard footsteps and muffled voices. She waited as they came closer. Rebecca thought it must be Ben and Jonah, or maybe Ben and Adam. She placed her right hand on the door.

At the sound of the first rap of knuckles against the wood, she tore open the door and sucked in her breath. Her eyes locked on Ben. "Thank God you're okay," she exclaimed, exhaling a sweet sigh of relief and joy before leaping across the doorway and wrapping her arms around him. "Where have you been? I've been sitting here waiting for you, worrying how things went. I don't know what I would have done if…"

"Shhhh…" Strong arms gathered Rebecca close and held her tight. "I am well," he whispered in her ear.

For a second Rebecca thought she heard a deep sadness and a catch in Ben's voice. She attempted to step back, wanting to see his face, but he drew her to him and rested his chin gently on her head. "I am sorry you worried. I was preoccupied. I didn't consider your concerns. I should have come sooner. My apologies, Rebecca."

Rebecca leaned against his chest, and inhaled all that is Ben. *Yes,* she thought as she felt the beat of his heart and heard him breathe in the scent of her hair. *I could stay in this moment, embraced by Ben, for the rest of my life.*

From somewhere outside her perfect world Rebecca heard the clearing of a throat.

Ben stepped back abruptly and disentangled their arms, obviously chagrined.

"Benjamin, would you care to introduce me?" a man asked.

Rebecca jerked her head toward the strange voice, suddenly aware that there was another person in the hall, and the other person was neither Jonah nor Adam. Ben looked from Rebecca to the man and dropped his gaze to the floor. He shook his head as though clearing away a fog. Rebecca reached for his hand, afraid the man before her was the magistrate come to take her away. Ben pulled his hand away. Rebecca's heart seized. She paled, feeling the world slipping away, the distance multiplying between them.

Rebecca shrank under the stranger's acute stare. This man was watching every move they made like a hawk eyeing its prey. He didn't necessarily look mean, just very, very observant of the interaction between Rebecca and Ben.

Finally Ben stepped forward. "Rebecca, I would like you to meet my father, Eli Reed. Father, this is Mrs. O'Neill, the woman I mentioned earlier."

Rebecca gaped, jaw open, tongue-tied. Her mind raced. His father? She could see where Ben got his good looks. She should have seen the resemblance the instant she opened the door. Well, maybe she would have if she hadn't been focused on Ben. *What did Ben tell his father about me? What will Eli Reed think of me? What does he know about me?* She remained motionless, unable to move beyond the swirling mess inside her head.

The silence became noticeable. Trying to recover, Rebecca extended her hand. Ben's father appeared puzzled. Rebecca quickly realized her mistake, drew her hand back, and curtsied.

"Pleased to meet you, Mr. Reed. Ben has spoken fondly of his family."

Mr. Reed offered Rebecca a warm, friendly smile in return, and she instantly relaxed. He took a few steps in her direction, walking past her and into the room, placing himself just to her left. Ben followed him in. Rebecca didn't move. Her feet felt glued to the spot where Ben had left her.

"Benjamin has told me some of your story, Mrs. O'Neill, though I believe he has omitted portions," Mr. Reed said, raising an eyebrow at Ben.

Rebecca watched with mild amusement as Ben turned various shades of red. Rebecca knew this wouldn't be the ideal moment to laugh at his discomfort, though she was tempted to. She coughed politely into her hand and raised her eyes to Mr. Reed, avoiding the temptation to smirk at Ben.

Ignoring Rebecca completely, Ben stepped closer to his father. "Mrs. O'Neill is the stowaway I conversed with you about last night." While Ben spoke without a drop of emotion, Rebecca noticed his father wore an expression of amusement, more than one of analytical interest.

Ben continued as though he hadn't observed his father's behavior. "I believe her innocent, Father. She is frightened at times, though I do not believe her fear is based on being caught in a web of lies. I do believe she is lost. When I came down to her cabin that first morn, she was praying reverently to go home. She believed she was alone. Her words were earnest and heartfelt. She was, in truth, rather annoyed when I startled her and made my presence known."

Mr. Reed merely nodded. "You are protective of her, Benjamin."

Ben sputtered, "She is in my care, Father."

"Ah," his father said and chuckled. "You are not ready to admit it yet. Your mother is going to enjoy this."

Ben shook his head. "Father, what are you talking about?" He sounded as perplexed as Rebecca felt. What *was* his father talking about? What was Ben's mother going to enjoy about Rebecca's current situation? Rebecca waited for the answer during the pause in conversation. After an overly long silence, she could almost hear the laughter in his father's voice when he spoke.

"Nothing, Benjamin, nothing at all." Then he did laugh and Rebecca wondered what was so funny. She certainly didn't feel like laughing. Nor did she feel at liberty to ask Mr. Reed what he was laughing about.

"Will you talk with her, Father? We must decide what is to be done with her."

"Yes, Benjamin, of course."

Rebecca sucked in her breath. Done with her? Did Ben, her Ben, just say "done with her"? Who was this man, and what had happened to the Ben who had held her close only minutes before?

Anger mixed with fear and Rebecca strode into the room. "You can stop talking about me as though I'm not present here in the room, as though I can't hear you. I am not invisible."

Both men turned their full attention to Rebecca. She realized women in their era probably did not speak to strange men, never mind so assertively. Well, too bad. She had feelings and opinions, and right now she wasn't too happy with Ben, and Mr. Reed wasn't too high on her list either. Whether Ben knew her history or not, he should be appreciating the fact that she traveled over two hundred years to be with him, not standing there asking some stranger, even if it was his father, to decide what should be done with her. Rebecca wagged her finger at Ben as she geared up for a tirade.

Ben's father stepped forward and captured her hand between his two. "My apologies, Madam. We were most rude." He bowed and released her hand.

Rebecca looked to Ben who mouthed, "Sorry."

Although she was still annoyed, especially with Ben, Rebecca offered an apologetic smile to Mr. Reed. "I'm sorry I snapped at you. My grandmother would not be happy with me."

The tension in the room dissipated. Mr. Reed clasped a hand to Ben's shoulder. "Perhaps we could start over, Mrs. O'Neill, and you could fill in some of the blanks Benjamin neglected?"

Rebecca knew an olive branch when she saw one, and she knew intuitively that this branch was one she wanted to accept. "I would like that, Mr. Reed."

"You are a gentle woman, Mrs. O'Neill, quick to forgive. I suspect your grandmother would be proud after all."

Ben's father offered Rebecca his arm, and they headed toward the saloon. Rebecca glanced behind to see that Ben was following, which he was, though she could not read his expression. He looked very serious but oddly pleased—a strange mix Rebecca did not have time to worry about. Maybe he was glad his father was being nice to her? Or maybe he was glad his father was around to decide what to do with her?

Stop it, Becca. You've got enough to think about without adding Ben's thoughts into your head.

Once in the saloon Mr. Reed suggested Rebecca take the inside bench. He took Ben's place at the table and was about to say something to Rebecca when Jonah descended the companionway.

"Good Morning, Father. Ben." Jonah appeared somber before giving Rebecca an impish grin. "How are you this morning, Mrs. Reed?"

Ben rolled his eyes. Rebecca blushed from head to toe as he exaggerated the *Mrs. Reed.* Mr. Reed stared from Ben to Jonah to Rebecca and round again. Jonah simply grinned at them all. "Father, have you not been introduced to Ben's wife?"

"Enough, Jonah." Ben was clearly struggling to maintain his composure. He turned to his father after glaring at Jonah. "Father, Jonah is distorting an incident yesterday where Mrs. O'Neill bravely and smartly acted a part to divert the attentions of a British captain intent on boarding the *Shenandoah.* Nothing more."

If Rebecca hadn't flinched at his last words, if Jonah hadn't guffawed, Mr. Reed might have believed Ben's story. Instead, he directed his attention to Rebecca and watched her squirm a little too much for Ben's "nothing more" to be the whole truth. Without shifting his focus, the reverend instructed his boys.

"Now Jonah, I'm certain you'll add color and comedic light to the events of the last few days. Please sit down and join Mrs. O'Neill and me at the table. I expect you to be respectful of the lady and her feelings at all times. Hold your tongue if you must."

"Yes, Father," Jonah replied with deference and admiration. Jonah sat across from Rebecca. He gave her a friendly wink while his father turned toward Ben.

Rebecca loved the little scoundrel, even if he did tease her incessantly. She imagined Ben felt the same, but probably not at this moment, as he currently appeared eager to strangle his little brother.

Mr. Reed looked up. "Benjamin, I believe you have much to do on deck before breakfast. I have heard your account of the past few days; now I shall discuss the recent events with your brother and Mrs. O'Neill. I desire to hear the rest of the story. Please ask Adam to bring us all a mug of coffee before you head up."

With a nod, Ben walked toward the kitchen where Adam was hard at work making breakfast. *Wow,* thought Rebecca. It was clear his sons adored and respected him and he them. She knew he had just admonished them both, but his words were said with such love and gentleness there was no sting or hurt to be felt. She hoped he would be as kind to her.

Steaming mugs of coffee soon appeared. Rebecca was thrilled to see that Adam, too, was alive and well. She was full of questions about last night but knew they would have to wait until much later. At least everyone and everything appeared to be well.

"Thank you, Adam." Mr. Reed took a sip of his coffee.

Rebecca waited for his first question. A nervous flutter twitched inside her stomach. She opted not to drink the coffee. She blew on the hot liquid, wrapped her hands around the mug, and prayed silently for the words to convey to Ben's father what was going on without having to tell him what was going on.

"You appear nervous, Mrs. O'Neill. Please relax. I am convinced my sons are rather fond of you, which is testimony enough to your innocence as well as your need for our help. Why don't we start at the beginning?"

Rebecca took a deep breath. She *was* innocent, and she definitely needed help. She wished she could just tell this kind man the whole truth, but her life wasn't that simple. So she began with her arrival on the *Shenandoah* that first morning and her encounter with James Packer. Mr. Reed listened intently, asking questions here and there and nodding occasionally. Jonah remained fairly quiet until Rebecca relayed her victory at cards.

"You should have seen Ben's face, Father," Jonah threw in. "He was flabbergasted."

Mr. Reed joined in the shared laughter. "Well done, Mrs. O'Neill. Benjamin is rarely bested."

Rebecca desperately wanted to skip over the hours after their card game and her night of sleeping on deck and waking on Ben's shoulder, but Jonah didn't let her. He did have the decency not to bring up all of the morning's events, for which Rebecca would be eternally grateful. She sensed Mr. Reed suspected there was more to that portion of the story, but he let it go. Rebecca told of the British ship in great detail. Jonah made sure Mr. Reed was clearly impressed. When she tried to gloss over her idea and her role in the farce, Jonah elaborated with extensive details. "She did the Patriots proud, Father."

Rebecca basked in their appreciation. "It was rather awesome, wasn't it, Jonah? Almost as good as the Sox sweeping the Series in '04." She clasped her hand to her lips. As soon as the words were out of her mouth, she knew she had given herself away. They wouldn't know who or what she was talking about, but they would know something wasn't right.

Then a miracle happened as simply as her grandmother said they did.

Jonah slapped his knee and laughed. "She talks a lot like Aunt Missy."

Mr. Reed eyed Rebecca carefully. "Aye, she does, Jonah. As well they should, having arrived from the same location, and, if I'm not mistaken, perhaps in the same fashion."

Rebecca sucked in her breath. *He knows,* she thought, *he knows in a good way. Somehow, someway he knows. Now what?* Rebecca didn't have time to ask any more questions as the ship's bell rang and the crew descended for breakfast.

Ben entered the saloon, and his father slid over next to Rebecca to yield the captain's seat to Ben. He patted her right arm gently. "All will be well, Mrs. O'Neill. We shall finish our conversation after the meal. I believe I might have a story to share with you as well."

Rebecca could only nod as her stomach knotted and flipped. Plates of food were passed in front of her, yet she did not dare eat a bite. Ben's father accepted a platter from Rebecca and glanced at her plate. As though he read her mind, Mr. Reed placed a biscuit and a small portion of eggs on her plate. "Do eat, Mrs. O'Neill. You need sustenance for the day ahead. You have naught to fear now. I believe I understand what you have not yet stated. A simple solution is within reach."

Rebecca didn't know what the solution could be, if he really knew who she was and where she was from, but she trusted him. She picked up her fork and took a bite of eggs.

*

Ben kept his eyes on his plate. He wondered, *What the devil is Father talking about? What solution is he referring to? And what did Rebecca and Jonah tell Father when I was out of the room?*

124

He made the mistake of glancing at his father, who immediately grinned, then drew close and murmured, "You have chosen well."

Ben stabbed his eggs with his fork. "I know naught of what you speak, Father." He shoved the forkful of eggs into his mouth as his father chuckled. Ben cast a seething glance at Jonah. He would strangle him later if he found out Jonah told his father about the other morning.

He stole a glance at Rebecca. She appeared more relaxed. Something had been said, and he was going to find out what.

18

JAMES PACKER SCRAPED HIS PLATE into the garbage pail and walked toward Ben. Throughout breakfast Rebecca had remained fully attuned to where Packer was. She had seen him enter the saloon before breakfast and had subtly slid a little closer to Mr. Reed. She had caught him sneering at her a couple of times and had averted her eyes, praying he would leave her alone. So much for that idea!

Packer strode over now, resembling a psychopath in a horror movie, his murderous glare never shifting from Rebecca. With furtive glances she scanned the room. Where was Jonah? Rebecca felt the need for protection; something similar to the New England Patriots' defensive line might be comforting. She gulped and wished like crazy she could somehow maneuver herself between Ben and his father.

Packer stopped to Ben's left. He glowered daggers at Rebecca while he addressed Ben and Mr. Reed. "I am sorry for your loss. Magnus was a good man," Packer said, eyes focused on Rebecca and seething with hatred.

Shock rippled through Rebecca. She fought for air. "What did you just say?"

"You heard me, Tory. Another good man is dead at the hands of the King's Men. I would gladly hang you myself in retribution."

Rebecca felt the room spin. She heard voices but couldn't make them out. Someone hollered a warning. She gripped the table and lowered her eyes to the floor. She'd forgotten about Magnus. When she saw Ben this morning, all she could think about was how happy she was he was alive and standing there before her. She hadn't given a thought to his father's arrival and what news he would bring. No wonder Ben had held her so tightly earlier. *Oh, Lord, why did Captain Roberts have to be right? Poor Ben. Poor Jonah.* Tears misted Rebecca's eyes. She folded her arms and dropped her head to the table.

"Spare me your tears, traitor. You'll be crying for your life before this day is over."

"James!" Rebecca heard Ben roar. The room grew eerily silent, and tension charged the air to the point where no one breathed easily. "I cautioned you twice. You are discharged from my ship as of this moment. William will take you ashore immediately. Gather your belongings."

Packer took two aggressive steps toward Ben before William and the burly Donald Blake grabbed his arms. Like a caged animal, he howled, "Your own brother dead at the hands of the King's Men, and here you sit, defending their spy. You should be hanged along with her."

Plates crashed to the floor. Rebecca snapped her head up. Ben charged at Packer, sending some dishes flying and setting the table to teeter like a child's seesaw. William and two others continued to restrain James. Jonah appeared and moved in front of Ben, pushing with both hands on his chest. Adam parted his way through the crew, mallet in hand.

Rebecca started shaking. "No," she yelled but heard not a sound. She opened her mouth again, and still nothing came out.

Mr. Reed placed a hand on her shoulder and rose. "Benjamin! James!"

Everything and everyone ceased to move. All eyes turned to the reverend, startled at his vehemence.

Mr. Reed placed both hands firmly on the table, steadying the rocking motion from Ben's blast. "You disrespect Magnus with this division amongst you. He died defending a cause he believed in. One you too believe in, Benjamin. And one you also care about, James. I will ask you both to cease at once. Division amongst ourselves will serve no good purpose."

The reverend stood tall and leveled his gaze at Packer. "James, I have known you since you were a lad. Your father and I fought side by side at Bunker Hill. When I tell you Mrs. O'Neill is no enemy of yours, I pray my words will give you the assurance you need to trust the lady is one of us."

Packer stumbled back, as though he'd been shoved. "How would you know this, sir?"

"In conversing with Mrs. O'Neill I discovered we have a mutual acquaintance who I hope will board later today to speak on her behalf."

Rebecca's mouth went slack in shock.

Mr. Reed gave her hand a fatherly pat. "I am going to send a rider to Milton at once and see if she and her husband can join us posthaste."

Jonah smiled and nodded as though he knew exactly whom his father was talking about. He elbowed Adam and whispered something to him. Adam, too, smiled and nodded. Rebecca could have sworn Adam said, "Of course."

Ben just kept staring at her, his expression once again unreadable.

Rebecca dared to look at Packer. She couldn't tell if Mr. Reed's words had had any impact on him at all. He wasn't yelling, and he no longer appeared ready to throttle Ben, but his eyes still brimmed with anger.

The reverend turned his attention to Ben. "Benjamin, Mrs. O'Neill is rather distraught. Perhaps you could take her down to her cabin and have a word with her as she is in your care. I will ask to speak with her again shortly. I would like a moment with James before his departure, if I may?"

Neither Ben nor James moved. Rebecca wasn't the only one holding her breath. Almost simultaneously Jonah laid a hand on Ben's shoulder, and William gripped James by the arm to lead him down the hall.

Ben yielded first. "Yes, Father, of course. Please speak with James while I attend to Mrs. O'Neill."

The room instantly became habitable again. The crew began to disperse. Mr. Reed slid out from behind the table and waited for James to leave. A couple of men started picking up the broken plates and mugs. Adam ordered someone to retrieve a pail and mop. Rebecca stood on wobbly legs and paused for Ben to indicate what she should do.

William and Donald escorted James Packer to his cabin. Rebecca assumed they were gathering his belongings and, essentially, guarding him until someone rowed him ashore. Mr. Reed followed the three of them. Rebecca hoped he could talk some sense into Packer before he disembarked the ship.

When James left the room, Ben held out his hand to Rebecca. She moved slowly around the table and offered him her left hand. He clasped her fingers tenderly in his and drew her to him. Rebecca wanted to hug him, to collapse into his arms, but knew she couldn't. Instead she picked up his right hand and stood with both her hands in his, holding onto his strength, speaking to him with her eyes. She had been terrified James would start a fight, or worse. Ben wasn't even breathing hard. Her heart was pounding, and he hadn't even broken a sweat. "You are the epitome of 'Never let them see you sweat.'"

He regarded her quizzically, then chuckled. "I am relieved, Mrs. O'Neill, that you have regained your sense of humor…even if your colloquialisms are rather odd."

They both laughed, a little louder and harder than the joke called for, but it felt good, and necessary, to release the strain of the morning's events.

"Allow me to walk you to your cabin, Mrs. O'Neill."

Ben offered Rebecca his arm and she looped her left arm through his. They walked side by side until the passageway narrowed, and Ben gave Rebecca the lead. He followed her into the cabin, closed the door, and gathered her into his arms.

Rebecca lost it. She wrapped both arms around his waist and burst into tears. Ben held her and let her cry it out. Seconds became minutes. The emotions she'd contained so carefully all morning burst through the floodgates like a river through a broken dam. Ben's hand smoothed her hair. Her body relaxed, and the tears subsided. She eased back just enough to gaze into his earthy brown eyes and felt herself floating away. *I'm lost,* she thought and rested her head on his chest.

"I know."

"What?" Rebecca looked back up.

"I know you are lost."

"Did I actually say that out loud?"

Ben stroked her cheek with his right hand. "Yes, you did. Please do not worry. I am going to help you, Rebecca. As it appears is my father. May I ask what you said to him? And, pray tell, whom do you know that my father is acquainted with?"

Rebecca wished with every fiber of her being that she could tell Ben everything right there, right then. He had already been through enough in the last twenty-four hours learning that Magnus had died, moving the gunpowder and supplies safely to shore, and the scene with Packer moments before. The last thing Ben needed was her bizarre, unbelievable story. "I will tell you later, I promise. Right now I want to tell you how sorry I am about your brother."

Ben squeezed her tight and kissed the top of her head. "Magnus was a good man. I will miss him and his political vision. He loved this land more than I love the sea. How sweet you are to think of me when you have experienced so much trouble these past few days. You are a treasure, Rebecca. Thank you for your condolences."

At the sound of her name on Ben's lips, she sighed and stepped deeper into his embrace. She rested her cheek on his chest again, hugged him tightly around his waist, and inhaled his scent of sea and male and wind. "I have never met anyone like you, Ben."

She felt his ribs expand beneath her hands as he drew in a deep breath. Exhaling slowly, he then placed a finger beneath her chin. "You captivate me, Rebecca. I want that which I should not want."

Every muscle in her body tightened. She ached for his kiss. Could he possibly know how she felt? What he did to her? "I know how you feel," she said so softly he had to lean down to hear her.

"Say it again, Rebecca. Tell me once more."

"I do, Ben, I know how you feel. I want..." She surrendered the last words to his lips. Rebecca melted into him, wanting nothing more than everything he gave. He kissed her lightly, sweetly, and then drew back. "I should not have."

Rebecca blushed. "I wanted you to."

Ben ran his hand under her hair. He wrapped his fingers around the back of her neck, drew her to him, and pressed his lips to hers again. His kiss took

Rebecca to the moon and beyond, flying through the stars. She never wanted to land. She leaned into Ben and laced her fingers in his hair. He deepened the kiss in response, and Rebecca soared.

A knock on the door startled them both and drew them back to reality. Rebecca felt as though her feet were still hovering above the ground. Ben opened the door to his father. Rebecca couldn't meet his eyes for fear he would be able to read her thoughts.

Ben stepped aside to allow his father entry. "Did you speak with James?"

If Mr. Reed suspected they had been kissing, he didn't mention it. He addressed Ben as though Rebecca was expected to be in the room, as though she was a part of Ben's life. "Yes. I cannot judge whether my words reached him or fell on deaf ears. I will offer my worries to the Lord and trust Him to handle what I cannot. William is preparing to take James ashore. I wondered if you would care to be on deck when he departs?"

"Thank you, Father. I will head up now. Did you wish to speak with Rebec…Mrs. O'Neill?"

"Aye, Benjamin, I would."

"I will leave you then." Ben bowed before Rebecca. "Until later, Mrs. O'Neill."

Heat rose to Rebecca's checks. She needed to create a diversion or start a conversation before Ben's father asked her what was going on. "What will happen to Packer now?" she asked as Ben headed out the door.

"I do not know. He is angry, filled with resentment and hate. I pray he will find the proper way to deal with his pain. War can be a terrible place for a man unable to confront and acknowledge his own fears and demons. The opportunity for violence is great, as is the chance that one will lose hope and give up. I am concerned James will take too many risks without heed to the danger, or worse, seek out the danger and the potential loss of life."

Rebecca clenched her hands into fists. "Oh, no. I don't wish anything bad to happen to him. I'm just worried he'll do something crazy to us. You don't think he will seek revenge on Ben, do you?"

"I cannot say for sure. I hope not. We can pray about it and trust that God's will, not ours, will be done."

"Can I…"

Jonah burst into the room before Rebecca could ask her next question. "Father, an officer from General Washington's command post has asked to come aboard. Ben has requested you and Mrs. O'Neill proceed to the deck. Hurry!"

19

REBECCA AND REVEREND REED FOLLOWED JONAH up the companionway. When they arrived on deck, a man dressed in what Rebecca guessed must be officer's clothing was boarding the ship. The reverend positioned himself in front of Rebecca.

With the exception of William, the crew stood either fore or aft. William was stationed a few feet in front of Ben and off to the right of the ladder's opening to assist those boarding, should it be necessary. Four men were in the skiff, but only one came aboard. Mr. Reed and Jonah moved a few paces nearer to Ben with Rebecca following closely behind.

"Good morning, Captain Reed. Private Richard Smithfield at your service. I have come with an urgent message from His Excellency, General George Washington."

Ben extended his right hand. "Welcome aboard, Private Smithfield. Would you care for a mug of coffee or beer after your journey?"

"No thank you, Captain. My message is brief, and I must depart promptly with your reply."

Everyone on board waited in expectation. Rebecca realized the men were standing perfectly still, like she'd seen soldiers do in the movies. The moment felt surreal, even more so than the last four days had.

Captain Reed extended his right arm, gesturing toward his cabin. "Should we go below deck to my quarters?"

"I do not believe that will be necessary, Captain. The general has sent me on ahead this morning to inform you that he should like to call upon you early this afternoon." The soldier paused and took in the number of men on board. "If you agree, His Excellency will wish to speak with you privately when he arrives."

Ben clasped both hands behind his back and stood taller. "Please inform General Washington I am humbled by his request and will await his arrival."

Private Smithfield saluted Ben. "I shall convey your message to His Excellency. Good day, Captain."

No one moved until Washington's man was in the skiff and being rowed to shore. Mr. Reed walked over to Ben and clapped him on the shoulder a couple of times. "Word of your success has reached General Washington's ears. He comes to ask for assistance, Benjamin. He wants the *Shenandoah* in his fleet. There are many who have already signed up for the Continental Navy. He honors you with a personal visit."

Jonah shouted a loud "yes!" and hustled over to Ben. "We can help to save our country, Ben. We can do this for Magnus."

Ben was somber. "I am honored, Jonah, and I will serve as I am called to do. The next trip I take will not be as easy as this one, though. Washington's presence in Boston means the battle has begun. No Patriot will be safe; no ship will be safe. Our home is also now at risk. There is much to consider." Ben looked directly at Rebecca as he spoke those last words.

His father clearly caught his gaze. "Benjamin speaks most accurately, Jonah. Our lives are changing and will alter further still with the advent of a declaration of war against the King. No decisions should be made lightly."

Rebecca saw the disappointment in Jonah's eyes. She wondered if he sensed, as she did, that Ben and his father were hinting that Jonah could not or should not go with Ben.

The four of them stood quietly reflecting on Mr. Reed's comments. The crew was standing about, excitedly waiting for Ben's orders. James Packer took advantage of the moment to slink toward Rebecca.

"Well, I for one am thrilled General Washington is on his way here. As soon as William rows me to shore, I will seek him out and tell him of the spy on board the *Shenandoah*," Packer sneered, only inches from Rebecca.

Rebecca sucked in her breath. The men turned to face her. Jonah and Mr. Reed each placed a hand on one of her arms. Ben took three very deliberate, very slow steps toward Packer. Packer assumed a fighting stance. All two hundred and fifty pounds of Donald's muscles stepped closer to Packer.

Keeping his eyes focused on James, Ben spoke to William. "Take him below and put a guard on his door. He is to remain there until General Washington has departed."

Packer bolted to the rail, but William and Donald grabbed him and wrestled him to the deck. Rebecca watched the men thrashing about in horror. Packer took a swing at William and missed. Donald landed a blow to Packer's chin, which must have stunned him. He went limp. William and Donald hoisted him up off the deck before he started resisting again. They marshaled him below, Packer yelling, "You'll be sorry, Ben. Your spy is going to be caught if it is the last thing I do."

Rebecca felt the blood drain from her face.

Ben reached for her. "Steady now. You are safe. I will let no harm come to thee." Ben spoke the words softly, so that only Jonah and their father could have heard what he said, but Rebecca sensed he was saying so much more. She wondered if the reverend and Jonah heard the something else in Ben's words, too.

So much was happening so quickly. Rebecca regained her footing, tilted her head up, and searched Ben's eyes. She saw everything she needed and more. She smiled timidly, still shaken by Packer's vehement hatred, yet trusting Ben to protect her and care for her. When he smiled back at her, Rebecca knew his words held greater meaning than the moment allowed.

But just as she was ready to breathe easy and relish her security in Ben, she noticed Mr. Reed was shaking his head. "What is it?" she asked.

He looked at Ben and Rebecca and Jonah and then motioned them closer. Rebecca's nerves tightened from her head to her toes. They stepped into a tight huddle.

"James presents a serious threat to Mrs. O'Neill and to Benjamin and the crew of the *Shenandoah*. If he can convince even a single Patriot that Benjamin is harboring a spy for the King of England, then trouble will find its way to wherever you are." He paused and intently studied each one of them. His words sunk in as he did. "Something must be done immediately. I must ride to Milton at once."

Ben lifted his right hand, signaling his father to stop. "Father, you spoke of this before. I do not understand. What or whom is in Milton that will ensure Mrs. O'Neill's safety?"

The reverend glanced fondly at Rebecca. She sensed he did not wish to disclose whatever he knew to Ben or Jonah. She didn't know exactly why he was covering for her, but she was grateful.

"Father?" Ben asked again with a hint of impatience.

Mr. Reed nodded at Rebecca and faced Ben. "I have reasons to believe Rebecca is acquainted with Missy. I feel it is of extreme importance that I ride to Isaiah's at once and ask them to travel back here with me today. We will not arrive before General Washington, though I hope to return well before nightfall. If there is any trouble, please inform the general I am on my way."

Ben appeared stunned. He was probably wondering why Rebecca had never mentioned Melissa to him. He probably had a lot of questions Rebecca couldn't answer right now. Fortunately, he had a ship to prepare for George Washington, and that should take priority over Rebecca's secrets. At least she hoped it would.

As if he read her mind or sensed her uneasiness, Mr. Reed suggested as much. "You have much to do, Benjamin, to prepare for General Washington. We can discuss these matters at a later date. Time is of the essence." The reverend laid an affectionate hand on Jonah's shoulder. He bowed to Rebecca and then placed a hand on the left arm of the still speechless Ben. "Prepare your boat, son. I trust Mrs. O'Neill is as eager to talk with you as you are with her. There are, however, more pressing matters for us all."

Ben seemed to hear his father at last. He draped an arm around his shoulder and walked him to the boarding ladder. "Safe journey. God's speed, Father."

When Mr. Reed climbed down the rope ladder into the rowboat with Samuel, Ben turned toward his waiting crew. He called out orders and details that sent the men into a flurry of activity.

Rebecca stood in the middle of the ship, people hustling all about, and felt useless and ignored. "May I help, Captain?"

Ben stared at her long and hard. Rebecca's heart ached for him. Of course he was hurt or angry or both. She would be, too, if the shoe were on the other foot. She figured Ben probably thought she had told his father everything. Rebecca couldn't tell him that his dad had guessed that she was from another century. Truth be told, she wasn't sure he knew that for a fact. She simply knew that he knew something about her appearance on the Shenandoah, that she had a similar story to Missy's and that whatever he believed he knew was, at present, saving her butt.

She inched closer, conscious of the crew all around, yet wishing so much to reach for Ben's hand. Instead she turned both hands palms up to Ben. "I can scrub, polish, swab, or help in whatever way you'll let me," Rebecca said, trying to be lighthearted. Her heart sank when Ben didn't even crack a smile. "Please, Ben, don't be mad."

"I wish you had trusted me, Rebecca, as you did my father."

She did trust Ben. How could she explain to him now, with the men milling about and General Washington on his way, that she trusted him with her life? She could only hope he gave her a chance to explain everything later.

"I do trust you, Ben. I trust you with my life."

She saw it then, the flash in his eyes. He loved her. She knew it. She had heard it in his words moments ago and had felt it in his arms this morning. She smiled for him, offering her heart and willing him to hear the words she could not say just yet. When he grinned back at her, Rebecca's heart leaped like a shooting star lighting up the night sky.

Ben inspected her hands. "I believe, Madam, that your small fingers may be well-suited to polishing brass. What say you?"

She was so happy, she would have scrubbed the deck with a toothbrush, had he asked. "Sounds wonderful, Captain."

134

Ben went to the supply chest and brought Rebecca the items needed to polish. He collected all the lamps on the deck and placed them beside her on the rooftop deck. He set her about the task and left to inspect the crew's progress.

There was excitement as well as tension in the air. Jonah occasionally led them in song, but most everyone worked as though the president were coming to dinner, which, in an odd way, he was. Rebecca giggled quietly at her own joke and continued polishing.

A few hours passed. The ship shone like a new car in the midday sun. Adam served lunch, which everyone except Ben ate heartily. Rebecca nudged Jonah.

"Don't worry about Ben, Mrs. O'Neill. Whenever he is in a quandary or making a grand plan, he forgets to eat until he has mastered his situation. Father always assured Mother he would not starve to death, and he never has."

Rebecca laughed, grateful once again for Jonah's friendship. "I'll leave him be, then. Wouldn't want to nag the man."

Jonah gave Rebecca one of his looks again. "I wager you are looking forward to seeing Aunt Missy. When she arrives, you two will be able to understand each other."

You have no idea, Rebecca thought before stating casually, "I am looking forward to her arrival. It has been years since I heard any word from or about her."

Jonah nodded as though he felt this was completely natural. "Back to work for me, Mrs. O'Neill. I expect it shan't be long now before we see the general's party."

Rebecca looked to shore and up along the coast as far as she could see. There didn't appear to be much activity. Rebecca had no idea what road or trail Washington and his company would be on. She leaned back against the post and closed her eyes, trying to recall everything she knew about George Washington. She had no idea how much time had passed before Ben gently shook her awake and informed her Washington was minutes away.

She jumped up, startling Ben a bit, and dashed to the cap rail. She peered toward the shore as if she were a child gazing at a decorated tree surrounded by presents on Christmas morning.

Another solemn expression replaced Ben's usual smiling and teasing eyes. "I must ask you to join Jonah and Adam by William's doghouse."

Rebecca couldn't help her momentary disappointment. "Of course, Ben. I understand this is official business."

Ben's shoulders relaxed, and his face softened slightly. "Thank you, Rebecca. This visit will change the life of each man on board."

Rebecca nodded, a twinge of anxiety mixed with pride. She wished once again that she could tell Ben everything she knew, everything that could or might make a difference in his life. Most of all, she wished she could hug him and wish him the best in his meeting. Instead, she behaved as was expected. "I know, Ben. Good luck."

She smiled at Ben and moved toward Adam. She stood on tiptoes trying to glimpse George Washington. Adam was much calmer than Rebecca. He seemed amused by her eagerness. Of course, he had no idea who was *really* coming onboard.

Rebecca watched in awe as the small rowboat approaching the *Shenandoah* grew in size. She knew she should be nervous or scared. Even if she ignored who he *was,* which she couldn't, the man coming aboard could order her imprisoned or worse. She did feel nervous, jittery even, though more for what she was about to experience than in fear for her life. The event was so unreal. No one would have believed her back home. Heck, she didn't quite believe what was happening to her even as she was living it.

As the boat drew closer, Rebecca knew in an instant which man he was. She had seen countless pictures of him throughout her life. She carried him around in her wallet daily. Now, in this moment, Rebecca knew no artist had done him justice. Although he wasn't standing in the boat as he had been depicted while crossing the Delaware, General George Washington looked every aspect of presidential.

20

"WOW!" REBECCA SAID AS MUCH TO HERSELF AS TO ADAM. "This is totally amazing. I can't believe George Washington is coming here, and I'm here to witness his visit."

Rebecca considered all her father's history books she had read over the years and the countless classes she had taught on the American Revolution. "My father would just love this."

Adam looked at her sideways. "Your father knew of George Washington before he passed? Did you visit the Virginias?"

Yikes, thought Rebecca, *I've done it again.* "We never visited Virginia, but my father loved history and this country. He'd be so excited for me right now if he was still alive. I bet he's watching from heaven and grinning from ear to ear."

Adam nodded. "I suspect many folks would enjoy an opportunity to meet General Washington, though I doubt few would be as enthusiastic as you appear to be."

Truer words had probably not been spoken. Never in a million years had Rebecca thought she'd meet George Washington, *the* George Washington. Who in their right mind living in the twenty-first century would consider that a possibility? As the boat was rowed closer and closer, Washington's very existence became a reality. Rebecca felt her sharp intake of breath as Washington stood for the last few yards of the boat's approach.

"He did it. Did you see that, Adam? He really stood in those boats," she exclaimed, goose bumps rising over her arms. She realized Adam was peering at her in puzzlement, but she didn't care. She had just experienced one of the great moments in history. Okay, the *Shenandoah* boarding wasn't a moment in any history book she had read or knew of, but Washington standing in a boat in all his regal splendor was "A" moment.

The skiff pulled up alongside the *Shenandoah,* and the crew bustled into position. Ben stood tall and proud as William lowered the rope ladder for General Washington's ascent. The crew drew to attention, and goose bumps tingled on Rebecca's arms again.

In a few seconds General George Washington, the first President of the United States of America, would be standing within twenty feet of her.

Rebecca wished she had her camera or her cell phone. This had to be the most unbelievable and one of the most spectacular moments of her life. And she had no way to document it and no way to share it with anyone.

Washington boarded the boat without fanfare, yet Rebecca noticed that she and everyone else grew a smidgen taller as all stood ready to salute. Ben looked incredibly handsome as he greeted the general.

The general's cream-colored breeches appeared freshly pressed, as did his white shirt. His tailored navy jacket let everyone know he was important. Rebecca remembered that he had his clothes custom-made in England, but she decided to keep that information to herself. None onboard the *Shenandoah* or the skiff were dressed as finely or projected an image that demanded attention before a word was spoken.

He was taller and more fit than Rebecca had envisioned. When he removed his tricorn before shaking Ben's hand, Rebecca found herself fixated on his hair. She had forgotten that many men wore wigs or powdered their hair in Colonial times. After days on the *Shenandoah*, where none of the men did anything more than tie their hair back, Rebecca caught herself, mouth open, gawking not at the first president of the United States of America but at his shocking white hair.

Rebecca could not remember whether Washington wore a wig or powdered his hair. It was startling at first to take in the awkwardness of Washington's perfectly coifed hair after he'd just ridden all the way from Boston. For a moment, forgetting this was real and not a dream, Rebecca thought Washington more resembled an actor playing Washington than Washington himself.

She pondered whether or not Washington might have fixed his hair or adjusted his wig before getting into the rowboat. Why had men worn wigs in the first place? Why had they powdered their hair? Rebecca couldn't remember a single history lesson on men's hair. Jonah nudged her and brought her back to the present as General Washington shook Ben's hand.

Formal introductions were made. Rebecca watched Ben introduce William as his first mate. She wished Ben could introduce her. She wished for pen and paper, too. She could imagine how much a George Washington autograph would be worth at home. *Money I'll never see.*

Rebecca remembered reading in one of her father's books of the naval fleet Washington built with some of the finest schooners ever made. Such a position would be an honor for Ben. She wished she could hear what they were saying. She guessed from Ben's pleased expression and Washington's approving look that Washington was thanking Ben and praising him for the delivery of the gunpowder and supplies. Rebecca so wanted to eavesdrop.

Ben and Washington turned to head toward his cabin at the same moment James Packer called out from the window in his cabin below, "Captain, are you going to turn in the spy?"

Everything, even the air, stopped moving. Washington finally broke the spell, rotating around to locate the man who had called out. James could not see out and remained quiet. Rebecca thought he was probably waiting for the lynch mob to seize her. She noticed Donald moving toward the companionway and going below, undoubtedly to silence any further remarks from James.

Ben's crew seemed to collectively hold their breath. When no other sound was uttered, Washington pivoted on his heel and faced Ben. "You have a spy for the Regulars on board? Bring him forward."

Rebecca saw Ben visibly falter. Her heart pounded so hard her chest hurt. She watched Ben's face as he carefully considered his words.

"The man in question is actually a woman, Your Excellency, and I do not believe the lady is a spy. A stowaway perhaps, lost for certain. She has no memory of how she came to be onboard the *Shenandoah*," Ben said, his voice like a soothing balm over Rebecca's raw nerves. "My father has spoken with her and believes he knows an acquaintance of the lady's."

Washington stepped closer to Ben. "Reverend Reed has spoken with your prisoner?"

Ben gave a single nod. He probably wasn't surprised General Washington had researched his background. Surely General Israel Putnam had mentioned to Washington his meeting with the Reed family. And Rebecca had learned from Jonah that Ben's father was well known for his numerous sermons on Patriotism and freedom.

"Yes, General. He spoke with Mrs. O'Neill this morning."

Ever so subtly, Washington scanned the crowd. "Is Reverend Reed still aboard, then?"

"No, Your Excellency. My father rode to Milton to bring Mrs. O'Neill's former neighbor to meet with us later today." Ben searched the faces, settling with a smile on Rebecca. The tension in the air evaporated amidst the warmth of his smile.

Rebecca exhaled slowly, feeling his love and protection wrap around her like a soft blanket.

Washington followed the direction of Ben's gaze, noticing Rebecca for the first time. "Please ask the lady to step forward. I should like to speak with your prisoner," General Washington said.

Ben flinched. Rebecca's eyes widened. What was he going to say to the President of the United States? Okay, he wasn't the president yet, but he would be and Ben needed to tread carefully and with high regard at all times. Rebecca didn't want him getting into trouble on her account. She could easily disappear tonight, and Ben could be stuck in jail for the rest of his life.

Ben extended his right arm toward Rebecca. "With all due respect, Your Excellency, I do not consider Mrs. O'Neill my prisoner."

Silence followed Ben's correction of the country's highest-ranking official. Rebecca twisted her fingers until the general spoke.

Washington glanced from Ben to Rebecca a couple of times, as though he was sizing up the situation. "Very well, Captain Reed. I would ask to speak with you and Mrs. O'Neill privately."

All eyes focused on Ben. He motioned for Samuel Marsh to bring Rebecca forward. Samuel, a kind young man ill suited to battles and war, gently placed his shaking hand on Rebecca's elbow and walked her over. Ben introduced Samuel to General Washington. Samuel stuttered a reply, bowed, then quickly retreated. Washington eyed Rebecca while Ben attempted introductions.

Rebecca, forgetting her place and acting like a starstruck teenager, spoke not only before Ben had said her name, but also before General Washington had spoken to her. "General, Your Excellency, I am honored, truly honored, to be here. You can't imagine what a thrill it is to meet you."

Washington looked at Ben, Rebecca guessed, for confirmation that she wasn't mentally ill. Ben shrugged, as if equally uncertain of Rebecca's outburst, and then offered Washington a weak explanation. "Mrs. O'Neill has been particularly on edge, often forgetting herself and common courtesies while she's been detained with us."

Rebecca picked up on the subtle hint, fumbled through a quick curtsy, and cast her eyes to the floor. She offered up a silent, desperate plea. *Dear Lord, help me not to screw up. Please put the right words in my mouth so I can speak with this great man without sounding like an idiot and without getting myself or Ben into trouble.*

Washington gave the impression of being at least momentarily appeased by Ben's response and Rebecca's attempt at manners. He gave a curt nod to Rebecca. "Thank you, Madam, for the compliment. Please be so kind as to state your family name and from whence you come."

She looked him in the eye. "Rebecca O'Neill, Your Excellency. I live on Martha's Vineyard."

"Mrs. O'Neill, can you tell me how you came to be aboard Captain Reed's vessel?"

Rebecca answered honestly, "I don't know. One minute I was sleeping in my bunk on Captain Roberts' ship off the coast of Martha's Vineyard, actually off of Tarpaulin Cove, and the next thing I knew a man was dragging me across the floor by my hair."

"What?" Anger and disgust flared in Washington's eyes. "Who would dare to treat a woman so?" Washington cast accusing eyes over the crew. Rebecca gulped, hoping Donald was down below with James Packer and would help Packer keep his mouth shut for once.

Washington brought his focus back to Rebecca, waiting for her response.

"Your Excellency, with all due respect, I would rather not say. The matter is done and settled. I need no enemies aboard this ship, or elsewhere."

"Well spoken, Mrs. O'Neill. Your reply, however, does not fully answer my previous question."

Rebecca winced. She knew everyone within earshot was waiting on her response. "I realize that, sir, but I don't have an explanation. I wish I did. I went to bed one night, and the next morning someone was calling me a stowaway."

Washington regarded Rebecca with disbelief. He put his right hand on his hip. Rebecca tried to contain the smile at the familiar image she had seen in numerous paintings. Washington scrutinized the change in her expression. Rebecca immediately wiped off her grin. There was no way she could explain to either General Washington or Ben that she'd seen Washington depicted in that pose in numerous paintings in books and museums all over the world.

Ben interrupted their conversation. "Your Excellency, perhaps now would be the opportune moment to move this conversation to my private quarters?"

The general and Rebecca both surveyed the crowd of expectant faces.

"Yes, Captain Reed," the general announced. "I believe we should continue this discussion privately."

Ben offered his arm to Rebecca, and together they led General Washington to the stern of the boat. They descended into the main cabin. Ben motioned for them to sit around the small table in his room. He held a chair for Rebecca, allowed General Washington to sit, and then took his own seat.

The conversation resumed as soon as the three of them were seated. "And where is your husband and your family? Will they not be searching for you?" Washington's voice sounded kinder to her.

Two pairs of eyes focused intently on Rebecca. She considered her answer quickly, yet carefully, knowing how important her words would be when Ben and General Washington heard them. "My parents died years ago, and my grandmother passed away last spring, sir. There will be no one in my family looking for me."

Rebecca felt better knowing she had only partially lied. Her family was gone. Captain Roberts and the students would be looking for her if she did not return, but even they weren't aware she was missing now, at least she didn't think so. She hoped they hadn't found out about her secret evening travels yet. All she needed was time to figure out what to do, or more accurately, what she wanted to do. Either way she knew she could not leave the *Shenandoah*. "If I could just stay on board, I believe I shall be fine."

Washington looked aghast. "On board? You wish to remain onboard? Pray tell, Mrs. O'Neill, why would a lady desire to remain aboard a naval vessel?"

Rebecca glanced at Ben. and her heart leapt. She had discovered this morning that he loved her. And, much to her surprise and wonder, she found herself in love with him, too. She knew without a doubt that she had to be on the *Shenandoah*, in her cabin even, to return home to the twenty-first century, but her heart wasn't in the twenty-first century. The thought of never seeing Ben again ripped her heart in two. He was her home now. Where he was, she wanted to be. Rebecca couldn't say those words aloud to Ben or Washington, but she couldn't allow President Washington or anyone else to tear her away from Ben.

"I beg you, General, I believe the only way for me to get back where I belong is aboard this vessel. My only hope is that whoever or whatever brought me here will bring me home."

Rebecca looked General Washington in the eye. He was so tall, so powerful. Even now, years before he would become President, Rebecca could see the strength and wisdom in this man. How odd to find oneself face to face with history, knowing the paths he would take, the victories and the losses, the date of his death even. . In many ways she knew more than him, though her knowledge had come from history books and his from life's lessons he had and would experience.

Rebecca could fully understand how a country would look to this man for guidance and leadership. He exuded a strength both regal and commanding. Yes, *commanding* was the best word. Not so ironically, Washington had just been appointed Commander-in-Chief, a term that would later describe the President of the United States. But at the moment, he could command her future, and that was Rebecca's primary concern.

While Rebecca pondered Washington, and Washington pondered her fate, Rebecca kept her eyes from drifting back to Ben, afraid any glance in his direction would expose the main reason she wanted Washington to allow her to stay.

She could feel Ben watching her. She had no idea what he was thinking or feeling. This morning he had held her so tenderly and kissed her as she had never been kissed before. She wondered if he felt half of what she was feeling—if he wanted her to stay. If he knew the torture she was going through, perhaps he would say a few words to assure her of his desire to be with her. Rebecca wished like crazy that he would say something.

"Madam!" Washington's sharp voice cut through Rebecca's reverie.

Rebecca realized he had been speaking to her while she was thinking about Ben like a teenage girl in the middle of study hall. She shook her head. She had no idea what he had asked her or said to her. "I'm sorry, General."

Rebecca didn't know what else to say. How could she explain to the future President of the future United States of America that she was from the twenty-first century and if she left the boat she might never get back to her present-day life? Never mind mixing those fears with her rampant, ongoing thoughts that not going back might be a good thing, perhaps the best thing to ever happen to her.

A flash of compassion appeared in Washington's eyes. "I appreciate how frightened and nervous you must be, Madam. I have heard great praise for Reverend Reed and have seen firsthand the service Captain Reed has done for the Cause. I have no reason to doubt their words or their judgment. Therefore, I must conclude you are no threat to our mission."

Washington paused. He glanced at Ben, hard. "However, I cannot, no, will not, consent to a woman onboard a naval ship. If Captain Reed accepts my appointment into the Continental Navy, you will disembark the *Shenandoah* before she departs on her mission. In the meantime, I shall leave the decision of your remaining on or disembarking from this vessel to Captain Reed." Washington glanced between Rebecca and Ben. She felt his eyes reach into the secret places in her heart. "Your life, Madam, is in Captain Reed's hands. I suspect that is as it should be."

Ben remained motionless. Rebecca wanted to shake him. Why didn't he say he wanted her to stay? She knew his business with General Washington was far from over, but surely he was feeling something.

Seconds passed, but it felt like hours to Rebecca.

Washington broke the silence. "Mrs. O'Neill, if you will excuse us. I must speak with Captain Reed privately."

"Thank you, General," Rebecca said. She searched Ben's face for some reaction and saw nothing. She got up and walked toward the stairs, heart heavy with doubt and longing. Why hadn't Ben told her, and General Washington, that he wanted her on the *Shenandoah,* or at least that she could stay onboard?

Rebecca climbed the first two steps. Out of nowhere she thought about the cannons at Fort Ticonderoga. Images flashed before her eyes. Images of the great storm, of Dorchester Heights being fortified, images of men hauling and pulling cannons and weapons through rain and mud. She halted midstride. Did she dare divulge what she knew? Should she? Was her knowledge of the past the reason she had traveled back in time?

21

REBECCA PUT HER HANDS TO HER HEAD to help stop the world from spinning. She didn't know if her being there on that day on the *Shenandoah* in that room with General George Washington was the key to changing history or if traveling to that moment in time was nothing but a glimpse into another era. Was it possible that she was a fundamental source to Washington's success? Was she supposed to be helping write history, not rewrite it? What if she was always destined to travel to this place and time and was supposed to tell General Washington what she knew? What if this was all a bad dream? How was she to know? Her head pounded. She had no answers and too many questions...and two very important men waited for her to collect her thoughts.

Knots formed and twisted in Rebecca's stomach. She felt Ben and General Washington staring at her. She also felt the impulse—no, the need—to explain to the first great leader of her country what she knew about a turning point in his life. Rebecca realized she was still holding her head and probably looked as crazy as she was about to sound. She lowered her hands, took a deep breath, then turned to face Ben and the soon-to-be first president of the United States. "You're probably going to think I'm crazy, but here goes nothing."

Ben stood abruptly, scraping the table across the floor. "Think before you speak, Rebecca. I beseech you."

Rebecca could see the desperation in Ben's eyes. He must have sensed she was going to jump off a cliff. She wanted to appease him, to assure him that everything was happening as it was meant to happen, but she wasn't so certain herself. Her gut was telling her to speak to General Washington. She felt it deep within, through the knots and between the butterflies.

"I must say this, Ben. Please trust me, whatever you hear, no matter how unbelievable it may sound. Please believe in me."

Rebecca's heart clenched. For a moment she wanted to climb the steps and forget everything she'd read in all those history books filling the bookcases in her home. But she knew she couldn't. Her Da had often quoted to her: "Courage is not the absence of fear, but rather the judgment that something else is more important than fear."

Rebecca had spent too many moments in fear on this ship. Now, standing before General George Washington, she knew there was more than just her life at stake. She had no idea whether or not her conversation with General Washington would or could affect the Patriots' eventual victory, but she did know crucial, significant facts that could alter the future of a nation, *her* nation.

Her mind made up, her heart convicted, Rebecca squared her shoulders and marched down the steps and over to the table where General Washington remained seated. Ben slowly sat back down.

"Your Excellency, if I could have a moment of your time." Rebecca paused. "Please."

"Speak quickly, Mrs. O'Neill. Time is of the essence today."

Rebecca faltered at his curt reply. "Um, General, I don't know if my presence here is meant to be or a bizarre twist of fate or an accident. There are things I know that I want to tell you, but I don't know if I am supposed to."

Impatience and frustration, as well as suspicion, flashed across Washington's face. "Madam, you are where you are meant to be, for reasons known only to the Almighty. If you have something to say, something you feel you must impart, do so now as time is short, and there is much to be done."

Rebecca stepped closer to Washington. A ripple of fear prickled down her spine. Women had been burned at the stake in history for less than she was about to say now. She heard her Da's strong voice telling her to be brave. Rebecca cleared her throat. "Henry Knox and Nathanael Greene will be two of your most loyal and capable officers. Though they are young, both will show great skill, bravery, and judgment beyond their years and experience."

The walls felt like they were closing in. Washington and Ben wore blank, stunned expressions.

Rebecca hesitated for a second then charged ahead. "Henry Knox, if he has not already done so, is going to ask you to allow him to retrieve the guns at Fort Ticonderoga. Let him. He will succeed, and the cannons will be a critical factor in later battles."

General Washington stood and slammed his fist on the table. "How do you know these things?"

Rebecca stammered, "I can't explain. I just do. I know it sounds crazy, and you have no reason to trust me, but I am telling you the truth."

General Washington's eyes narrowed. "Madam, I am about to reconsider my earlier decision that you are not a spy."

Something snapped inside Rebecca. Her spine stiffened. She was no liar and no spy. "Sir, I assure you I am no spy. I just...the future...I know it for reasons I do not understand and cannot explain. You may convict me of treason, but the words I spoke to you will still come to pass as truth."

General Washington leaned forward and stared intently at Rebecca. "Madam, no one knows the future."

Rebecca shook her head. There was simply no way she could explain that she didn't know the future. She knew her past, which just happened to be their future. Perhaps she had said enough, at least enough to help. And that's all she wanted to do, all she could do, and she had done it.

"Yes, General. Forgive me if I overstepped. I only wish to help."

The look she received in return told her General Washington did not believe she was sane, never mind helpful.

"I have heard what you had to say, Madam. I will consider your comments not only as to their merit but also to ascertain how you acquired knowledge which only a handful are privy to." Washington cast a glance at Ben and returned to his chair.

Rebecca, knowing she was dismissed, walked to the steps. She could feel Ben's eyes burning holes into her back. How would she ever explain to him what had just happened? Would he ever look at her the same again? Rebecca was about to exit the room when she remembered the storm. She felt that same gnawing in her gut she'd felt about the cannons.

Since she was already neck-deep in the hole, should she tell him about the great storm on March 5, 1776? Those days and events had such an unreal quality to them already, even before Rebecca entered into the picture. General Washington's campaign to take Dorchester Heights and ensconce the Colonial troops there would depend on his timing. The men must begin building the redoubts and moving the cannons from Fort Ticonderoga into place on Dorchester Heights after sundown on March 4. Had she always been destined to share that fact with the Commander? Whatever the answer, her moment to do so had arrived.

She knew the British would awaken on March 5, the anniversary of the Boston Massacre, to find the rebels entrenched in newly built forts, heavily armed with cannons. The British would plan an attack by sea, but an unusual storm of hurricane proportions would rage against the shores and hold back the British. Finding themselves surrounded by cannons, the British would immediately begin plans to leave Boston, scurrying to evacuate all Loyalists as quickly as possible. When they did leave on March 17, it would be General Washington's first major victory in the Revolutionary War. The knot tightened in her stomach.

Yes, Rebecca thought, *I have to do this.*

Once again she turned to face General Washington. Ben simply shook his head. Rebecca's inner strength built her up as she considered her next words. *I could go through the whole war and warn him of every mistake, every situation, but that doesn't feel right. It's just these two events. Something or someone—is it You, Lord?—is urging me to warn him.*

Rebecca contemplated how to share her knowledge before she opened her mouth to play fortuneteller yet again. She unconsciously tapped her forefinger against her chin. *Got it,* she thought, then held her finger up.

"General? One more thing, if I may?"

Ben was shaking his head.

Washington, too, looked as though his patience had been pushed to the limit. "I sense you feel you must, Madam."

Rebecca lowered her hand. "There will come a time when you decide to take Dorchester Heights. It is imperative you begin your move on the evening of March fourth. Gather every willing and able man to help. You will do in one night what an army of thousands could not do in a month. On March fifth and sixth there will be a storm like no other, and the enemy will be unable to attack and dislodge you. They will leave Boston shortly thereafter."

"Enough, Madam! You talk in riddles of things unknown."

Without thinking, Rebecca clasped her hands together and begged, "Please, General, I know I sound nuts, but remember the dates March fourth, fifth, and sixth. Remember to make your move after sundown on March fourth. I implore you."

Having pleaded the last words, Rebecca turned and literally ran from the cabin. She hadn't a clue what Washington and Ben might be thinking after her last outburst. Perhaps they both thought she was a witch? Washington was most likely going to have her arrested. Ben was probably regretting he had kissed her. Worse, he might allow them to take her away, away from him.

*

Little did Rebecca know that her warnings to General Washington reminded Ben of some comments his Aunt Melissa had made over the years. She, too, seemed to know things others did not. He remembered a family dinner in early April when everyone was talking about the King's Men and what their next move would be. His uncle Isaiah had asked about the spies who were reporting back on the actions and intentions of the Regulars.

Melissa had suddenly begun begging Isaiah not to join the militia. She had mumbled something about Lexington being fine, but the next one was out of the question. None of them had known at the time what Melissa was babbling about. She made Isaiah promise, there in the parlor, in front of his entire family, that he would not fight in June. There had been fear in her voice, and he recalled now that she had been trembling. Ben remembered being stunned when his uncle agreed, as though Isaiah felt Melissa's request bore credence instead of irrationality. With sudden clarity Ben realized Melissa had been referring to Bunker Hill.

Ben hadn't thought about it until now. Did Melissa and Rebecca know each other, as his father suggested? Was it possible they could know the future?

He figured it was a good thing his father was bringing Isaiah and Melissa to the ship. He had more questions than answers, and he hoped his aunt and uncle might shed some light on the darkness he was mired in.

*

Rebecca scooted around the roof of the cabin, slowing when she reached Adam's doghouse. He and Jonah were talking by the hatch of the companionway. Rebecca walked over, breathing in the fresh sea air. She filled her lungs and exhaled slowly.

Physically motionless, Rebecca's mind raced. Would Ben allow her to stay now, after what she had just done? Surely he wanted her to stay. He had to, right? He had to want her to stay as much as she wanted to stay with him. "Dear Lord, please," Rebecca whispered.

Adam murmured, "Relax, Mrs. O'Neill. Benjamin will not be sending ye away."

A small sob escaped Rebecca. "How do you know every time I'm worried about something?"

"I suspect it is the lines creasing your forehead, Mrs. O'Neill." Rebecca knew Adam was teasing her, but he was also telling her yet again in his very subtle way to let go and let God.

"You're right, Adam, you're right." Rebecca glanced back toward the captain's cabin, where Ben and General Washington were sequestered. "What do you think they're planning?"

Adam shook his head. "I cannot say for certain, though I suspect General Washington wants Benjamin and the *Shenandoah* in his fleet."

"Na," Jonah teased. "They are probably talking about you, Mrs. O'Neill."

Little do you know! Rebecca struggled to crack a smile for Jonah's sake. The three of them stood pensively. Rebecca considered the fact that they probably were talking about her, or about what she had just said. She knew Adam was correct and Washington was asking Ben to join his navy. He had said as much when she had asked to remain on board.

She remembered clearly Captain Roberts telling her about the lost ship's logs from 1775 through 1776. She had no way of knowing for certain if Ben would accept Washington's post, but she suspected he would. He was a man of honor. He loved his country and his family and the Lord. He would be compelled to serve and to protect and to lead. Pride swelled within her. Ben was a good man. Her father would have liked him.

About twenty minutes passed with Adam and Jonah distracting Rebecca with detailed accounts of the unloading of the gunpowder and supplies the night before. They both commented on how quiet she had been in her cabin.

Jonah teased, "I was surprised you didn't sneak up on deck or offer to help, Mrs. Reed."

"Occasionally I do as I am told," Rebecca quipped while thinking, *At least when I'm in my bed two hundred years away and unable to do differently.*

While the three of them were sharing a chuckle, Ben and General Washington appeared topside. Ben walked the general to the ladder. The two men shook hands. Rebecca watched General Washington disembark. She realized she would most likely never see him again, at least not in person. She wanted to run to the rail to watch him leave, but she remained by Adam. Ben stayed positioned by the rail.

When the rowboat became visible as it glided over the water away from the *Shenandoah* and toward the shore, Ben fixed his eyes on Rebecca and headed her way. "I would like a word with you, Mrs. O'Neill."

Jonah stepped in front of Rebecca before she had a chance to move an inch. "Aw, Ben, tell us what happened. What did the general want? Are we bound for battle?"

Rebecca didn't want to talk about war; she already knew the answers. She wanted time alone with Ben to explain, if that was possible, what she had said and why she had said it. Either way, she needed to erase the emotionless expression on Ben's face and replace it once again with a smile and eyes brimming with love.

Unfortunately, Jonah and the crew won out. Ben had business to tend to and, Rebecca noticed, with a thud in her chest, he was clearly annoyed with her. Rebecca lifted her chin and rolled her shoulders back. At least Ben hadn't sent her packing. She would wait, all day if she had to. And maybe Mr. Reed would return soon, and maybe Melissa would be with him.

22

THE MINUTES DRAGGED ON FOR WHAT SEEMED LIKE HOURS while Rebecca waited for Ben to finish talking with the men. She didn't want to go below deck since James Packer was still down there somewhere, so she walked toward the stern and sat on the roof of Ben's cabin.

She wondered how long it would take Mr. Reed to return. He had been gone almost six hours. She prayed Melissa would be with him. A minute of panic struck as she considered whether Melissa might be afraid to set foot on the boat for fear of being transported back to Vineyard Haven.

What if Melissa hadn't discovered it was the cabin, not the ship, which was the transporter or travel machine or whatever one should call it? If she thought it was the boat, Rebecca couldn't blame Melissa if she didn't come, but she had so many questions for her and desperately needed her to come. The day was getting longer by the minute. The waiting was torture.

The shore was busy with activity. Rebecca had never been to this area in present day, but it reminded her of Menemsha, the small fishing village on Martha's Vineyard. The last few years had seen more stores and snack shops popping up on the road to the beach, but the tiny village still looked much like it must have in 1775—a dock, a couple of fish markets, rows upon rows of lobster traps and fishing gear and dozens of boats. It was one of Rebecca's favorite places. Menemsha was also one of the best places to watch the sunset on the Island, and it drew large crowds all summer long. Rebecca scanned the cloudless sky and thought the evening would offer a gorgeous sunset.

The sun was warm, and the air was cool—the perfect beach day, if you loved sitting on the sand and soaking up some rays. Rebecca couldn't resist. She stretched out on the roof deck and closed her eyes. Lying in a floor-length dress with sleeves down to her wrist limited any chance of a tan, but the sun felt glorious on her face.

She tried to remember what Melissa looked like. Everyone knew everyone in town on some level or another, but Rebecca couldn't recall ever meeting Melissa in person. Any image she could conjure in her head was from newspaper photos, not from personal memory. She doubted Melissa would know her, either.

When Melissa disappeared, Rebecca had been a senior in college and had only been home for summers and school vacations during the three years prior. Melissa had taught up Island at the Gay Head Elementary School when Rebecca was young and attended Holmes Hole Elementary.

Rumors spread during Rebecca's sophomore year in high school that Melissa, then Mrs. Burroughs, had caught her husband cheating and had thrown him out.

The Island gossip mill churned rapidly, and soon everyone knew Melissa had divorced him quickly, taken back her maiden name, put the house on the market, moved to Tisbury, and applied for a teaching job at Holmes Hole. Two years later her ex-husband drove off the road and crashed into a tree. He died two weeks later. More rumors surfaced that he had a first wife, whom he had also cheated on, and even had an illegitimate child somewhere.

His third wife pointed a finger at Melissa, said she was stalking him and probably forced him off the road. A couple of articles in the local papers mentioned her accusations, but most reporters hinted the widow was crazed with grief. An Island paper suggested Bryce Burroughs was speeding home drunk after spending the evening with yet another woman. Few people questioned that story. Rebecca remembered Melissa was never so much as taken in for questioning.

Most of the teachers who taught with Melissa were still at school and spoke very highly of her work with the kids. There had been some discussion over the years about where she could be, if she had really killed herself or how she had drowned. Whenever the topic came up, as it did every year when the fundraising and planning for the *Shenandoah* trip started, most of Melissa's colleagues noted that she had never dated after her divorce, but nobody ever mentioned her being depressed or bitter.

Rebecca had never paid too much attention. *Hindsight really is 20/20,* she thought. *If I had known I was ever going to chaperone this trip* and *follow in Melissa's footsteps, I might have taken notes.*

A shadow covered Rebecca. She shaded her eyes with her right hand and looked up to see what or who was blocking her sun.

Ben was shaking his head.

"My sisters avoid the sun at all cost. They rarely leave the house without a bonnet and parasol. You appear to have no care for its ill effects. Do all the women on Martha's Vineyard expose their skin to the sun so?"

He has no idea. She tried to picture Ben on the beach with all the bikini-clad bodies and had to stifle a chuckle. His all-too-serious expression took the bubble right out of her giggle and she answered without thinking.

"Most of the beaches are littered with bodies from June through August.

Some people actually rate the summer by how tan they are."

"Tan? What is tan?"

Rebecca clamped her mouth shut. *I did it again. Now I'd better think of a good response before I blow it.*

She smiled at Ben. "Oh, tanning is when you lie out in the sun on the beach to get a golden glow to your skin." It sounded somewhat ridiculous to Rebecca's ears, but it nonetheless was true.

Ben stood gaping at her. "Incredible. How is it so many people can be so idle during the growing season? Does no one farm on Martha's Vineyard? Who tends to your crops and animals?"

His questions would be impossible to answer fully. She certainly couldn't tell him the Vineyard was a vacation destination for Hollywood celebs, business execs, and thousands of families every year, including U.S. presidents. Nor could she reveal that tourism was the leading economy, and farm stands and the Farmers' Market were something the tourists thought of as quaint. She needed to change the subject. "When will your father get back?"

Ben glanced over to the shore. "I expect him shortly. In the meantime William and Donald are going to row James to shore and deliver him to a constable in town. Donald will remain with James and the constable and aid in escorting him to the next county to detain him there until we hoist anchor. I shall not risk another confrontation. William will bring my father as soon as he returns."

"I would rather not see James again. May I wait in your cabin until he is off the boat?"

"Of course. And I would like a word with you in private before my father arrives."

Ben held out a hand to help Rebecca down from the roof, which was totally perfect in and of itself, yet completely unnecessary as she was only three feet off the ground. Rebecca placed her hand in his and again the tingles spread through her fingers and up her arm. She swung her legs over the side and hopped down to the deck, her eyes never leaving Ben's.

"A word would be great. Two might be even better."

Ben's smile sent Rebecca's heart fluttering. "I sense there is a fire in you, Rebecca, where at first I saw only a spark. Do you intend to burn me, Madam?"

Heat rushed through her. She was already burning, couldn't the man see that? "I have no such intentions, Captain Reed. Incinerating you would be counterproductive to the plans I do have."

A moment of surprise flashed across Ben's face. Rebecca was certain no woman had ever spoken so boldly to him before. She had forgotten how much fun it was to flirt. And flirting was much better than answering any questions about what she had said to General Washington earlier. Maybe shaking Ben up a little bit would jumble his thoughts and rearrange his focus.

He offered her his arm. "I am relieved to hear that, Madam. Shall we go below and talk then?"

Obviously it didn't rattle him too much. Rebecca gave it another try. "Is talking how you put out a fire?"

Ben didn't rise to the bait. Instead he walked her to his cabin and held her elbow as she descended the ladder. As soon as her feet hit the floor, Rebecca spun around to face the inquisition. "I can explain about what..."

"Later." Ben drew her toward him and wrapped his arms around her. Inches from her mouth he stopped. "First we shall deal with the fire."

When his lips took hers, Rebecca lost all thought of Washington, Melissa, and jail. She slipped into the mist and flew through a rainbow, swirling in reds and yellows and blues and oranges and the softest purple. She was in paradise.

"Captain?" a voice called down the hatch.

Ben pulled back, tracing a finger over Rebecca's lower lip before he answered. "Yes, Nathaniel?"

"William said to inform you he is ready to depart with James."

"Thank you, Nathaniel." Ben laid his right hand on her check. "I must see to James' departure. I will return momentarily, and then we shall have that discussion."

When Ben had climbed the steps, Rebecca placed her left hand on her cheek where he had laid his and put her right hand on her chest. Her heart was pounding like horses' hooves running the oval track of the Kentucky Derby. How could the man think about a discussion? She was hoping her pulse would stop racing before his father arrived and caught her flushed from head to toe once again.

Rebecca picked up a small map of the local area from the table and fanned herself. She needed that cool breeze on deck—heck, she needed Alaska right about now. She wasn't going up above with James there, so she sat in the chair General Washington had used, waving the paper back and forth, and waited for Ben.

He returned looking like a matchstick. *Well, not exactly,* thought Rebecca, but his tall, hard body, his full, incredibly kissable lips and those gorgeous brown eyes were making her temperature rise yet again. They really needed to talk about Washington if his father was due to arrive at any minute. The sparks between them would have to be extinguished until...Rebecca didn't know until when. She didn't want to dwell on the possibility of never.

She fought back the tears. "Is James gone?"

"Yes, they reached shore."

The tension between them was palpable, ignitable even. Rebecca stopped fanning herself, set the map on the table, and stood. "Ben, do you want to talk about General Washington?"

His smile disappeared. "No, Rebecca, I do not want to discuss General Washington though I fear we must. I heard you speak of events that have not come to pass. Why? How?"

She wasn't ready to have this conversation. She didn't know what to say. Her grandmother would tell her "the truth will set you free," but in this case the truth could land her at a witch trial.

"I want to tell you, Ben, I do. I just don't know how. Can you wait until your father returns?"

Disappointment, or perhaps hurt, registered on Ben's face. "I can wait, though I ask ye what light can my father shed on your conversation with General Washington?"

Rebecca visibly relaxed. He wasn't going to press her. "If your father brings Melissa, or has spoken with her, it will be much easier for you to understand."

Rebecca swallowed the lump in her throat. She considered her list of what ifs once again: What if Melissa refused to come? What if Ben's Melissa wasn't her Melissa? She hadn't considered that option before. Worse yet, what if Melissa refused to acknowledge her past?

Ben hadn't moved. They stood quietly, neither knowing what to say, yet both wanting to say so much. Minutes passed. Rebecca sat down, and Ben went to his desk and shuffled some papers. He turned suddenly. "I wish you would trust me, Rebecca."

She got up and walked to him. "I do trust you, Ben. This isn't about trust. It's simply that my story will be a lot easier to tell with Melissa present. I promise."

"Captain, your father is approaching."

Ben grimaced. Rebecca sensed he wasn't done talking. "We are not finished, Rebecca, but I expect more answers will be revealed shortly. Before nightfall, I hope you will have confided in me whatever your secrets are."

She smiled with all the love in her heart. "You've got a deal, Ben."

They reached the deck rail and Rebecca counted three people in the skiff with William. She glanced out of the corner of her eye at Ben and realized she wasn't ready for this. She needed more time, yet it appeared William was rowing at lightning speed. The little boat was approaching with extreme alacrity, and she wasn't sure Ben was ready to hear her story. And she wasn't ready to lose Ben if he couldn't accept who she was and where she was really from. She stepped back toward the companionway.

Jonah appeared at her side. "Oh good, Uncle Isaiah and Aunt Missy have traveled with Father. Ye must be pleased, Mrs. O'Neill?"

Rebecca nodded. Relief rushed through her, easing some of her apprehension. At least Melissa had come. Surely she had come to help. As they got closer, Rebecca observed Melissa and realized she would never have recognized her. She was the perfect picture of a Colonial woman in her blue dress and matching blue bonnet. She didn't look anything like her old pictures; she looked as though she belonged in the eighteenth century.

Reverend Reed boarded first, followed by Melissa and Isaiah. Ben offered Melissa his hand as she came aboard. She said a quick hello and then made eye contact with Rebecca. She dashed over to Rebecca like a mother finding her lost child. She wrapped her arms around the younger woman, and both women burst into tears.

"Oh, thank God you came," Rebecca choked out.

"Of course I came. I have not forgotten how terrified I was when I arrived. When Eli told me you were onboard, I couldn't get here fast enough. You must have a thousand questions, and I have a few hundred or so for you. Let's go down to Ben's cabin and talk. The men can do what men do."

23

"I CAN'T BELIEVE YOU'RE HERE. I never thought I would see anyone from the Vineyard ever again." Melissa wrapped her arms around Rebecca a second time, then stepped back to take a good look at her.

"How did you get here? Silly question, I know, but I figured it was a fluke, or a miracle, when I landed here. I never considered someone else would turn up."

Rebecca nodded vigorously. "Believe me, I didn't plan on visiting you when I was coerced into chaperoning the class trip. I didn't even want to be on the *Shenandoah* in the first place, never mind travel here to this one. I argued with Mark tooth and nail to stay home."

"Obviously Mark won out. How many days have you traveled here?"

"Four. Sunday night I just thought it was a dream. I was only here for a minute or two. Monday and Tuesday my 'dream' became a reality. Then on Wednesday I had to take a student off the ship to the hospital. I didn't make it back to the boat until Thursday morning and here I am."

Melissa was nodding while Rebecca spoke. "Same thing with me. The first night truly felt like a dream. Then I thought I was going crazy."

"Did you figure out it was the cabin?"

Melissa shook her head. "What do you mean? What was the cabin?"

Rebecca reached for Melissa's hand and led them over to Ben's bed. They sat down and huddled close. "Captain Roberts was talking one night after dinner about the restoration of the boat. He mentioned the current Cabin 8 is the only fully reconstructed cabin with every original board put back exactly as it was when the *Shenandoah* was first built. I think the location of the room got moved or something in the remodeling process because it's a storage room at the end—oops, I mean the stern—of the boat now in 1775, sort of where Cabin 1 would be on the restored boat if you remember the layout. Either way, the cabin is the time machine."

Melissa's eyes widened. "You're kidding me! How did you figure it out?"

Rebecca grinned at the tall blonde. Her hair was long and gathered in a loose bun typical of the times. She wore no makeup, her skin glowed with health, and she appeared ten years younger than she had in any photo published at the time of her disappearance.

"I was in my bunk one morning waiting for Jonah to bring me breakfast. I noticed a knot on the wall, and a light bulb went off. I knew I had seen that same knot in my cabin back home." She filled Melissa in on every detail she could remember and had discovered. She relived the mornings when she'd wake up uncertain of where she was and how in blazes she was getting from one place to another. She told Melissa about the week with Ben and traveling back and forth every night. "Except the nights I wasn't in the cabin. Then I stayed in 1775 or..."

Melissa put up her hand, halting Rebecca midsentence. "What did you just say?"

"Oh gosh, did I skip over that part? The only way to get back and forth is to be *in* the cabin at night. I figured that out the night we slept on deck, and I woke up on Ben's shoulder. It's not merely that the cabin is the portal or transport, but you actually have to be inside the cabin at night. I'm guessing you have to be sleeping, too, though I haven't tested that theory."

Melissa stared, momentarily speechless. "I didn't know. I thought, well, when Isaiah anchored the boat and we disembarked, I figured I would leave at night as I had the previous three nights, only that time just from wherever Isaiah was taking me. When I woke up in the morning still in 1770, I freaked out. He already thought I might be touched, so he asked his sister to 'speak with me.' I think Isaiah expected Elizabeth to ascertain my sanity, or insanity, and then have me put in the stockade or some such nonsense. I scared that man silly."

Rebecca tipped her head back and peered toward the hatch to be sure no one was standing nearby. She whispered, "So it wasn't love at first sight?"

Melissa patted Rebecca's hand. "Hardly. Is that the case for you and Ben?"

"No!" A blush tinted Rebecca's cheeks. "Really, no. The first time I landed in the storage room I heard Ben and Jonah talking, and I thought he was a terrorist. Then I just wanted a friend, and, well, I really have no idea how he feels, truly, none at all. I mean, I think he likes me, he acts like he might be interested, but nothing's been said. And, after this morning, he may never want to see me again."

Melissa nudged Rebecca. "That's not what I hear."

Rebecca could feel the blush on her cheeks deepen. "Why, what have you heard? And from whom?"

Melissa scooted a little closer. "Eli told Elizabeth, who told me before we departed, that Eli thought Ben had feelings for you. Elizabeth is eager to meet you. Benjamin has not shown any interest in marriage or settling down, much to his mother's disappointment. He has always been a restless one. Elizabeth confided she often worried for his happiness. She will be thrilled with you."

Rebecca's stomach tightened and put her hands to her ears in mock resistance. "I don't think I'm ready for this conversation. Let's skip over me and Ben and get back to you and Isaiah. What did you tell Elizabeth? And when did he fall in love with you? When did you fall in love with him?"

When Melissa's eyes twinkled, Rebecca knew the painful life she had known on Martha's Vineyard had been healed by love.

"I told Elizabeth the truth. She was startled at first. She asked a great deal of questions, many of which I couldn't answer because I simply didn't know. After an hour or so of talking, she accepted my story as fact. The good Lord blessed her with a kind and trusting heart. And once she knew my story, she developed her own plan for my survival in 1770."

"What do you mean?" Rebecca asked.

"I think Elizabeth suspected Isaiah was drawn to me the first day he brought me home to her house. She kept suggesting we keep my secret between ourselves for a few days and see what transpired. I wanted to tell Isaiah the truth and have him take me back to the *Shenandoah*. I was certain I would return to the Island at any moment. Elizabeth believed I was destined to remain. She was right."

Melissa glanced up. No one appeared to be within earshot. "Elizabeth concocted many situations for Isaiah to escort me places or to introduce me to a neighbor or to help me get some fresh air. She was a born matchmaker. She'll have Ben proposing to you before the week is out. I'm sure you'll be much easier than I was." Melissa chuckled and winked at Rebecca before continuing.

"I nearly blew her plans to pieces. A week passed and still I remained in 1770. One night I asked Isaiah if I could sleep on the boat. It wasn't so much that I wanted to leave, but I needed to know whether or not I was just going to disappear one day. Unlike you, I hadn't figured out how I was moving from century to century."

Rebecca interrupted. "You've never gone back, right? You've stayed here every day since you left the real world, right?"

Anxiety hung in the air. Melissa gave Rebecca a comforting look. "I have never gone back. Elizabeth was correct. This is where I belong. And I thank God every day for bringing me here and for allowing me to stay."

Rebecca exhaled. "So it all worked out?"

"Eventually, yes. After I asked to sleep onboard, Isaiah informed me that the *Shenandoah* had sailed for Maine to collect a shipment of timber. I sat down and wept. I told him I would never get home then, and I told him where home was. He was livid. I thought he would turn me in as a witch. When he stormed out of the house, Elizabeth confided he was licking a bruised ego. I guess the man had feelings for me and believed I had feelings for him, even though the fool had never given me a clue he had any inclinations of the kind. Suddenly I had hurt those feelings I didn't even know he had when I said I would never get home."

Rebecca rolled her eyes, and Melissa laughed. "Yes, men are still men even in the eighteenth century, though most have morals and values severely lacking in the twenty-first century. Isaiah didn't speak to me for a week. Finally Elizabeth gave him what I can only guess was a thorough talking to, after which he asked me if I would accompany him on a walk. He spoke barely a word, but he picked me wildflowers and held my hand. From there on out it was smooth sailing, no pun intended."

"I'm so happy for you, Melissa."

"Thank you, and please call me Missy. Everyone else does."

"Hey, does Mr. Reed know where you're from?"

Missy grinned. "Yes, Elizabeth told him the night I told Isaiah. They are a wonderful family. I wished for this all my life, and God answered my prayers." Melissa chuckled. "Not that I was praying for life in 1770, mind you. But He certainly knew what I needed and worked everything out for my good."

"Have you ever been back on the *Shenandoah?* Before today, that is."

"No. I didn't dare risk it. I was so nervous about the boat I asked Isaiah to give up sailing. Benjamin was already working as his first mate, and he loved sailing more than life itself. Isaiah gave the ship to Benjamin, and we settled down to farm."

Rebecca stood and paced the floor. "If you believed the boat itself was the transport home, why did you come today? You could have lost everything."

Missy took Rebecca's hands in hers. "I was in your shoes once, Rebecca. I simply had to come, and I had to trust the Lord had a plan and it was for my good, your good, and the good of all involved. I was nervous on the ride over, as I believe Isaiah was, too. He will be relieved to know that I must sleep in the cabin, which I will most surely not do."

Rebecca wrapped her arms around Missy. A lump formed in her throat. "Thank you, thank you from the bottom of my heart. I can't believe you would risk your life here for me. God bless you, Missy."

"He has blessed me, Rebecca, a hundred times over. I never imagined this life for myself, and I wouldn't trade it for anything in the world, not even for hot, running water and electricity."

Rebecca stepped back and looked into Missy's eyes. "So you're happy?

Truly and completely happy that you stayed? You don't miss the Island? Or cell phones? Or grocery stores? Or movies? Or teaching? Or, I don't know, everything, life as we know it?"

Melissa leveled her gaze at Rebecca, all traces of humor and jest erased. "No, not for a minute. There are conveniences I miss, I won't deny that, especially as a woman, but I don't miss the life I led there. Staying here was the best thing that ever happened to me. I love Isaiah. I wouldn't want to be without him, not for a day. This is my home now."

"How did you know? How did you know that Isaiah was the one and that you would be happy with him?"

Missy rubbed her hand gently over Rebecca's right arm. "I'm sure you know I was married once. He was a cruel man. Bryce cheated and lied and twisted the truth around until I lost sight of what was real and good. When I caught him cheating the third time, I found the courage to leave. Almost instantly a weight was lifted off my chest and I could breathe again. I thanked God for my freedom and vowed to trust Him to lead me. It wasn't always easy. I was lonely at times, but I would pray and ask God to send me a good, kind, honest, compassionate man. And he did. I knew in my heart and soul that God had brought Isaiah and me together. Is that how you feel about Benjamin?"

Rebecca twisted her hands. "I don't know. I mean I do know, but then I think about everything for too long and I can't think straight."

Missy placed an arm around her shoulder and drew her closer. "I understand your concerns. I promise to help you in any way I can, answer any questions you might have."

Rebecca swallowed hard. "I don't know what I want. You look so happy. I have fallen—well, Ben could be—I just don't know, Missy."

"Are you prepared to leave the boat today?"

Tears formed in Rebecca's eyes. "No. I love Ben. I do. There, I've said it out loud for the first time. But I want him to want me to stay, to ask me to stay. First, though, he needs to know and understand who I am and where I'm from. Then I need to return home and talk with Captain Roberts. He went through a great deal of bad press when you disappeared. I don't want to do that to him again."

"I wondered about that. I'm sorry for the troubles I caused him. If you decide to stay, maybe there is another way," Melissa said.

Rebecca tugged at her grandmother's ring. "If I stay, maybe there will be."

Melissa studied the ring perfectly situated on Rebecca's left hand. "Is it nerves, or do you have reason to believe Benjamin may not have feelings for you?"

Rebecca flinched. "I need for Ben to know who I am. This morning, when I met General Washington, I felt an urgency, a need if you will, to share with him things I knew. Missy, the feeling was so strong I couldn't ignore it. I felt as though God was yelling in my ear, 'Tell him X, Y, and Z.' So I did. Needless to say General Washington *and* Ben thought I was crazy. I ran out of the room. Ben wanted to talk after, but I couldn't. I was hoping Mr. Reed would bring you back here, and maybe you could help me make some sense out of all of this."

Melissa, eyes distant, reached for Rebecca's hands. Rebecca felt a moment of panic. What if she had said something wrong already that Ben's father had shared with them on the ride back? What if his father thought she was a liability because of James Packer?

Melissa sighed and wiped away a tear, her eyes welling as she tried to speak. "I know what you mean. There are things I, too, have felt compelled to share with Isaiah. I gave him my blessing when he went off to Lexington an hour later than he had intended, though exactly as I knew it should be as he would arrive *after* the shot was fired on the Green. Two months later I insisted he avoid both Breeds and Bunker Hill."

Melissa bowed her head, and her shoulders began to shake.

"What is it?" Rebecca asked.

"I didn't know about Magnus. If only I had guessed. I just wish I had told Elizabeth and Eli about the bloodshed at Bunker Hill, but I had no idea Magnus would be killed. If I had known, maybe I could have saved him."

Rebecca surveyed the room for a box of Kleenex and realized she wouldn't find one. "Darn it!"

Missy glanced up. "What?"

"I was looking for a box of Kleenex."

Melissa started to chuckle, and Rebecca joined in. "You don't know how many times I reached for something during my first year here and found myself biting back a word or two a lady of this century would never speak."

"I can only imagine."

Missy lifted the folds of her long skirt. "I never thought I'd say this because I hated them before and hardly ever wore them, but I'd love a few dozen pairs of pantyhose and tights. Stockings and garters are for the birds."

Rebecca erupted into a fit of giggles.

"Oh, you think that's funny? Have you ever put on a corset? I promise you I lost ten pounds in my first two weeks here just so that dang thing didn't pinch me every time I moved. We didn't know how liberated we were in the twenty-first century. Women's Lib had nothing to do with jobs, and everything to do with bodily comfort. I'll keep my bra and burn this baby."

A loud snort escaped Rebecca's nose. Missy cracked up. Rebecca lifted the folds of her dress. "I was hopeless getting into this dress—don't bring one of those torture devices near me," Rebecca squeaked out between belly laughs. "If they only knew that they're marketed as intimate apparel two hundred years later, every church community in and around Colonial Boston would have a corset-burning bonfire and you'd never have to wear one again."

Missy held her stomach. "Maybe you could bring back a catalog tomorrow and save us both."

Both women lost it. They collapsed back on the bed and laughed until their sides ached. At the sounds of footsteps overhead, they sat up quickly and returned to what the gentlemen onboard would consider a ladylike posture.

"Aunt Missy, Mrs. O'Neill, are you well?" Jonah called down.

"We are fine, Jonah. We shall be up promptly," Missy answered primly. She ran a finger under her eyes, wiping away any sign of the tears she'd cried earlier, and stood.

"I just love him," Rebecca confided.

Missy nodded. "I know what you mean. He can be quite the tease, but he is soon going to be the most eligible bachelor in town and one fine catch." She smoothed her skirts and reached down to pick up her bonnet. Rebecca passed it to her before standing. "That felt wonderful. Thank you for the laughter. All sorrows should be replaced with joy."

"If we believe our being here is God's will, we must also believe that the lives of others are being played out according to His will too, including Magnus."

Missy squeezed Rebecca's hand. "Elizabeth said those same words. I believe it's true. I know it's true. I only wish His will had been for Magnus to live." Missy put on her bonnet but left the strings loose. She rubbed her cheeks to erase any sign of her tears and flashed a smile. "Shall we go on deck and find out what the men are up to? Perhaps it's time for you to talk with Benjamin?"

A small sigh escaped Rebecca. "After supper could be an even better time."

Melissa squeezed Rebecca's arm. "You know what they say, 'No time like the present.'"

Rebecca laughed. "Unless, of course, the present is actually two hundred years earlier. Maybe I could wait a century or two to tell Ben?"

24

THE LADIES WERE STILL GIGGLING when they reached the deck. The men turned at the sound of their laughter. Isaiah walked over and introduced himself to Rebecca. "Have you had a nice visit? I'm sure you both had a lot to catch up on."

Rebecca knew he meant much more than he was saying. "It has been wonderful. Thank you for bringing Missy. Words cannot express my gratitude. The risk you took...I don't know what to say."

Isaiah pulled Missy close. "My dear wife insisted. I could not deny her. We had faith all would be well."

Missy nudged him with her elbow. "Although the ride over was a bit tense, faith and all, wouldn't you say, husband?"

"Hush now, woman."

The love between the two of them shone like the noonday sun. Turning to find Ben, Rebecca felt her own heart fill at the sight of him. He looked happy, almost jubilant, though why she hadn't a clue. *Maybe this isn't the time to tell him. Why ruin his good day? Tomorrow is soon enough.*

She stepped closer to Missy. "I can't do this. I can't tell him."

Missy rubbed her back and whispered, "Yes you can. And you must. Don't be afraid. Benjamin will understand. Any fool can see by the way he's looking at you that the man is head over heels in love with you."

Rebecca's stomach flipped. In a low voice she spoke into Missy's ear, "That's not comforting. He thinks I'm somebody else. He doesn't love me, not a girl from the twenty-first century."

Missy shook her head. "Look at him, Rebecca. He is grinning from ear to ear at the sight of you. Whether you are from this century or the next, you are the woman he's beaming at."

Missy placed her palm on Rebecca's back and urged her along like a parent would a small child. When she reached Ben, Rebecca's throat went dry. She swallowed and met his eyes. *Please say no, please say no,* she prayed as she asked, "Do you have a minute, Captain?"

Ben glanced at his father, who nodded. He smiled and offered Rebecca his arm. "Of course. Would you like to take a walk on deck?"

A walk? He couldn't have been serious. She didn't want to walk. Her legs were going to give out any second. And she wanted to be alone. She couldn't talk to him with everyone watching. "Can we sit down somewhere? Somewhere private?"

She heard Adam whistling in the galley. Two men stood by the bowsprit. Everyone else was below deck, probably in the saloon or their quarters. She knew the only place she and Ben would have privacy was his cabin. She waited for him to make the suggestion.

Ben turned to his family. "We would like a few minutes alone to talk. We will be in my cabin. Please don't leave before we return."

Rebecca's feet dragged every step of the fifty or so feet to Ben's quarters. She spied Adam in the galley, and he winked up at her. As they walked beside the rail, she fingered the top of each belay pin, slowing her stride as though they were the most fascinating things she'd ever seen in her life. Ben appeared not to notice their turtle-paced steps. She paused at the wheel and wrapped her fingers around one of the spokes.

"Would you rather talk here, Rebecca?"

The sound of her name on his lips felt like his hands were caressing her skin. She wanted to cry, she wanted to shout for joy, she wanted the conversation to be over and done. *Dear God, please don't let me lose him.*

He moved closer. "Whatever you have to say, I will understand."

She shook her head. "I don't know where to begin or how to tell you." Rebecca felt her legs wobble. "I think I really need to sit down."

Ben led her toward his cabin and helped her down the short ladder. He pulled a chair out for her, took a seat beside her, and waited while she composed her thoughts.

Rebecca twisted her hands together and apart, together and apart. "I have something to tell you; it's just so unbelievable, there's no good way to say it."

"Might I suggest at the beginning?"

Rebecca bolted up, hands raised and gesturing, and began pacing, two strides forward, two back, two forward, two back. "That's the problem; I don't know where the beginning is. Is your time the beginning or my time? If you go back in time, does the earlier time become the beginning?"

Ben reached for her hands as she passed in front of him. She stopped pacing. Her face twisted in exasperation, her fingers and toes twitching.

"I don't believe there is anything you can tell me that will change how I feel about you," he said softly.

She stopped fidgeting and focused on their hands, joined, interlocked, his comforting hers. *Okay, Benjamin Reed, it's now or never.*

Rebecca pulled her hands back and started talking at lightning speed, her hands punctuating every other word. "Well, if I tell you I'm from the twenty-first century, that I time-traveled to this *Shenandoah* from my *Shenandoah,* and I could zap back there tonight and potentially never come back to 1775, you might reconsider any thoughts you might have had about dating me. Most guys like younger women, but I think two hundred years is a bit much."

Rebecca paused to catch her breath. "Or am I older than you?" Then she added, "But, hey, at least I'm not married."

A brief smile graced Ben's face, though Rebecca couldn't tell whether he was happy, amused, or putting on a brave face until he could get her off the *Shenandoah.*

Dropping to the chair, she buried her face in her hands. She inhaled slowly, trying to steady her racing pulse. The sarcasm hadn't helped. The quiet didn't feel so good, either.

The cabin was still. Ben didn't move or speak. Rebecca kept her eyes closed and her head in her hands. An invisible clock ticked away the seconds. Minutes passed—they seemed like hours. The air grew stale, her mouth was dry, her heart was thudding, and she couldn't move. *Why doesn't he say something?*

Rebecca drew in a deep breath, filled her lungs, and exhaled slowly. She'd known this moment would come eventually. Hadn't she asked to come back one more time so she could say good-bye to Ben? Well, her wish had been granted. Time to face the music. She raised her head slowly, opening her eyes with dread.

Her jaw dropped. "You're smiling! You're smiling?" Rebecca stared at Ben's mouth. "Why are you smiling at me? Shouldn't you be calling for a witch hunt?"

"My father told me."

Rebecca narrowed her eyes. "What? Your father told you what?"

Ben looked a little sheepish. "While you and Missy were talking, my father and Uncle told me about Missy...and you, at least as much as they could figure out about your appearance on my ship."

At first relief washed over her, then a smattering of anger edged its way in, then more anger. "You knew?! You knew, and you made me sit here trying to figure out how to tell you, wondering what you were going to say, fearing you'd throw me out and never want to see me again? Ooooh!"

Rebecca shot to her feet and stomped to the ladder. She'd made it to the first rung when both feet left the floor, and her body was lifted and twirled about. Laughter filled her ears as Ben lowered her gently and gazed into her eyes. "I would prefer you didn't leave. Ever."

He lowered his mouth to hers, wrapping his arms around her and pulling her into the warmth of his embrace. Rebecca melted into him. His lips claimed hers, and she surrendered to his love and the love she'd held inside.

His lips traced kisses to her ear. "I love you, Rebecca O'Neill."

The tears came, joyfully overflowing and running down her cheeks. Ben tipped her chin up, kissed her tears, and waited. Rebecca moved her right hand over his shoulder and up to his face, resting her palm on his cheek. He turned slightly and kissed the inside of her hand. She smiled. "I love you, too, Benjamin Reed."

He kissed her again, sealing their fate, promising her everything and giving all. When air became essential, she rested her head against his chest and sighed. *Please, God, don't take me away from here. Let me stay forever.*

"I won't let you go."

Rebecca stepped back.

"I will hold you forever," Ben said, then drew her snugly back into his embrace. He kissed the top of her head. "Can you tell me what happened? I want to know everything about you. It was you a few nights ago in the storage room when I was speaking with Jonah, correct?"

"Yes. That was my first night onboard the *Shenandoah*, my *Shenandoah*, for the school trip. I thought I had dreamed you and Jonah, or so I tried to tell myself."

"How did you come to be here? Do you understand how you travel? Can you explain it to me?"

"I can try, at least as much as I've figured out. Should we find the others first, though? Missy is probably wondering if I managed to get the words out. And it might be easier to tell the story once."

Ben kissed her again, slow and deep. The boat rocked, or maybe it was just her imagination. When their lips parted, Ben squeezed her hand and winked. "Now we can go tell my family."

25

THEY STOOD IN REBECCA'S CABIN, or what she had come to think of as her cabin. All the crates and barrels of rice and supplies had been emptied out. The room seemed cavernous almost, another reminder that the journey had come to an end, that her time was up, that life was going to change one way or another, for better or for worse.

Nestled against Ben's chest, gathered tenderly in his arms, Rebecca didn't want to move, never mind leave Ben's side and risk going back to her time and not being able to return.

"I have never been more scared than I am now. In the last five days I've traveled back in time to 1775 and back to the future four times, met George Washington, been accused of treason, had my life threatened, had a child in my care fall and need a trip to the emergency room, and I confessed to you and your family who I am and where I'm from, yet none of that compares with leaving you tonight."

Rebecca took a tiny step back from Ben to look into his eyes. She saw everything she needed, everything she'd never known she wanted and all she could ever ask for. She recognized that the feeling of love she now felt was what her parents and grandparents had known in their marriages. The love was why her mother's heart had broken when her father died. She had never understood, had resented her mother and her broken heart, until this moment. Her mother had known something incredible, and Ben had given that same wonder to her.

Tears formed in the corners of her eyes. "What if?"

"Ssshh." Ben tugged her gently against him. Her arms went of their own accord around his waist, and her cheek found its place again in the fabric of his shirt. In his arms she was surrounded by love, home at last.

"I don't want to leave. I'm afraid, Ben, afraid this will be the time I don't come back."

"Sshhhhh." He put his fingers on her lips. "We will not allow ourselves to ponder the what-ifs. We must trust in the Lord, trust in His plan. If He has brought you to me, I must believe He shall bring you back again, for good."

"Your faith is so much stronger than mine."

"Nay, my love, I am frightened, too. I waited my whole life to find you.

You are about to go to a place where I cannot follow, where I cannot see you or hear your voice or know that you are well. I will worry, and I will pray. I know, as my father told us on deck, the prayer will do more good than the worry."

Eli had been wonderful when they'd rejoined Ben's family after Rebecca's confession to Ben in his cabin. She had explained to Eli, Isaiah, Jonah, and Adam, with Missy's help, her nightly journeys from the twenty-first century to 1775. When she'd finished her story, Eli had asked what her plans were.

Swallowing the lump in her throat, Rebecca had answered, "I have to go back. Tomorrow is the last day of the school trip. I can't abandon Captain Roberts. He went through terrible hardships after Missy disappeared—not just the rumors and gossip. It was worse than that. The Coast Guard, our naval police of sorts, shut down his operations not only on the *Shenandoah* but also on her sister ship, *The Lady Katherine*. He was devastated. I have to go back and tell him what I know and what I want and pray that there is another way, other than vanishing into thin air, so I can come back to Ben without hurting Captain Roberts."

Eli had gathered them in a circle and led them in prayer. He lifted the situation to the Lord and asked for His divine intervention and wisdom and protection. Rebecca had felt peaceful then. Standing in the cabin now, holding onto Ben moments before he would close the door and she would leave him, she felt as though she was trapped inside a tornado, spinning wildly out of control with no say as to where she would land.

Eli, Isaiah, and Missy had gone ashore for the evening. Although Isaiah had wanted to believe Rebecca's assurances about the cabin being the transport vehicle, he had insisted on taking Missy off the ship. He would not take any chances. They had hoped to find rooms at an inn nearby and had promised to return in the morning to be certain Rebecca had traveled safely back to Ben.

The light in the lamp flickered. Ben kissed her lips softly. "It's time, my love. Go now so you can come back to me. I will be here in the morning with arms longing to hold you for the rest of your life."

Rebecca didn't want to let go of Ben. She knew she had to, but every ounce of her being wanted to cling to Ben as though he was the source of her life.

He must have sensed her urgency and panic. He tipped her chin up and locked his eyes on hers. "I will wait for you, for as long as it takes. If you do not come back to me, I will find a way to come to you. I promise you, Rebecca, we will be together again."

A calm settled over Rebecca. Whether it was the look in Ben's eyes or his faith in their love, she suddenly felt at peace with what she needed to do. "I'm coming back to you, Benjamin Reed. You can't get rid of me this easily."

He smiled. Her heart skipped. "We are in agreement then, my love. I will see you again."

He kissed her quickly one more time, turned, and walked out of the cabin. Rebecca laid a hand on the door and listened as the latch clicked into place. She walked over to the cot and changed into her sweatpants. After folding the dress, she lay on her back. Her body tensed. She breathed in deeply through her nose and exhaled slowly out of her mouth. She repeated the exercise a few times until her body settled into the cot. Then she closed her eyes and asked for help.

"Stay with me, Lord. Carry me on angels' wings forward and back again."

*

Ben paced the floor in his cabin. He wondered how long it would take for Rebecca to fall asleep and, once she was asleep, when she would be gone. He wanted to stand outside her door, checking on her throughout the night, but he was afraid if he opened her cabin door that he would interfere with her time travel somehow.

Fear and worry coursed through his veins. He wished his father had remained on board. He needed his steady hand and absolute, unshakable faith. He knew he had to remain calm and focused. He still had a crew depending on him. His life was not his own. Sitting on the edge of his bed, he removed his boots. He knew of only one way to get through the night without losing hope. He dropped to his knees and folded his hands.

"Father, I know You hear me. I know You know my needs even before I ask. Please stay with Rebecca, Lord. Keep her safe and guide her path. And give me the strength to get through this night, to trust in You and to accept whatever answer the morning brings. Amen."

Ben lowered his head to rest on his hands atop the bed. "That's the hardest part, Lord, to accept whatever the morning brings." Time passed slowly. He talked to God. He fell asleep while praying, on his knees, his arms folded on the bed serving as a pillow for his head.

26

REBECCA KNEW BEFORE SHE OPENED HER EYES where she was. She felt the cotton pillowcase against her cheek, the smooth, satiny fabric an instant indication of where she was. Her arms snuggled under soft sheets. The comfort alone told her she was in the twenty-first century. She listened for the kids. The ship was still fairly quiet, so she knew she hadn't overslept. The time had come to rise and shine. Today was the day. Rebecca had to put a plan into action, well, think of a plan, and then get back to Ben.

A moment of panic seized her, and her body stiffened. "No, I will not give in to doubt. There is a way, I will find it, and I am going home to Ben!"

Images of Ben rolled on a screen in her mind. She closed her eyes and played the movie until peace settled into her bones. *I can do this. There is a way. I will not be afraid.* "Okay, Lord, we both know I'm a little scared, but I can handle that. Just show me the way, give me the answers so I can be with Ben without hurting Captain Roberts."

The sound of feet overhead alerted Rebecca to the time and the need to move. If she wanted to get in a workout before the kids woke and were in full force, she had better get moving. She picked up her mat, pulled a sweatshirt, on over her tank top, and exited her cabin.

Fifteen minutes later, as she was doing triceps dips off a storage chest, the sun's first rays shone into the orange-pink sky. Rebecca had never been able to decide what she enjoyed more, the sunrise or the sunset. Both could be equally brilliant and worthy of a great artist's canvas.

She finished her fiftieth dip, stood, and walked to the rail to admire the view while she stretched her arms. As she pulled her right elbow back beside her ear with her left hand, a chill ran down her spine. She shuddered, released her elbow, and shook out the arm. She turned around to do a couple of sets of push-ups off the chest and came face to face with Mike Natale. "Oh!"

"Caught you off guard?"

Rebecca reined in her anxiety. She had no desire to speak with Mike, not then and not later. Placing her hands wide on the storage chest, she kept her legs shoulder-width apart and straight out behind her and started her push-ups.

"Didn't mean to interrupt you." The words sounded empty.

Rebecca chose to play along. "No problem. I don't want to seem rude. I just want to get my workout in before the kids wake up." She counted "four" and lowered herself down for number five. Twenty more to go. She could drag them out if she needed to, go painfully slow and hope Mike took the hint and left, but she'd rather not have to torture her body. At the moment, he wasn't moving. Rebecca gritted her teeth and slowed her movements.

"How did you sleep last night?"

Rebecca heard the edge in his tone. She wasn't getting sucked into another go-round with him, especially with Hawk nowhere in sight. She plastered on a perky smile. "I woke up ready for the day, as you can tell. There is nothing like a great night's sleep."

She wasn't about to tell Mike she hadn't had a true night's sleep since she'd boarded the *Shenandoah*. And she sure as heck wasn't going to share with him what her nights had consisted of. She could honestly reply she wasn't tired, and her body felt good. She hadn't given it much thought, but it was ironic her nights here were filled with activity and she wasn't exhausted or in need of a nap. She maintained the perky look as she counted eighteen.

Another minute ticked by ever so slowly. Rebecca's arms were getting sore, and Mike wasn't moving. She had no desire to do extra push-ups, yet she didn't want to stop and be subjected to Mike's interrogation. She extended her arms on the twenty-fifth push-up and held the position, thinking what she could do next to keep busy. Stretching, which is what she wanted to do, would seem like nothing to Mike, and he would probably assume she was done. *There's never a bad time to do abs!*

Inhaling deeply, and loudly, Rebecca rolled up and then quickly dropped down onto her mat. She began with basic crunches. Mike didn't move. "Hey, Mike, why don't you grab a towel and join me?"

She glanced up at his face. He didn't even crack a smile. He stared back at her, giving her an uneasy feeling. "Why won't you tell me the truth?" he whined, sounding like a petulant child.

Rebecca tensed but kept crunching. "I have, Mike."

"I know you've seen Melissa. I know it."

The last time he'd accused her of meeting up with Missy, she'd been able to honestly tell him she hadn't seen Melissa. She couldn't give him that same answer. She hoped the minutes she took to do two hundred sit-ups would be enough time to think of a response. Lifting her knees up to a 90-degree angle, she kept crunching…and thinking.

When her abs began to burn, Rebecca closed her eyes, extended her arms long overhead and her legs straight out, and stretched. A few minutes later, knowing Mike hadn't moved but that she needed to, she took a deep breath in, hugged her knees to her chest as she exhaled, then rolled up to her feet in one fluid movement.

As soon as she was vertical, Mike stepped closer, too close. "Why won't you admit that you've visited Melissa?" he snapped.

Rebecca flinched and snapped back, "What is it about Melissa? Why is it so important that someone might have talked to her?"

Between the layers of anger, she saw pain register on his face. Rebecca was sure of it. What was the big deal with Mike and Melissa? She pressed a little harder, hoping he would confess whatever was going on. "What are you not saying, Mike? She's been gone for five years."

Mike backed up. Rebecca thought she had pushed a button until she heard Hawk's voice behind her. "Walk away, Natale. Now!"

Mike raised his hand, stabbing a finger at Rebecca, accentuating each word as he spoke. "I have a right to know."

Hawk stepped up beside her. Rebecca placed a hand on his chest and gave him a sideways plea with her eyes for him to step back and let her talk to Mike. "What do you want to know, Mike? I don't know anything about you or your mother or your relationship with Melissa. I didn't even know you before this trip. How could I tell you anything?"

He shook his head violently. "I don't want you to tell me anything. I need answers from Melissa. She knows. She has to. My mother won't tell me. I deserve to know. I have a right to know!"

She lowered her voice. "Know what, Mike?"

"Who my father is, okay?" The sentence seethed through clenched teeth.

Rebecca jerked back as if she'd been slapped. The Missy she knew couldn't be this man's mother, and she wouldn't be involved in anyone's affairs. Mike had to be mistaken or clutching at straws. Her mind racing, she asked, "I don't understand, Mike. How can Melissa help you?"

Mike shook his head. "She was married to Bryce Burroughs. Rumors are, that slime was my father. My mother won't tell me. Melissa has to know. He was her husband. He probably told her he'd been with my mom years ago. Or maybe she knew because she and my mom had been friends since high school."

Rebecca felt a wave of compassion. She'd never heard a kind word spoken about Bryce Burroughs. Missy had made it clear he was abusive. No one would want him for a father. "But Mike, why would Melissa know anything? As far as I can remember, she was only married to Bryce for a few years, and you would have already been born by the time they were married."

Mike shook his head. "I know that, but maybe he told her. Maybe he was bragging one night while he was drunk. Someone has to know. I can't stand to think that bum was my father. But I have to find out. I thought, I hoped, by working on the boat I could somehow find Melissa and ask her. Pete swore to me she was alive and living in another century."

Hawk walked up to Mike. Josh, Dave, and Brian were all on deck waiting to oversee morning chores. "Listen, I've got to start the generator and get the kids up on deck scrubbing. I'm sorry, Mike. Melissa is gone. No one has seen her in five years. I know you want to believe Pete's story, but there's no proof Melissa is alive. Rebecca can't help you. Hopefully your mom will. Why don't you go down and grab a cup of coffee?"

Rebecca reached for Mike's hand, but he yanked it back. "I don't want your sympathy. I want answers."

"I don't have any answers, Mike. But I'll keep you company down below if you'd like."

Mike's hulking frame looked fragile, as though he would break, or break down, at her touch. Rebecca placed a tentative hand on his upper arm and gently maneuvered him toward the companionway. The kids were lined up ready to charge. "Let's try the companionway down by the boys' cabins."

"Hey, Miss O'Neill, can we come up yet?" Raz hollered.

"Did you hear the generator?" she said jokingly.

"Aww, give us a break. The girls went up early twice this week," Nick whined. Before Rebecca could reply, the generator kicked in and the stampede hit the ladder. Rebecca guided Mike in the opposite direction.

He stopped before they reached the hole. "I don't feel like coffee or talking. Tell Hawk I went to my cabin."

Mike wove his way through the kids, shoulders hunched, eyes to the deck and, Rebecca was sure, with a broken heart. She watched him brush by Hawk without a word and head toward the bow where the crew's quarters were located. Rebecca walked to the aft companionway and headed down, making her way quickly to her cabin. Safely inside, she closed the door and collapsed onto the bed. A long sigh eased past her lips.

"Well, I guess that explains a lot. I wouldn't want to be him. Nor would I want to be me if he found out I had seen Melissa. I've got to formulate a plan and get out of here and back to Ben without anyone finding out."

Rebecca stood to change. "Oh no, I forgot my mat on deck. Now it'll be soaked." She thought about that comment for a second, then smiled. "Well, with any luck I won't need it tomorrow anyway."

27

THE KIDS AND CREW GATHERED IN THE SALOON FOR BREAKFAST. Rebecca noticed Mike was nowhere to be seen. Hawk sat at the head of the portside table and whistled to get everyone's attention.

"This is our last day at sea. We head home today and tie up to our mooring ball in the harbor for our last night." Hawk paused as many groans and sighs erupted. "I'll take your response as a sign you've had a great time. You've been a wonderful crew, and today promises to be another perfect day on the water."

Kayla raised her hand.

"Yes, Kayla?"

"Is it true there's a treasure hunt today and a party tonight?"

Hawk grinned. "Now who would be telling such tall tales?"

The popular blonde smirked. "I heard it from my friends on the Oak Bluffs class trip."

"Well, Kayla, I guess the cat's out of the bag then. Later today, after we've tied off and all the chores are done, you'll break off into your work groups. We'll give you all a list of clues, and you'll hunt for treasure. The first team to gather all the clues and find the buried treasure wins a prize." Hawk winked at Rebecca as the kids became excited. Then he added, "The winners will sing and dance at the captain's dinner tonight."

"No way!" "Sweet!" "I'm not dancing!" "Oh, this is going to be so much fun," were a few of the louder comments overheard in the room. Hawk waited until the kids calmed down. "Actually, there are some great prizes and you'll all have fun. Singing and dancing will be optional."

Rebecca scanned the room, all the smiling faces, and sadness ran through her. She'd known most of these kids since first grade and now, if she left forever, she wouldn't see any of them grow up. If she returned to Ben, she would probably never teach again, either. The last thought really hit home. She hadn't considered it before…hadn't considered what she would do with herself all day if she weren't teaching.

She tried to imagine what her life would be like in 1775. Would she stay home all day and take care of a house, or would she be able to sail with Ben? There sure wouldn't be any gyms or yoga classes. And running would be out of the question, even if she could bring or wear her favorite pair of running shoes back with her. She should've asked Missy how she spent her time.

"Miss O'Neill?...Miss O'Neill?"

Rebecca shook her head. Ashley was standing before her. "I'm sorry, Ashley, what were you saying?"

"Are you coming swimming with us? Can we race around the boat one last time?"

Rebecca realized the children were dispersing—one could guess to put on bathing suits.

"One last time," Ashley had said. If Rebecca left for good, it would be one last time for her. She smiled at Ashley, burying her doubts. "Of course I'm going swimming. Just try to keep me out of the water. We'll have a couple of races, and maybe I can get Hawk to scrounge up a prize for the fastest swimmer. How does that sound?"

Ashley's sparkling eyes said it all. "Great!"

As if on cue, Hawk sauntered over. "Did I hear my name?"

"Guilty as charged. I have a favor to ask."

"You sure were lost in thought. You seemed to drift off when I was talking about final bunk inspection. Thinking about Mike? That was some confession. What's the favor?"

Rebecca nodded. It was some confession, but not what she had been thinking about. She'd been thinking about how drastically different her life would be if she stayed with Ben in 1775, not that she could share that with Hawk. "I just told Ashley we would have one last swimming contest. Any chance you might have an extra T-shirt or hat to give out as an award to the fastest swimmer?"

"Sure thing. I've got a box full of hats."

Nick and Raz ran by and jumped off the rail into the water. Rebecca spotted Mike at the bow. "I feel bad for him," she said, pointing toward Mike. "I knew his mom was a single parent, but I had no idea she had ever been with Bryce. Yuck. I hope she'll tell him one way or the other who his father is. He does deserve to know."

Hawk placed a hand on Rebecca's forearm. "You're right. He does deserve to know the truth, and I feel sorry for him, too, but I think there is more on your mind. Can I help with anything?"

Rebecca looked into his blue eyes and saw a depth of kindness. She wished she could tell Hawk about Ben and her doubts and hopes, but she didn't dare. "Thanks, Hawk, but I really need to talk to Captain Roberts. I was hoping he'd be at breakfast."

"He was on his cell to Katherine. From the sound of it, Tess was in trouble, or something like it, again last night," Hawk said as he stepped back and shoved his hands into his pockets.

"Oh, gosh, not again. Tess is a spitfire, that's for sure. Three boys and Tess, and I think Captain Roberts has his hands full with Tess. I do love her, though. We've been friends since we were kids. We hung out in high school and always had fun. Even then she could kick it up. These last few years we've had the best time, sort of grown up some, I guess. Though I doubt Tess will ever be boring."

Hawk winced. "I'm just glad she didn't convince her father to let her work on the boat this summer. She sure gave it a run for the money in the spring. I don't think I could handle Tess on the ship 24/7."

Rebecca heard something in his voice. She watched his face and thought she detected a slight blush creeping up his neck. The longer she stared at him, the deeper shade of red his cheeks turned. *Interesting. I wonder if Tess knows he still has feelings for her?*

Rebecca chose to ignore Hawk's reaction, at least enough to let him off the hook and not grill him about it. "Thanks for the heads-up about Tess. I'll let Captain Roberts have some peace before I bother him with my problem. I'm going to swim with the kids and catch up with him later." She turned and headed toward her cabin, calling over her shoulder, "Maybe Tess will come to the captain's dinner tonight." She didn't turn around or wait for Hawk's reply.

28

THE MIDDAY SUN FELT GREAT. Rebecca stood mid ship by the White Hall rowboat as Hawk awarded Jessica Andrews a *Shenandoah* T-shirt for her victory in the swimming contest. Two seconds later, Brian performed his favorite galley boy job and rang the lunch bell. The kids raced by her as they formed a line and grabbed plates.

Dave had laid out another fabulous meal: all the fixings for tacos, including spicy beef and tortillas, as well black beans, a huge bowl of salad, and a plate of sliced watermelon. By the time Rebecca made it to the front of the line, some of the students were behind her ready for seconds.

Josh carried a plate over to Captain Roberts. The captain was clearly engaged in a lively conversation with Hawk and Tim. Rebecca had yet to find a time to present him with her dilemma. She hoped the kids would go below deck after lunch to prepare for cabin inspection while they sailed the last hour toward Vineyard Haven Harbor.

After creating her own taco salad with heaps of lettuce, black beans, and all the taco fixings, Rebecca took a seat on the cabin roof beside Sharon.

"I don't know how you do it," Sharon said as she raised a bite of lettuce to her mouth.

"Do what?"

Sharon pointed to Rebecca's full plate. "Eat all that food and stay so slim."

Rebecca refrained from rolling her eyes. Noticing that a couple of the girls nearby had overheard Sharon's comment, she stabbed some beef and black beans and lifted her fork. "Well, it's easy when the food is this good and good for me. How can I not enjoy a gigantic salad of lettuce, tomatoes, cucumbers, black beans, onions, beef, and a little salsa and guacamole? This is better than Marco's Deli."

Sharon shook her head. "I don't know where you put it."

"I just swam for an hour. I'm starving," Rebecca said, working really hard to keep the irritation out of her voice. The last thing she wanted to do at lunch on their last day was talk about food again.

She took another bite and motioned for Kayla to have a seat by Ashley. "We've had the best weather all week. Can you believe how lucky we've been? I hope you've enjoyed the sail."

Sharon put down her fork. "It's been better than I hoped. Thank God for the sunny days. I was terrified we'd be stuck in our cabins like the Edgartown School was two weeks ago. I heard nightmare stories about those kids and parents going crazy being cooped up below deck for three days straight. All in all, I can't complain."

Rebecca pushed a piece of lettuce back onto her fork and then shoveled on some beans and guacamole. "I'm glad you've enjoyed yourself. I had the best time. I don't ever want to leave. I think I could stay on this boat forever."

Sharon laughed. "All the more power to you, Rebecca. I'm looking forward to a hot shower as soon as I get home. Then I'm going out to lunch at Slice of Life, ordering my favorite salad, and then I'm heading to Nail Bliss for a pedicure and a manicure. An afternoon of bliss."

The girls had moved closer. Kayla was practically sitting in her lap. Alexis was inching her way between Sharon and Rebecca.

"I agree with you, Miss O'Neill. I would loooovve to stay onboard for another week," Alexis chimed in.

"Me, too," Kayla said. "But maybe I could go home and take a shower and come back."

"I had fun, but I miss my dog and my baby brother," Ashley said. "I wouldn't want to be gone for another week, even if we did get to miss school."

"Hey, maybe we could have school on board the *Shenandoah?* What do say, Miss O'Neill? Then you really could live on the boat." Kayla looked rather pleased with her suggestion.

"I think your parents might have something to say about that, Kayla."

The girls took over the conversation and chatted about what they liked best about their trip and what they missed about home. Rebecca finished her salad and looked around for Captain Roberts. He was still talking with the crew. Her future with Ben would have to wait a little longer. She rose and walked over to the compost bucket, scrapped her tidbits in, and placed her plate and fork in the dish crate.

When Brian called for Galley Crew 3, everyone started clearing out. Rebecca stayed put and hoped Captain Roberts would soon be free. She borrowed a couple of towels left by the kids on the rooftop, rolled one up for a pillow and stretched out atop another. Her golden-brown skin soaked up the sun's rays as she let her mind contemplate the possibilities and probabilities of the choices before her.

She was trying to figure out what to say to Captain Roberts when Hawk called her name. "Rebecca?"

She rolled onto her right side. "Hey, Hawk."

"I mentioned to Captain Roberts you needed a few moments of his time. He's headed down into his cabin now and said he'd be available if you're still keen to talk."

Rebecca swung her feet over the rooftop and dropped down onto the deck. Whether she was ready or not, she had to tell Captain Roberts what was going on and ask for his help. "Thanks. I'll head down now."

Hawk offered a hand as she stood. "No problem. Good luck."

Rebecca took in a deep breath. "Thanks, I need it."

"Doubt it." Hawk grinned, "Oh, and just in case you were wondering, Tess won't be coming tonight."

Rebecca chuckled and walked toward the stern and the captain's cabin. Hawk may have avoided Tess for the last two years, much to Tess's frustration, but he clearly felt something for her. Maybe in time Tess would get that elusive date with Hawk.

29

REBECCA KNOCKED ON CAPTAIN ROBERTS' OPEN DOOR. She was certain her heart was pounding louder than her hands on wood ever could. He poked his head out from behind a bookshelf and motioned her in.

"Is this a social visit, young lady, or do we have a problem?" His voice was warm and steady. Years of chartering children and adults had probably prepared him for just about any and every problem. *Almost any situation. Surely I'm the first to request an early departure off his boat to travel back in time to 1775.*

"I want to leave," Rebecca said. Her voice sounded shaky to her own ears.

Captain Roberts stared at Rebecca and asked calmly, "Today? Why? Is there an emergency on Island? Is there a problem with one of the crew or the children that I don't know about?"

Rebecca shook her head slowly from side to side. She should have rehearsed the conversation more. She didn't have a clue how to tell him what she wanted or, more accurately, what she needed.

"Oh, no, the crew is great, all of them. The kids have enjoyed an incredible week. They've really been rather well behaved, minus one or two minor incidents. I...um...I want to leave for different reasons...personal...I don't even know how to explain..."

The captain removed his glasses and lowered them to the table he was sitting at. "Why don't you have a seat and tell me what's wrong?"

She moved slowly to the seat across from Captain Roberts. Placing both hands on the table, she laced her fingers together, her index fingers tapping against each other. Rebecca kept her eyes on her hands and whispered her secret. "You won't believe me, and I understand why you wouldn't, but I know where Melissa is because—because I've been there, I've seen her, I've talked with her, and I want to go back. I want to live where she lives."

She felt his hands encompass hers, squeeze her gently, and heard his deep sigh. His voice was laced with concern when he spoke. "I cannot imagine how difficult your life has been, Rebecca, with your father's death, and then your mother passing two years later. Now your grandmother has joined them. I know you must be lonely, but you must have faith that life will get better. There are people you can talk to. I know Katherine would be glad to spend some time with you, and Tess could certainly make better use of her time. Maybe the two of you could…"

Rebecca smiled at Captain Roberts, at his warmth and compassion. "You're so kind, Captain Roberts, and I appreciate your concern. You've always been wonderful to me. I don't want you to worry. I'm not depressed, and I'm not thinking about dying…far from it, trust me."

His shoulders relaxed, and he sat back in his chair, releasing Rebecca's hands. "I am relieved to hear that. So why, then, are you wishing to join Melissa in an early grave?"

She struggled to inhale around the lump lodged in her throat. "There is no easy way to say this: Missy isn't dead. Pete Nichols was right. Melissa did travel back to 1770, and she stayed there, though not by her choice. I have seen her and talked with her and…"

He held up an angry hand. "Why are you saying this? I've never known you to lie or fabricate stories, Rebecca. All those years running around with Tess, and you were always the voice of reason. Why are you saying this? How could you pretend to know this with such certainty?"

Rebecca looked into his eyes and held the contact. "Since boarding the *Shenandoah* on Sunday, every night that I have slept in my cabin, I have traveled back in time to the original *Shenandoah*. I've seen Missy, and I've met Benjamin and Jonah Reed and their father, Eli, and—" She stopped when she saw his expression.

Acceptance, or maybe recognition of truth, registered in the captain's eyes. "I've wondered. It hadn't seemed possible, so I tossed it aside."

"What?"

He offered her a half-hearted smile. "First, believe me when I tell you that Melissa is the only person to ever disappear off the ship. But, back in the days when we offered adult cruises, numerous passengers mentioned or talked about vivid dreams, all of them set on the original *Shenandoah*. No one ever said they physically went back in time, only that they'd dreamed, vivid dreams, of being there."

"But why didn't you or anybody mention it, especially after Melissa disappeared?"

He looked away, remembering or contemplating, Rebecca couldn't tell. "Think about it: no one wants to look foolish. Talking about dreams on a ship is one thing. Suggesting your dreams might have been real is quite another. And, when we started taking the kids out, we changed the cabin numbers. Melissa's Cabin 8 would have had little meaning to anyone who might have experienced a dream thirty-some odd years ago."

"But surely someone…"

He shook his head. "Melissa was the first adult in years to stay in your cabin. No child ever even mentioned having dreams. Honestly, after fifteen years, I wrote it off as overactive adult imaginations. I saw many unique interactions on those adult cruises. People do and imagine all sorts of fantasies on a cruise ship."

Rebecca's mouth must have been hanging open. Captain Roberts reached over and tapped a finger softly under her jaw. "Is it more unbelievable to think I didn't mention anything about thirty-year-old dreams, or that Melissa Smith traveled back in time and chose to remain there? Even I, knowing of the dreams people supposedly had years ago, didn't believe Melissa time-traveled."

"Well, she did, and I have, and…"

He interrupted her. "You really have? All dreams and joking aside…how does it work? Do you know when you're leaving? Can you feel your body shifting or moving?"

Rebecca laughed. Captain Roberts was your typical guy: forget the romance, focus on the sci-fi mechanics. "No, I can't feel anything. I travel only when I'm sleeping. The first night I traveled, I thought it was a dream. I was gone only for a couple of minutes and the time just seemed like a very real, very vivid dream. The next night I was there for a day and returned here when I went to sleep there. I don't know if I've come or gone until I wake up."

Captain Roberts just stared. Rebecca took a deep breath. She needed him to believe her as much as she needed his help.

"I can tell you this, though: Cabin 8 is the ticket. The night I spent off the boat, on Wednesday after Starr Gates's accident, I didn't go back. Same thing happened one night when I was on the original *Shenandoah*. Everyone, including me, slept on deck because it was so hot and humid. The next morning I was still there. I hadn't come back here. It's crazy because time kind of stands still on either end—at least it has for these nightly sojourns. Missy has aged in the five years she's been there, and time has certainly moved on now that she is permanently gone."

"Why would you want to leave, Rebecca? Your life has always been here. Has Melissa enticed you somehow?"

Rebecca felt the blush spreading across her cheeks. "Ben."

The captain rose and moved to his bookshelf. "I assume by 'Ben,' you mean Captain Benjamin Reed?"

For the first time in her life, Rebecca professed her undying love for a man. "Oh, Captain Roberts, I love him, and he loves me. I finally understand what my parents and grandmother were talking about. He's waiting for me right now. I simply *have* to go back. I *have* to be with him. He is my life. Please try to understand."

The captain reached to his right for a book, a finely bound leather journal. He thumbed through the pages. "I gather this means you would disappear tonight?"

Tears welled in Rebecca's eyes. "Yes. I'm sorry. God knows I'm sorry. I don't want to hurt you or Ms. Katherine or Tess. But I have to go. I love Ben with all my heart. I have no one here and everything there. I'm sorry, truly, truly sorry." Tears streamed down over her cheeks and dropped onto her lap.

Captain Roberts shook his head, walked back to the table, and placed the journal in front of his seat. "I could force you to stay, but I don't have the heart to. Nor would Katherine or Tess forgive me if I did."

He turned another page in the journal. "Do you understand how this works, Rebecca? Do you have to go to bed at a certain time or fall asleep by an exact hour?"

"I don't know. Why?"

He sat down and ruffled through the pages of what Rebecca could see was a captain's log. She noticed the pages were well worn and dated from five summers ago. "I'm thinking, Rebecca...trying to figure out how you can leave without having you disappearing from the *Shenandoah*. These are the logs from the night Melissa vanished. There is nothing out of the ordinary. I've read through these a hundred times. Everything was in order."

Rebecca looked at Captain Roberts sympathetically. "There are no explanations, at least none we can reason or prove. I don't know how it happens or why me or why Melissa, but I know I have to leave tonight before the cruise is over."

"I understand, Rebecca. Do me a favor, please. Give me some time to think. Don't go to bed without coming to see me first, okay?"

"Of course, Captain, anything you want." Rebecca rose from the seat cushion. She stopped at the door and turned. "I'm so sorry. I wish I had a twin sister or a double or some sort of magic power to create two of me." Rebecca went up the small ladder, leaving the captain huddled over his log with her confession and intention weighing on them both.

The crew maneuvered the ship safely onto her mooring ball in the harbor. The kids walked around chatting excitedly about the remaining activities. Rebecca felt the afternoon drag by, her thoughts always drifting back to Ben and wondering if he was getting any sleep or just pacing the floor of his cabin.

Rebecca forced herself to laugh and join in the fun as the kids read clues and hunted for treasure. By late afternoon the girls were trying on outfits to wear to the "Captain's Dinner" and practicing their performances for the talent show. The boys were either in the saloon playing cards with Kevin or up on deck hanging with the rest of the crew.

Just before dinner, Hawk knocked on her door. "Captain asked you to stop by for a second."

She rose slowly from her bunk, heart in her throat. "Thanks. I'll head right up."

Hawk let her go up the companionway first. "He seemed pretty happy. What's up?"

Rebecca brightened. "Really? Wow. Maybe he's thought of something I can do, some way to get there, even."

Her feet hit the deck, and she rushed down to the captain's quarters, mindless of the ferryboat passengers waving as they passed or of Hawk trying to ask her a question about where she was going.

30

REBECCA WAITED FOR THE FERRY'S WAKE to settle before descending the steps into the captain's quarters. "Knock, knock," she called.

"Come in, Rebecca." She noticed he looked much more relaxed than when she'd left a couple of hours ago.

"Hawk said you wanted to see me? Did you think of an idea?"

"Perhaps, Rebecca, just perhaps."

Rebecca's heart filled with hope. "Really?"

He motioned for her to sit. "Your comment about a twin gave me an idea, however crazy or farfetched it might be. Andy will be motoring out later with a package for me as he usually does on Friday nights. He'll time his trip this week to pass Brian and Josh as they row the dogs to shore for their nightly walk. Tess will also be in the boat, covered by a tarp and unseen."

At the mention of her friend hiding in the boat, Rebecca held her breath. "When Andy gets here, he'll maneuver close to the stern, and Tess will climb on board, using the chains and ropes under the yawl. God willing, no one will see her. Andy is going to come starboard and distract all attention to his landing. He'll have my favorite bagels and donuts for Saturday's breakfast, and it will be one big joke with the crew as it always is. I'm known for this; they're expecting it." He paused, and his face became serious.

Rebecca cut in. "But why is Tess…"

He continued on with his train of thought as though he hadn't heard her. "I'll need you to fetch some of your clothes and a hat and bring them to my cabin. Be discreet. Come like you're going to wash and brush your teeth before heading off to bed."

Her eyes widened. "Are you thinking what I think you're thinking?"

He almost smiled before his eyes grew pensive again. "You mentioned wishing you had a double. Tess is so much like you in body type that we might be able to pull off a switch without getting caught. It's a stretch, and I haven't worked out all the details, like where you're going and why and how, but it's the best I could come up with on such short notice."

Captain Roberts looked at her and, for the first time in her life, she saw fear in his eyes. A chill of anxiety swept over her. His plan had to work, or her departure would probably ruin his business that he loved so much. He pointed to a world map on the wall to his left. "We still need to figure out a place you can go to, someplace your friends and uncle will believe, or at least think plausible. Your uncle may have moved back to Ireland, but he'll still be worried about you. I don't want Paddy to fly over here in a rage and start a search for you."

A cautious bubble of hope and excitement rose inside her. His idea could work. She could leave and pretend to go someplace far away, and nobody would get hurt. Leaning over, she gave Captain Roberts a hug. "Thank you. Thank you for caring, for understanding, for helping me do something I imagine you think is pretty crazy."

He patted her back and settled once again into his chair, clearing his throat before he spoke. "I've been married to Katherine for more than forty years. She might tell you that I love this ship more than anything, but she knows I would be nothing without her. When you find true love, it's worth everything. You move mountains if you have to."

As Rebecca smiled and wiped away a tear, he masked his sentimentality with a curt, "Let's just hope the plan works."

"It will. It has to." Rebecca stood, knowing the conversation was over. "I can't wait to see Tess. I'll finally be able to tell someone all about Ben." She giggled when she saw his raised eyebrow. "I meant a girlfriend."

He gave a short, gruff chuckle. "I knew what you meant. Why don't you head below, and I'll see you after dinner?"

Rebecca left his cabin optimistic and eager for the night ahead. The captain's dinner was a veritable feast of roast beef, roasted potatoes, green beans, salad, and Dave's famous rolls. Rebecca vacillated between sheer happiness, worries about what her life would be like in 1775, and doubts that their scheme would work.

The kids were having a wonderful time, however. The mood grew festive during the talent show and even the boys performed. The captain applauded them all and encouraged everyone to keep up the good work. He joked that fame and fortune were sure to follow.

Hawk drew a loud round of cheers and whoops when he passed out the awards for bunk inspection. Cabin 11 won the Best Cabin Award, while Cabin 2 earned extra galley duties in the morning for having the messiest cabin.

At long last it was time for the kids to head to bed. Rebecca dressed in a second set of clothes underneath her sweat pants and sweatshirt. She tucked her Red Sox cap into the pocket of her hoodie and headed up on deck to wash her face and brush her teeth.

The deck was still a flurry of activity. The kids had gone to bed, but some of the crew was on deck milling about and helping tie off the motorboat. Andy had arrived. He passed Hawk the boxes of donuts and bagels before he climbed up the ladder from the skiff. Within seconds they all started calling out their favorites. Rebecca thought they sounded like her students arguing over who would get what cookie. No one saw Tess climb over the cap rail and slip into her father's cabin.

"You eat that blueberry bagel, and I'll toss you over," Tim joked to Dave.

"Don't look at me. You'll be fighting off Josh come morning. If I were you, I'd be the first one down to breakfast. Or you could slip the cook a twenty and I know for a fact he'll stash that bagel someplace safe for you." Dave winked at Rebecca as he held his palm out to Tim.

Rebecca smiled and walked over to the portside pump. While Rebecca was brushing her teeth, Andy purposely bumped into her just like he had when they were kids and she was playing with Tess. She gave him a mock glare. "You'll never grow up."

He responded with a lopsided grin. "Let's hope not. Some of us were meant to be teachers, and some of us were meant to be class clowns. So, how's life for the teacher? Had a good trip, I hear."

She nearly choked on her toothbrush. He winked. "Wonderful," she replied, wanting to spit the toothpaste at him instead of over the railing.

"Want to go down to Dad's cabin and catch up on what you've been doing this summer? I've hardly seen you."

Rebecca noticed Hawk was watching them. "Sounds great. I heard you've been dating Molly Parkinson. Are those rumors true?"

Andy rolled his eyes and Rebecca chuckled. "Ah, I guess she's one more in a cast of thousands."

"You wound me, Rebecca. Hundreds? Maybe. Thousands? I haven't had time."

They were both laughing and shoving each other back and forth as they walked to Captain Roberts' quarters. Rebecca went down first and had to keep herself from squealing when she saw Tess. She hugged the captain's daughter tight before Tess pulled her down beside her on the bed so they could sit in the back corner of the room and talk.

Andy watched them slip into the dark. "You have five minutes to gossip. We have a limited amount of time to put this plan into place before Rebecca has to go to bed," he said before ascending the ladder and leaving them to talk.

The two women huddled close.

"Tell me everything," Tess urged. "Don't leave out one juicy detail."

Rebecca blushed. Tess was never one to mince words. "Remember all those nights we'd sit on the beach and talk about who Prince Charming really was or who he should be?" Rebecca watched Tess nod. "Ben is all that and then some."

"Becca, give me more than that, will ya? What does he look like? What kind of accent does he have? How long is his hair? Does he wear a wig?"

Images of Ben talking, of Ben standing at the helm, of Ben leaning down to kiss her flashed before her eyes. "He has brown hair that's not quite to his shoulders. When he's at the wheel and the wind is blowing, his hair lifts like the sails, and I just want to run my fingers through it." They both giggled like schoolgirls.

"And?" Tess asked.

"He's strong."

Tess smiled. "Good. I wouldn't want to hear about a knight in shining armor who didn't have moral character. We'll just skip over the last two guys who asked me out. They thought strength was in their biceps. Neither one had met my father, or yours for that matter." Tess paused. Rebecca knew what the next question was going to be. It was the one question they had determined years ago that would make or break a committed relationship.

"Would your dad have liked him, Becca?"

Rebecca never thought she'd hear Tess ask her that question. A mix of sorrow and joy filled Rebecca's heart and spilled out as tears. "Da would be proud to call Ben his son. He would respect him as a man of faith and virtue and honor. And he would have loved his sense of humor. Ben pokes fun at me with the same affection my dad used to. I hope he can see me, Tess. I hope he and Mom and Gram know how happy I am."

"I'm so happy for you, Rebecca. And I bet your family is, too."

Over the remaining minutes Rebecca told Tess as much as she could.

Her friend loved the story about George Washington. She said she wished she could meet Adam and Jonah and Melissa. And she joked that Donald sounded rather tempting. They giggled quietly and cried softly until Andy and Captain Roberts descended the ladder into the cabin.

"Time's up," the captain said. "Andy, fill them in on the plan. I'm going up on deck to talk with the men and keep everyone away from this end of the ship. Rebecca, come say good night before you, ah, leave."

Tears welled in her eyes. "I will, Captain Roberts. Thank you. From the bottom of my heart, thank you."

Tess squeezed her hand.

Captain Roberts' gravelly voice cracked as he said, "Be happy, Rebecca."

"I promise."

The captain left, and Andy went on deck for a minute so Rebecca could undress and give Tess her hidden layer of clothing. Rebecca pulled down her sweats.

"Oh no, you didn't!" Tess exclaimed. "You're finally going to give me the best pair of jeans you've ever owned?"

"They're all yours."

Tess ran her hands over the stonewashed denim. She'd talked Rebecca into buying them a year ago for a hot date she had fixed up for her. The date was a total flop, but Rebecca had loved the jeans and refused to ever let her borrow them. Tess hugged them to her. "I'll keep them forever. Whenever I wear them, I'll think of you."

"I can't take anything with me, but you'll be in my heart for the rest of my life."

The two friends sat on the bed, holding hands, sharing memories without saying a word.

When Andy returned, he gathered them close around the table. "Here's the deal: Tess will sleep in Dad's cabin. I'm leaving, but I'll be back early. I'll make sure no one's on deck, and Tess will climb down into the motorboat dressed as you. I'll head down to your room to get your bags and, well, to check that you're actually gone."

Tess interrupted. "Are you sure, Rebecca? Absolutely, 100 percent certain Ben is the one? No doubts about leaving? No doubts about Ben?"

Rebecca didn't hesitate. "Ben is the one. I would be lying if I didn't say I had a few doubts about what my life will be like and how I'll adjust to it, but I have no doubt that with Ben is where I belong."

"Awwww," Tess sighed.

Andy just stared at them as if they had two heads. "Okay, can we get back to the plan?"

Tess huffed. "There isn't a romantic bone in your body. Are you sure we're related?"

He gestured dramatically. "I'm romantic."

Rebecca snorted. "Of course he is. Just ask any girl on the Island over the age of twenty."

"Funny, Rebecca, very funny. Now, can we please get back to your life?"

Andy explained his idea to get Tess off the boat, onto the ferry, and up to Logan Airport. "We'll need credit cards, your email account, a list of people you would have sent—make that, will send—a quick note to and a location that you're going to, if you've thought of one."

Rebecca looked at her two friends, for all intents and purposes the last two people she would see and talk to in this century. "You guys are wonderful. I just want you to know I appreciate everything you're trying to do."

They both nodded, and nobody spoke for a moment as the magnitude of their endeavor and Rebecca's choice settled over them. After a minute, Rebecca said, "Africa. What do you think of Africa? Some remote village with no mail or phones where I could volunteer and literally disappear."

"I like it," Andy said.

"Me, too. It's perfect. And so *you.* You're always volunteering. No one would doubt that you'd dedicate your life to helping underprivileged kids," Tess said.

Rebecca jotted down her email address, password, and a list of people "she" would contact. She handed the paper to Andy. "I'll guess you'll be online tonight searching for that mission in Africa?"

"Lucky for you I already cancelled my hot date." He grinned before taking on his father's serious tone. "Okay, it's settled. Time for bed, at least for you two."

Rebecca stood. Andy walked over and gave her a hug. "Good luck, Girlie. I'll miss your beautiful smile."

"Be good to yourself, Andy. And be nice to Tess."

After a muffled laugh, Rebecca turned to Tess. Her friend was crying. "No tears, Tess. It's all good. I'll miss you, though, and I'll always remember you. You've been the best friend."

Tess hugged her tightly and released her quickly. "Go, go before I'm a sobbing mess. Everything will work out on this end. Just be happy."

Rebecca nodded as she moved toward the ladder. "Love you."

"Love you, too."

31

REBECCA AMBLED TOWARD THE BOW OF THE BOAT where Captain Roberts was chatting with Hawk, Tim, and Dave. The captain saw her and excused himself. They walked back toward the companionway together.

"Everything all set?" He slowed his long legs to match her stride.

"Yes. Andy has everything under control. He's a master planner. Maybe he should work for the government."

"I don't think the state or federal world is ready for Andy." He placed a hand on her shoulder. "Are you ready?"

His single question was loaded with a million unasked questions. "Never been more ready."

"Well, then, I'll say good night and good-bye."

Rebecca took a small step, turned left, and wrapped her arms around the tall, burly captain. "You're the best. Thanks again."

"God bless you, Rebecca."

She stepped back. She had a few things left to do, but the hard stuff was done. Walking to the pump, she picked up her basin and toiletries she'd left by the hatch. As she placed a hand on the top of the ladder, she thought of her father. "You know, Captain Roberts, this really is a magical boat. My father was right all along. She's a beauty and definitely one of a kind. I bet Da's looking down and loving all this. He always loved to be proven right."

Rebecca listened to the captain's laughter as she descended the rungs of the ladder and moved toward her cabin. She closed the door and punched her arms toward the ceiling. "Yes! Yes! Yes!" she shouted silently. "Thank you, God."

After a few near-soundless jumps for joy, Rebecca set about the task of packing up her cabin. She moved all the school supplies into two large shopping bags. She labeled one for the classroom and one to be returned to Jackie. She packed her big duffle for Tess to pretend to take to Logan. Tess and Andy could donate the clothes to a shelter while they were in the city. She organized all her personal items—wallet, keys, journal, address book, and tubes of lip gloss and sunscreen—in her backpack for Tess to keep.

Within half an hour she had everything stacked and prepared for Andy. She stared at her bags. Not one item would travel with her. She eased down onto the lower bunk and let the reality of her eminent departure sink in. She was leaving, truly and permanently leaving. Never in her wildest imagination had she dreamed her life would follow the path she was about to take. She couldn't believe she'd fallen in love, couldn't believe her heart's desire lived in 1775, and couldn't believe in a few short hours she would be returning home to Ben. Forever.

Rebecca started to climb up to the top bunk, then thought of something she needed to do. She knelt in front of the lower bunk and came eye level with her bags. "Dear Lord, please bless Captain Roberts and Tess and Andy. Help them to do whatever needs to be done so no harm comes to any of them. Watch over all these kids, too, please. Help them to grow up to be men and women who make a positive impact on the world. And, please, help me go home to Ben. Amen."

Rebecca rose, climbed up onto the bunk, and lay on top of the sheet and blanket. She reached over the side, dangled her flashlight just inches from her duffle, turned it off, and let it fall to the bag, where Andy would find it in the morning. Everything was done. It was time to close her eyes. Time to go to sleep. Time to go home to Ben.

*

"What's up, Andy? You're here early. You playing bellman today?"

All six-foot-two of his lanky frame spun around the small cabin to face Hawk. "Morning, Hawk. Just grabbing Rebecca's bags. She's leaving now, already in the motorboat waiting for me. She's headed up to Logan this morning. Guess she talked to Dad about some big idea yesterday."

"Wait. She's leaving now?"

"As soon as I bring her gear up." Andy saw Hawk begin to bolt for the companionway. "Oh, Hawk, the captain asked for you to bring him a cup of coffee—right away."

"You're kidding, right? The captain's up at this hour?"

"Yup. He just said good-bye to Rebecca. Now you know why he wants that coffee immediately."

"I want to see Rebecca before..."

"Get the coffee. I'll wait for you."

Hawk left for the galley, none too happy. Andy grabbed Rebecca's duffel, the two shopping bags and her backpack, and scurried up the companionway. His father waited by the ladder.

"You'd better get downstairs, Dad. Hawk is on his way up to see Rebecca.

Oh, and he's bringing you that coffee you asked for, if you get my drift."

Captain Roberts patted Andy's shoulder. "Thanks, son. Good luck. I'll see you tonight. Godspeed."

"Later, Dad. I'll call from the road."

Andy climbed down the ladder and into the motorboat as Captain Roberts descended the companionway to intercept Hawk.

Tess, dressed in Rebecca's jeans and sweater with her hair tucked up under the Red Sox cap, sat with her back to the *Shenandoah*. Andy started the motor and pulled away from the vessel. They came around the stern and headed toward the dock.

Right as they were about to disappear from view behind their sister ship, Hawk called out, "Rebecca!"

Tess stiffened. Andy waved to Hawk and spoke calmly to his baby sister. "Just raise your hand and wave, Sis. Don't turn around." She lifted her arm and said good-bye to Hawk seconds before the little skiff went behind the seventy-five-foot sailboat.

Tess exhaled. "That was close."

Andy grinned. "Are you kidding me? That was perfect. Now Hawk *saw* Rebecca leave. We couldn't have planned that any better if I had choreographed it myself. Now all we have to do is get you to the car, on and off the ferry, and up to Logan without anyone else seeing us."

He eyed his sister. Rebecca was gone. He knew Tess felt like crying, but she was tough enough to refuse to give in to tears, as she had yesterday.

"It's pretty amazing, isn't it?" Tess said slowly.

Andy brought the boat alongside the dock and tied them off. "That's an understatement. Who would've thought Pete Nichols was right?"

A strange, faraway look come into Tess's eyes. "Rebecca's so lucky. Her life is better than any reality show. I wish…"

Andy put down the duffle he was about to hoist onto the dock and snapped his fingers directly in front of his sister's face. "Snap out of it, Tess. This isn't *Fantasy Island* or *The Love Boat* or *Survivor.* Don't get one of your harebrained ideas running around in your head. The *Shenandoah* has seen her last day as a time-travel machine. Dad said we're changing some of the boards in that cabin tomorrow."

Tess flashed an indignant look at her brother. "I wasn't…"

"Save it, Sis. Leave your plotting to whatever fantasies you have about Hawk."

32

A KNOCK ON THE DOOR WOKE HER. She didn't hear the stove. Rebecca realized in an instant where she was. "Thank You, Lord!" she shouted and flew to the door. "Ben?"

Before her hand was on the handle, the door opened. Ben stepped into the room, and she jumped into his arms. He wrapped his hands around her hips, lifted her off the ground, and twirled her about. She laughed and tossed her head back, her hair flying out behind her. Ben slowed their spin and set her on the floor.

"Rebecca." He uttered her name as though it was sacred.

He took a step back. Rebecca felt her knees go weak. He appraised every inch of her in quiet, reverent appreciation. Even in her sweat pants and tank top she felt like a bride walking down the aisle toward a man whose eyes absorbed every moment, every nuance, every feature with love and passion.

He moved a stray strand of hair behind her right ear. "You are more precious to me than life, Rebecca. I do not know what I would have done if you had not returned."

Tears of joy pooled in her eyes. "Oh, Ben, I was so worried. I thought the day would never end. First I had to tell the captain, then we had to come up with a plan, and after he thought of a plan, a really good one by the way, then I had to wait for lights out to go to bed."

"I understand, for that was the longest night of my life. Please, do not ever travel again where I cannot go."

Rebecca traced a finger along the side of his face, touching him, assuring herself of his presence, and feeling the stubble of his normally shaven skin. "Did you get any sleep?"

Ben pressed her hand to his cheek. "A little. It matters not. You are here. All is well."

He lowered his lips to hers, drew her close, and took her breath away. She swayed into him, losing herself in the warmth of his embrace.

"If you kiss me like that every morning, Benjamin Reed, I will never get out of the house, never mind leave your sight."

Ben gazed into her eyes. "Then I shall make a habit of kissing you just so each and every day. Of course, I feel you should first do me the honor of becoming my wife."

Rebecca sucked in her breath. "Are you asking me a question, Benjamin Reed?"

Ben released her and reached for her right hand. He knelt on his left knee and smiled up at her. "Rebecca O'Neill, I have waited my whole life to love you. Will you marry this humble man and stay with me forever?"

Tears rolled down her checks, her heart raced, her mind sifted through a dozen responses until only one remained.

"Yes."

* * *

"For I know the plans I have for you,"
declares the Lord, "plans to prosper you
and not to harm you,
plans to give you hope and a future."

JEREMIAH 29:11

Author's Notes

The *Shenandoah* is a real and magical ship, though her magic lies in her ability to transport you back in time through your imagination, not in actuality. Captain Robert S. Douglas dreamed of, designed, and commissioned the 108-foot square topsail schooner in the early sixties. She was launched on February 15, 1964, from the Harvey Gamage Shipyard in South Bristol, Maine. I took the liberty of dating the fictional ship's origins to 1770. Captain Douglas actually created the *Shenandoah* to resemble the fast U.S. revenue cutter, *Joe Lane*, from the nineteenth century, "America's Golden Age of Sail."

The *Shenandoah*, moored in the Vineyard Haven Harbor and sailing from Martha's Vineyard, is truly one-of-a-kind. She is the only non-auxiliary square topsail schooner in the world, and she boasts the longest-standing captain and schooner tandem in the nation. The kids' cruises depicted in the book are the *Shenandoah's* primary function. Captain Douglas offers every elementary school on the Vineyard the chance to sail for a week at half the cost of the chartered cruises booked through the remainder of the season.

Island fifth graders raise money all year long and then enjoy a special week on the water between the summer of their fifth-and-sixth-grade years. The kids learn a variety of essential knots on a ship, the art of coiling tight lines, how to raise and lower sails, what it means to flake, the importance of wind direction, the indications if there is enough wind to sail, the strength and teamwork needed to raise and lower the anchor, and the effort involved in keeping a beautiful boat ship shape. The children, with no electricity or modern conveniences to distract them, work hard and play hard, spending hours in the water swimming, diving, jumping, and even catching the occasional baby sand shark. As my youngest daughter can tell you, sailing on the *Shenandoah* is an unforgettable experience. To learn more: **www.theblackdogtallships.com** or **www.shenandoahfoundation.org.**

All the characters in *Shenandoah Nights* are fictional, though some of the names used are those of family and friends. I attempted to be as accurate as possible with the historical references and the time frame of the setting. Any errors are mine. The story, however, is a work of a fiction, and I took great liberty creating relationships between General George Washington, Captain Reed and Rebecca O'Neill. General Washington was real, of course, and many of the events described in the book happened during the Revolutionary War. Anything relating to the *Shenandoah* in the eighteenth century is merely a product of my imagination.

Acknowledgments

Shenandoah Nights would not have been written if Captain Robert Douglas had not designed the schooner *Shenandoah* and then graciously extended a discounted charter rate to all the elementary schools on Martha's Vineyard. My chaperone experience on the *Shenandoah* was unforgettable. Thank you to the captain and his son, Morgan Douglas, for allowing me to use your beautiful ship in my story, for answering my questions, and for sharing in my enthusiasm.

I am indebted to Kelsey and Kristina Ivory. To Kelsey, for the many hours you stayed with Kayla while I went to Writer's Group on Wednesday nights. And to Kristina, for reading through *Shenandoah Nights*—eagerly. I am blessed to call you my neighbors.

A warm thank you to my publisher, Ramona Tucker, for her enthusiasm for *Shenandoah Nights* and for encouraging and believing in my story. Many thanks to Les Stobbe, my agent, for taking me on as a client and believing my story would make it into print. I am grateful, also, to Linda Nathan for her keen editing skills.

A huge thank you to my Wednesday night writers' group led by mystery writer Cynthia Riggs. Emily Cavanagh, Catherine Finch, Amy Reese, Sarah Wyatt Smith, Valerie Sonnenthal, and Cynthia encouraged, critiqued, tweaked, and applauded throughout the writing of *Shenandoah Nights*. Wednesday night is truly my favorite night of the week!

Hugs to Tammy and Brian Cohan and your beautiful daughters, Alexis and Ashley. The years of love and friendship and your insistence, Tammy, that I should write because I *would* get published, inspired me to keep going. I just had to put you all in the book as a small way to thank you. Hugs for Brant and Starr Skyler, too. I hope you like your characters. Thanks for cheering me on.

Much love and thanks to the best grandparents my girls could ask for, Betty Belcastro and Jack Kobelenz. I appreciate your constant love and support and the many trips you make to the Island to visit us, to cheer on the girls at all their functions, and stay with them as I pursue my passions and hobbies. You are God's gift to us. I love you.

I am blessed with two amazing daughters, Kayla, to whom I gave birth, and Ashleen, who chose us as we chose her. You girls are my inspiration. You are both so amazingly talented. The house is filled with the fantastic sounds of your singing and dancing and acting. Your creative juices keep me at the computer long after I want to go outside and play or call it a night. Please forgive me if you ever felt neglected when I was late to pick you up when I got lost in the story. I'll do better!

No love story, real or imagined, would be possible without our Heavenly Father, the Creator of love. It is with a humble heart that I try to serve our Lord and Savior, Jesus Christ. I pray daily for inspiration and guidance to serve Him and hope this story will touch your heart and God's light will shine on you.